Branded

Ignite Trilogy #2

TARA SIVEC

Other books by Tara Sivec

PROLOGUE

I KILLED HER.

The beautiful, smartass firecracker that exploded into my life with the force of an atomic bomb – she's gone because of me.

All those moments spent fighting with her were a waste of time. Time that could have been better spent getting one of those rare laughs that were just for me, memorizing every freckle on her nose and showing her just how much she meant to me, even though I fucked it all up in the end when she needed me the most.

From the very first time I tasted her lips, she was mine. With that cherry red lip-gloss and her hands on her hips, all sass and snark and attitude – she was mine, but I fucked things up with her *that* time, too, at that damn graduation party.

Who the fuck knows at eighteen-years-old that the girl he felt up at a party would turn out to be his entire world years down the line? I sure as hell didn't. I drank too much and I didn't even get to remember what should have been the best fucking night of my life. I kissed those perfect lips, slid my hands up her tight shirt and tried not to blow my load when she moaned into my mouth. Then I blacked out, forgetting all of the important things, and walked away the next morning like the cocky little punk I was and tried to forget about her. I thought I'd done a pretty good job of it until four and a half months ago, when she walked back into my life. All that bullshit I'd spouted off to my best friend about how it's unnatural to spend your life with one woman...fuck, what I wouldn't give to go back and beat the shit out of that stupid asshole who thought he knew everything.

Eighteen weeks spent fighting her continued brush-offs and fighting with *her* when I should have been on my knees begging her to never leave me.

Eighteen days spent learning about what made her into the woman she was and trying my hardest to prove to her that she was worth more than she thought.

Eighteen minutes spent praying to a God I'd never believed in, begging Him not to take her from me.

Eighteen seconds too late.

I've counted each and every minute with her these last few months, the good and the bad. 181,440 minutes that I would give anything to do over. Sitting here with a half-empty bottle of whiskey in some dive bar I don't even remember the name of, I count the drops of condensation on my glass as they slide down, each one fading away and disappearing into the napkin underneath it, just like every moment I spent with her. I had her and I let her slip through my fingers. I should have held tighter, fought harder, gotten there sooner.

I'll never run my fingers through the long, crimson hair that reminded me so much of fire when the sun hit it. I'll never feel the heat of her body pressed to mine again, or the way she'd whisper my name against my lips right before she came.

Fuck, that goddamn sigh...it was like she just *breathed* my name, as if it were the oxygen in her lungs that gave her life. I can still hear that fucking sound every time I close my eyes, and it completely guts me.

She branded her name on my heart and I know I'll never be the same. I'll never get the chance to tell her that I don't fucking care about the scars on her body. I don't care about anything but seeing her smile and hearing her laugh.

Staring up at the clock on the wall behind the bar, I realize it's been eighteen hours since I last saw her alive. In my mind's eye, I see her standing there, a flush on her cheeks and determination in her eyes as she told me to go. I did as she asked because I was angry and I knew she was hurting. I couldn't stand the thought of causing her any more pain than I already had. It seems that all I've ever done is hurt her.

She told me to go, and I did.

If only I would have stayed.

Phina

Eighteen days earlier…

SERAPHINA ROSALIA GIORDANO. I know, it's a mouthful and I have hated it since the day I learned how to speak, which is why everyone just calls me Phina. Like, Feena, long *e*. The boys in school got a kick out of chanting, "Seraphina, you're so fine-a" whenever I walked by.

Hilarious.

I perfected the art of the resting bitch face, however, and one nasty look from me shut them right up. It probably didn't hurt that, on the first day of high school when my name was announced and my fellow classmates snickered, I told them my name means *fiery one* and they shouldn't piss me off or I'd burn their asses. I may or may not have also said something to the effect of my family being in the mob…what can you do? High school is a bitch, and so am I.

Standing in front of the full-length mirror behind my bedroom door, I stare at my body. As bodies go, it's not a bad one. Some might even

4

say it's pretty damn hot. There's a pun hidden somewhere in there that has everything to do with a few well-placed scars I keep hidden beneath the right pair of lace boy shorts. It's gotten a little tricky over the years, but I'm nothing if not resourceful. I'm not a slut by any means, but I like sex. I like being in control and bringing a man to his knees. I like the salty taste of a man's skin against my lips and that initial burn when he thrusts inside of me. I'm not opposed to a firm smack against my ass and I've been known to demand a little hair-pulling here and there, too. No one gets to see me fully naked though, that's where I draw the line – underwear stays on or the lights go off. Until the other night, I'd never had any man argue over my weird little demand. They see my flat stomach, sculpted by hundreds of crunches a day, my long legs, toned through an abhorrent number of squats and lunges, and my 36C all-natural breasts, straining against a miniscule piece of lace, begging to be touched. With my long hair, big green eyes, thick black lashes and full, heart-shaped lips, I am the total package and they care fuck-all about anything else outside of getting their dick inside me. They don't mind moving my underwear to the side or blindly feeling around in the dark. They do as I ask or they leave. Period.

Why the fuck didn't he leave the other night?

I didn't mark my body for attention. It's not a cry for help or a result of some lingering childhood trauma, regardless of what one or two of my former shrinks might lead you to believe. I like pain, that's all there is to it. So many things about life can make you feel dead inside, and the sting of burning flesh and the throb of pain makes me feel alive.

My name is Seraphina Rosalia Giordano, and I like to brand myself.

I realize that sounds a little sick and twisted when you say it out loud, but I don't mind. I like people thinking I'm a little fucked up in the head. It forces them to keep their distance and helps avoid attachments. There are only two people I just couldn't shake and my best friend, Finnley, is one of them. Honestly, she's the only person I didn't mind allowing into my life because she's genuinely good, through and through. She's never tried to use me for her own personal gain and she would give you the shirt off her back if it meant your happiness. Still, I've never let her see the truly dark side of myself. That's something no one needs to see, especially someone as decent and sweet as Finnley. When we met, I almost hoped that some of her goodness would rub off on me, but even at fifteen years old, I was already a lost cause.

For the first time in my life, staring at the scars on my hips, running my fingertips over the small circles of rough, uneven skin pisses me off. My best friend, who means the world to me, almost lost everything in a horrible house fire four months ago. Her estranged husband died, the love of her life almost died and she *did* die. For seventeen seconds, Finnley's heart stopped beating. When she came back to life, her legs, her hips and part of her stomach were covered in burns. Burns she never asked for and scars that she'll have for the rest of her life because of some sick fuck who couldn't let her go. Finnley, ever the optimist, is just grateful to be alive, but I've seen what those scars have done to her self-esteem.

Then you have me, a woman who willingly puts these marks on her body just to feel alive. I should be disgusted with myself; I should hate myself more than I already do. Unfortunately, all the guilt and self-flagellation have only made me angrier. I can feel the rage simmering just below the surface, building up inside of me, making me crave the burn. I know that eventually, I'll be forced to light a cigarette and add a few more ugly marks to my skin just to relieve the pressure. It's been so long since I've done it; I've been distracted with Finnley and trying to be a good friend to her. I've been at war with myself for months, not wanting to dishonor her by adding to my scars and yet, needing it so much it almost hurts to breathe.

My hands itch with the need to feel the searing burn on my flesh. My throat tightens with a locked-away scream, dying to get out and take all my frustrations with it as I blister my skin. The pack of Marlboro Smooths and the yellow BIC lighter are only seven steps away from me in the top drawer of my nightstand, taunting me. Seven steps across my plush, cream carpet where I can flick my BIC, take the one drag off a cigarette needed for the end to glow with red embers and then…*bliss.*

Instead of doing what I need, what I *want*, I walk seven steps in the opposite direction, stopping in front of my closet. Tonight is Finnley's night and I refuse to voluntarily mar my skin with the kind of scars she has to look at day after day on her own body, wishing they weren't there. I have so many reasons to add another brand to my body, especially after what happened the other night, but I won't. I will take a deep breath, put on the dress I bought for the art gallery event tonight in Finnley's honor and proudly stand by her side as the rest of the world is introduced to the beauty that she creates. My best friend is an artist and tonight, we are celebrating her recovery and her first show. I will don a smile, drink champagne and pretend like everything is okay. I spent the first eighteen years of my life learning how to hide my pain and the marks my father left on me, and then honed my skill for the next fifteen, concealing the misery and the darkness inside me; tonight will be no different.

And yet, I know *everything* is different now. I crossed a line two nights ago and I can never go back. I should have known better than to let him back in, the *him* in question being the second person – and the only man – that has crossed my path in my thirty-three years that I just can't shake.

I'm not the woman he used to know and the things that happened in this very room just forty-eight hours ago are proof of that. I wanted something and I took it, just like he did when we were eighteen years old. He wanted to know what my fantasy was and I told him. He was only too happy to oblige, although looking back on it now, I'm sure he had no idea what he was getting into. If I close my eyes, I can still feel that hard, firm chest that I rested my back against, strong arms holding me in place and callused hands sliding over my breasts. If I open them again, I see someone else's head between my thighs at the same time. I always wanted to know what it was like to be with two men at once, and he gave me my fantasy.

I'm not a slut, let me just remind you of that. This wasn't some skeezy, porn-style double-penetration. One only held me, his dominant presence a soothing, calming foil to the other, a man whose touch brought me more pleasure than I've ever felt before. On the surface, it felt exactly how I thought it would feel, but on the inside, the experience left me feeling hollow...empty. I had more orgasms in one sitting than I'd ever had in my entire life and my body was on fire as one licked and pushed and sucked while the other's hands roamed over my shoulders and slid through my hair. The fire was all on the outside, though. My skin was covered in sweat and flushed with pleasure, but on the inside, I was a cold block of ice that nothing could thaw, not even multiple orgasms.

I suspect my inability to let go of the past and my desire to live out one of my fantasies has something to do with my love of power. My current shrink will tell you that my need to control everything around me along with my penchant for always keeping a pack of cigarettes in my top drawer when I don't smoke is because of my childhood. It's always because of your childhood, isn't it?

A quiet, pleasant teenager who helped old ladies cross the road takes a gun into his high school and blows away twenty-five of his peers. *"His parents must have done something wrong."*

That nice, older man who waved to everyone and always brought chicken parmesan to the neighborhood block parties had seven mutilated corpses buried in his basement. *"I bet you he was abused by his mother."*

The college student on a full scholarship who always made the dean's list, volunteered at homeless shelters on the weekends and was the head of his youth group at church drugged and raped seventeen girls on campus. *"His father probably let him play those graphic video games when he was younger."*

The sweet, beautiful girl who loved to dance and draw pretty pictures for her mother to hang on the fridge likes to brand her skin. *"I bet you her mother skipped town and her father liked to take out his frustrations on her by stabbing a lit cigar into the smooth, pale skin of her eight-year-old body."*

Sometimes the shrinks are wrong, but in my case, they're probably right. I couldn't stop my mother from leaving, I couldn't stop my father from using me as a punching bag and an ash tray until I was old enough to fight back and I couldn't stop the boy I thought I was in love with from taking something from me and then running away as fast as he could. But this, this I can control. I say when, and how and why it's going to hurt. I administer the pain myself because it's better than letting someone else do it. If someone else hurts you, they have all the power. I refuse to give up my power.

Borderline personality disorder, depression, anxiety, post-traumatic stress, daddy issues, mommy abandonment issues...I've been given all the typical labels at one point or another, but I refuse to let them define me. I'm Sicilian. I have a temper and an attitude and I like being in charge. So what if I've carried on my father's discipline tradition? Who cares about a few burns here and there when I feel like life is going too well for me and I need to bring myself down to earth? My father was a genius at knowing exactly when things were looking up for me so he could knock me down a few pegs. An optimist is a fool, and I am no one's fool. I'm a realist. Some people just aren't meant to live happily ever after and float away on clouds full of rainbows and puppies.

I was born on October 15, 1981 to Rosa and Antonio Giordano and, for eight years, we had a nice, normal life living in the suburbs. Then my mother decided to fuck the principal of my elementary school and skip town, never to be seen again. My father used to get a cheap thrill out of telling me all about how she got remarried and had a new daughter. A better daughter. An obedient daughter. One who didn't make her mother want to run away.

Good for her.

She was smart to run away. According to my father, I was nothing but a burden, deserving of every bad thing that happened to me and the root cause of all the bad shit that happened to him. The burns are a way for me to never forget that fact. I'm nothing if not consistent.

I slide the slim, royal blue dress up my body and run a hand through my thick, wavy red hair. The dress is a little on the tight side through the chest and hip area, but that's exactly how I like it. My cleavage pushes up perfectly in the dress and I add a light dusting of shimmer powder to bring even more attention to that general area. After a spritz of my favorite spicy perfume, some nude lip-gloss and my four-inch blue stilettos with rhinestone straps around the ankles, I'm ready to go.

My scars are perfectly hidden for a night out in public and my dark thoughts are pushed far enough back in my mind that I do believe I'll have a rather pleasant evening. No one sees the real me because that's how I like it. What's the point of masks if you can't use them to your advantage?

2

DJ

I KNOW IMMEDIATELY when she enters the room, even from twenty feet away, halfway through my second bottle of beer and with some chick whose name I forgot as soon as she said it prattling in my ear.

Christina? Melissa?

"It was nice talking to you, Melissa," I tell her with a smile as I turn and walk away from her.

"It's Clarissa!" she shouts angrily to my retreating back.

Oops.

I bump into people standing around staring at artwork and don't even apologize. My eyes are glued on the woman who stands by the door, bringing a glass of champagne up to her lips. I pause when she pulls the glass away and runs her tongue over her bottom lip. Memories from the night I spent in her bed overwhelm me, and my dick instantly hardens in my charcoal dress pants.

Lying on my stomach between her legs, I slid the black lace that covered her to the side and ran the tips of my fingers through her, spreading the wetness around. It was hard to take my eyes off of the gorgeous fucking sight spread out before me, but I wanted to see her. I wanted to see the effect of what I was doing to her written all over her face. I glanced up and our eyes met. Her cheeks were flushed with desire and her tongue darted out, wetting her full bottom lip.

Then I think about the guy who had his back resting against the headboard, holding her between his own legs and my dick instantly softens. As hot as that entire night was, I'm pissed off that I had to share her with anyone. I'd wanted that damn woman for as long as I could remember, and the only way I could have her is if someone else was there with us.

Her rules: Both men in the room at all times. If the lights stay on, so do her clothes and if the lights are off, her panties stay on but everything else could go. No passing her back and forth like a game of hot potato, and no penetration aside from a few fingers and one tongue. I needed a damn flow chart just to keep everything straight.

So many fucking rules to be with that woman it blew my goddamn mind, but I jumped at the chance to finally have her. Even after I had a taste of her, I was dying for a second.

And a third.

And a motherfucking fourth.

My hand clutches onto the bottle of beer in my hand so hard I'm surprised it doesn't shatter as I close the distance between us. She drains the rest of her champagne and holds the empty glass in front of her, lifting her chin along with one of her eyebrows when she sees me approaching, clearly gearing up for a fight.

That's fine with me; I'm in the mood for a little fight. I'm pissed that I can't get her out of my system and I'm pissed that she probably knows it.

"DJ, it's nice to see you again," Phina tells me with a smile.

The smile is fake and it makes me angrier. I have a vague recollection of her giving me a few genuine smiles back in the day when we were in high school, young and most definitely dumb, and this is not one of those. There are no crinkles around the corners of her eyes and fuck if those green orbs don't get darker as they stare me down instead of getting brighter. The smile is closer to a smirk, like she's mocking me.

"Nice to see you again, too, Fireball," I tell her with a tip of my bottle in her direction. "The dress is a nice touch, but you look much better half-naked, screaming my name."

That stupid smirk falls as I bring the bottle to my lips and tip it back, letting the cold microbrew chill me the fuck out. This woman has gotten under my skin and I feel like it's only right to repay her in kind. She hates it that I've given her a nickname, and told me repeatedly over the last few weeks to stop saying it. She should have realized that only makes me want to do it more, just to piss her off. I still remember that day in high school when she moved to town and told the entire fucking class off after they laughed at her name.

She was full of fire and piss and vinegar even back then. Now all of that fire is intermingled with something dark and twisted. It should make me want to run in the opposite direction, but I'm a fireman. We like to race right into the flames, not giving a shit if we got burned. Something tells me if I spend any more time with Phina, she's going to leave me with more than a few scars.

She takes a step closer to me and I inhale the spicy perfume she wears as she lowers her voice to speak to me. "It's so cute how you seem to be forgetting the fact that I brought you to your knees. Literally."

Her hot mouth wrapped around the tip of my cock and she leaned forward, taking all of me at once. My legs gave out and I sunk to the floor of her bedroom, her body following mine and her lips and tongue never stopping as I dropped to my knees.

I shrug, taking a step back from her. "I'll give you that one. Best almost-blow job I've ever had."

Phina stops a waiter passing by, setting her empty glass on top of his tray and grabbing another full one.

"It's not my fault you couldn't handle my mouth and had to push me away," she replies cockily.

Dammit! I hate that she's right. A few minutes of having her mouth wrapped around my dick and that damn fantasy of hers was almost over before it started.

"So, how come I don't remember you being such a kinky little shit in high school?" I ask once the waiter has walked away. This earns me another glare and I ignore it as I polish off the last of my beer.

"It seems there's quite a lot you don't remember about me from high school," she replies vaguely. "How about we just pretend like the other night never happened? It was fun while it lasted, we got it out of our systems and now we can just move on."

Funny, but her words don't mirror the look on her face. Her lips are pursed and I can see the whites of her knuckles as she clutches tightly to her glass of champagne. She's definitely pissed about something and I'm going to guess it's the fact that she's feeling the same as me. She hasn't had her fill, and it's annoying the fuck out of her.

"You expect me to just move on now that I know you're into three-somes and there's a lot of kinkiness buried underneath that hard exterior you wear so well? Maybe if you'd have been a little sluttier in high school, I would have fucked you back then and you wouldn't have needed to wait so long to get a piece of me."

The smack across my face is quick and pretty fucking painful. Phina's got some power in those small hands of hers. I flex my jaw and calmly set my empty bottle down on a side table next to me even though my blood is boiling.

"You're a fucking asshole," she seethes before stepping around me and walking away.

"Right back at you, fiery one!" I shout to her, ignoring the questioning look from all the art enthusiasts scattered about the room.

Shit. I AM a fucking asshole. This night is for Finnley and I just made a scene.

Glancing around the room, I see my best friend, Collin, standing next to one of Finnley's pieces hanging on the wall and I head over in his direction.

"Everything okay over there?" he asks when I walk up next to him and he hands me a fresh beer.

I clap him on the back, grab the beer from his hand and nod. "Don't worry about me and my bullshit. How's Finnley?"

Collin glances over to where she stands, currently surrounded by a group of art critics as she explains one of her pieces on the wall next to them. His face lights up as he stares at her, and all I can do is shake my head at him. What a fucking schmuck. I love the guy, but I still can't believe he got back together with his high school girlfriend and is so damn blissfully happy. His hands nervously fiddle with something in the pocket of his pants and I know it's the engagement ring box that's been burning a hole in there the whole fucking night.

"Finnley is amazing. Jesus, I'm so proud of her. Can you believe she's about ready to sell almost every damn print in this place? Blows my fucking mind," he tells me.

Now, that I can believe. I may not be on board with the whole happily-ever-after, tied down to one woman for the rest of your life bullshit, but it's apparent how talented Finnley is. Collin and I are in agreement on that part, at least.

"She's doing good, man. You're looking good, too. When do you come back to work?"

Collin gets a huge smile on his face. "Next week, thank fucking God. I can't stand sitting around with nothing to do. I need to be back at the station getting shit done."

Collin and I both work for the Franklin Fire Department, and I've been filling in for him as captain since the fire that almost cost both his and Finnley's lives a few months ago. Bureaucratic bullshit and babysitting grown ass men have worn me down and I've had enough. I'm anxious for him to come back to work and take his job back.

"You still set on taking some time off after I come back?" he asks.

"Yeah, going to take on some extra hours with the paramedic squad. Need a change of scenery," I tell him with a laugh.

It's bullshit and I'm pretty sure Collin knows that, but he doesn't say anything. Ever since that damn fire where I had to race up a ladder and yank Collin out of a window with flames shooting out of it, I've had a hard fucking time going on calls. Every time I get on a ladder, all I can think about is the fact that I had to toss my friend out of a second story window and let him drop. I can still see his body bounce off of the bushes and smack against the ground, his leg pinned beneath him at a weird angle. I didn't know if he was alive, I didn't know if he'd ever walk again and instead of racing down there to make sure he was okay, I had to ride the fucking ladder down with the house when it collapsed and try not to get myself killed.

I can't get those images out of my head. He's fine outside of a few broken bones and he'll be back to work soon, but I relive the memory of him flying through the air and plummeting to the earth hundreds of times everyday. Before I drive myself crazy or fuck something up at work, I decided I would take some time away from the station and go full-time at my side paramedic job as soon as Collin returned to duty. As a fill-in captain for the station, those men need me to be a leader. They need to have faith in my ability to step in and take charge without being paralyzed by nightmares when I'm supposed to be shouting orders and saving lives. I am not a weak fucking man, but I know when I've reached my limit and need to call it quits for a while.

"So, you're really going to propose to Finnley, huh?"

Collin smiles, his sights still zeroed in on his woman.

"As soon as she's finished talking to those critics."

He turns to face me. "I know you don't agree with this, but I'm happy. She makes me happy. I can't spend another minute without her and I want her to be my wife."

I clink my bottle with his glass of whiskey and return his smile. "You're a better man than me, McDaniels."

He shakes his head at me and laughs before taking a drink. "One of these days, man, you're going to find a woman who brings you to your knees."

I choke on my sip of beer and Collin has to pound me on the back before I can breathe again.

Looking across the room, I see Phina talking to Dax Trevino. Aside from Collin, he's the best man I know. I used to like the guy. He works as a detective for the Franklin Police Department and I've known him most of my life. We share the same manwhore status, one woman never being able to keep hold our interest for more than a few hours, and we've both been known to like our sex a little darker than vanilla. A few nights ago, we even shared the same woman. Sort of. He mostly sat there and watched while I did all the work, but both of us got equal joy out of watching Phina come apart in front of us.

Phina's head tips back and she laughs, the smile she never gives me lighting up her face over something Dax just said to her. I suddenly have the urge to kick Dax's fucking ass.

I'll be damned if I let that woman bring me to my knees ever again.

3

Phina

I ARCHED MY *back, the feel of his lips and tongue between my thighs almost too much for me to take. I wanted more; I couldn't take anymore. Unfortunately, the brick wall of Dax's chest against my back made it impossible for me to go anywhere. His arms tightened around me, holding me in place so D.J. could continue the sweet torture of his mouth.*

I wanted this.

I asked for this.

I had no idea it would be like this.

My body was on fire and my skin flushed and glistened with sweat from so many orgasms. Three? Four? I have no idea how many times he brought me to release in the hour that the three of us had been on this bed, I only knew that I was dangerously close to another one and my body was shaking with a mixture of need and fear. I hated that he knew exactly how to touch me to give me what I craved. No one has ever known my body so well and for a moment, I thought about pushing him away and kicking him out of my bedroom. After one too many drinks when my defenses were down, he coerced me into telling him one of my fantasies. What woman hadn't thought about what it would be like to be touched and pleasured by two men? I thought for sure my revelation would throw his ego into overdrive and he'd smirk at me, explaining that he was man enough to take on the job of five men. Much to my surprise, the corner of his mouth tipped up in a boyish smile and I found myself focusing on the dimple in his cheek, barely paying attention to his words when he told me he had a friend he trusted who would be more than happy to make my fantasy a reality. I watched his tongue trace over his bottom lip and imagined it gliding over my skin while I thoughtlessly nodded my head in agreement to whatever he was saying.

The plans were set in motion right there at the bar while I was still under the spell of vodka and his fucking sweet smile. Even after I sobered up the next morning and read the text he'd sent me in the middle of the night confirming that he would make my fantasy come true, I couldn't change my mind. I couldn't show him any weakness or he'd take it and run with it. Months went by and the chaos of what happened to Collin and Finnley consumed all of our lives, but DJ had never forgotten. He set up the time and the place and I had to follow through with this for the sheer purpose of shattering any 'good girl' illusions he might have about me. Phina the good girl died right around the same time my father first pressed a cigarette into my skin. As it continued through the years, and after a particularly brutal evening with my father and his cigarettes, I foolishly ran to DJ one night for comfort and he took everything I had to give without another look back.

He pumped two of his fingers inside me over and over, and it obliterated all of those painful memories from so many years go. I couldn't help but clutch tightly to Dax's arm banded around my chest, trying to anchor myself in place as I felt the past forced further back into the recesses of my mind with each push of his hand. I felt like I was in a dream where I was falling, the butterflies and anxiety building in my stomach as I held my breath and waited for the crash.

The slapping sounds his hand and fingers made, combined with how wet I was should embarrass me, but I didn't even care. I wanted to know what it was like to be pleasured by one man while another watched and this was the result. I've turned into a mindless puddle of need on this bed and the only thing I cared about was the next release that had me teetering on the edge. The moans, screams and curses he'd pulled from my body sounded inhuman when they passed my lips and disappeared into the candlelit room. Every time I made a sound of pleasure, Dax hummed his approval in my ear and DJ did the same between my legs, the vibrations of his voice while his lips were around my clit like the shock from a live wire.

I felt like a whore with my back pressed against Dax's naked, muscled chest as I stared down between my legs at the top of DJ's head. Two men have watched me come nonstop for the last hour, but only one was actively participating, so I refused to let the label I'd given myself have any meaning. Dax's presence certainly increased my desire and the knowledge that his eyes never left my body while I writhed and screamed and begged made my orgasms that much sweeter, but it's DJ's lips and DJ's tongue and DJ's fingers that brought me those releases, one right after another.

As I stared down at the top of his head, he glanced up and his eyes met mine, his tongue swirling faster around my clit. My thighs opened wider and I rocked myself against his mouth, refusing to look away from what he was doing.

"Come on, sweetheart, I want to watch you come again," Dax whispered in my ear, his hot breath skating over my skin like a cup of warm water.

I felt DJ growl angrily between my legs, and if his mouth weren't buried in my pussy, I'm guessing he'd be baring his teeth like a rabid dog. He shot a glare in Dax's direction over my shoulder before bringing his eyes back to meet mine. I felt the rumble of laughter in Dax's chest pressed against my back, but I ignored whatever silent bullshit communication was going on between them. DJ agreed to this entire night and handpicked Dax to participate. He should have checked his fucking jealousy at the door.

Dax slid his palm down the front of my body, resting his hand below my stomach, his fingers just barely dipping below my panties, touching my little landing strip of pubic hair. I ignored the warning look DJ sent him and let my head fall back against Dax's shoulder while I thrust my hips faster, reaching desperately for that moment of bliss that would make me forget everyone and everything around me.

"That's it, Phina. Just let go," Dax muttered against my neck.

I'd like to say that it was Dax's encouraging words that pushed me over the edge one more time, the feel of his muscles tensing against my back and the heat from his arms against my skin as he held me closer to him, but I'd be lying. Staring into DJ's eyes, seeing them darken with desire as he fucked me with his fingers and sucked my clit into his mouth is what did it. Focusing on DJ and his single-minded intent to bring me to orgasm was what made the tingling between my legs turn into a wave of pleasure that washed over me. I wanted to close my eyes and drown in the release, but I couldn't look away from his eyes. They held me captive almost as much as the sight of his tongue sliding through the plump, wet lips of my pussy.

I lifted my hips from the bed and held my body suspended against DJ's mouth, coming harder than any time before. I shouted DJ's name over and over as the tip of his tongue flicked my clit rapidly, prolonging my orgasm until I was practically sobbing his name. My body jerked against both men as DJ flattened his tongue and languidly licked every inch of my pussy, swallowing every drop of my wetness while he continued to groan and hum his approval against my sensitive skin...

"PHINA!"

The loud bark of my name being shouted pulls me out of my daze. I quickly bring one hand up to my cheek, feeling its warmth, and I know if I look into a mirror right now I'd find my face flushed with desire and possibly embarrassment. Having a daydream about the almost-threesome you had in your bedroom a week ago isn't really proper workplace etiquette.

I glance up at Suzy, one of my new employees, and take a deep breath, pushing the memories from my mind.

"Sorry, I've got a lot of things going on," I explain to her with a shake of my head as I grab the inventory sheet I had been working on before I zoned out and my thoughts were once again consumed by the events that happened in my bedroom a week earlier.

"I'd say," Suzy says with a laugh. "I called your name about six times before you finally heard me. I just wanted to let you know I finished refilling the six mobile blood units on the floor. We're getting low on infant heel lancets and tape."

Grabbing a pen, I make note of the needed supplies on my chart and send Suzy off to check the mobile units in the outpatient labs. As the phlebotomist manager of the hospital, I'm directly responsible for the twenty-five phlebotomists who work here, including the ones who currently staff the two outpatient labs. It's a mind-numbing job filled with endless paperwork and staff meetings and when I accepted the management position a few years ago, I thought it would be a nice change of pace.

Being a phlebotomist wasn't exactly my little girl dream come true. When I thought about my future all those years ago, my dreams only consisted of escaping the nightmare of my reality any way I possibly could. After I graduated high school, I closed my eyes and randomly picked a job that required the least amount of schooling. I didn't have a penny to my name and there was no way in hell I'd take a handout from anyone, even though Finnley's family was more than willing to help. I worked full-time as a waitress at a local strip club, pulling in enough tips to go to school part-time until I got my certification. After I was hired at the hospital, I worked my ass off, taking on as many extra shifts as I could, and eventually climbed my way up the hospital's corporate ladder, going back to school in the evenings to get my bachelor's degree in medical management.

It might come as a surprise, but I don't enjoy inflicting pain on other people. The first time I had to stick a needle into the pudgy little arm of a screaming baby, I almost threw up all over the frantic mother pacing back and forth next to me, and it never really got better. I probably should have quit after my third panic attack during my first week of work, but I wasn't a quitter. I sucked it up and imagined it was my own skin I was piercing time after time. I pretended like the sharp prick of the needle sliding into skin and vein was happening to *me* instead of my patients. I took their pain and their quick, indrawn breaths and made them my own. I was fast and efficient and never needed more than one try to get the needle where it had to go. Now, my days are filled with staff meetings, making sure all shifts are covered, performance evaluations, continuing education and ordering stock. I rarely interact with patients unless we're short on staff and there's an emergency. It's perfect for me since it seems that over the years, my bedside manner has gotten worse instead of better. I like to think that maybe it's because I'm a woman in my thirties and age has made me irritable, but I know that's not it. I'm angry every time I have to inflict pain on someone else. I'm pissed that I'm not on the receiving end of all those needle pokes because more often than not, I'm deserving of the pain, not the patient. Whenever I do something new to fuck up my life, I want to pick up a needle from the mobile unit and slam it into my skin, not smile at the nervous person in front of me and assure them it will just be a tiny pinch and over before they know it.

Pain isn't just a tiny pinch and it shouldn't be administered to the innocent. It is a living, breathing thing that latches on and spreads like poison ivy, making you claw at your skin and want to scream at the top of your lungs.

When I close my eyes, I can still feel the ghost of lips and fingers between my thighs and I have to cross my legs under my desk. I fucked everything up the other night. I wanted to push him away, but all I did was light the fire and now it's raging out of control. My heartbeat quickens and I take a few deep, ragged breaths, squeezing the pen in my hand so hard that it snaps in half. I need to get out of here. I need to go home, to my bedroom, to the drawer in my nightstand and grab the items inside that will bring me the relief I need. I want the pain. I *deserve* the pain.

I can't have the pain.

Thoughts of Finnley bombard me and guilt overwhelms me. My best friend, my sister, the woman who has always been there for me even when I didn't deserve her love and support...the burn scars that take up most of her hips and thighs that make her self-conscious...I can't do this. I WON'T do this. I refuse to disrespect her like this, but I need to do something to take the edge off.

My hands shake with the need to pick up the phone and call DJ, ask him to come over so I can have another turn, tasting, licking and sucking. I want stroke his cock, feel him thrusting inside of me and see the look on *his* face when he comes. He only let me have him in my mouth for a few minutes before he dragged me up from the floor and tossed me on the bed.

I stand up from my chair so quickly that it almost topples over. I still have an hour and a half left on my shift, but I don't care. Suzy can handle things in my absence. If I don't get out of here now, I'll make yet another mistake and DJ will see right through me. I can't let that happen.

Grabbing my purse from the top drawer of my desk, I race out of my office and down the hall, shouting to Suzy as I go that something came up and I have to leave. I barely keep my car under the speed limit as I drive home, swerving around slow drivers and gunning it through yellow lights. I shouldn't go home, there's too much temptation in that house. If I look at the bed I'll remember every bad decision I made that night and every time I shouted his name as I came. If I look at the nightstand, I'll think about the sweet relief lying right inside the top drawer, calling my name. Home is the last place I should be, but home is the only place I can go right now. I would never burden Finnley with my problems, and even I know that going to a bar alone for a few drinks right now would only end in disaster.

I'll take a bath. I'll fill up my Jacuzzi tub with hot water and bubbles and, for a few moments, I'll pretend that I'm just a normal woman who had a one-night-stand and has a bright future filled with possibilities ahead of her, instead of a fucked-in-the-head person who needs to harm herself simply to feel alive.

I think about the smell of vanilla and lavender bubbles instead of cigarette smoke and burning flesh as I walk up to my front porch. A note taped to the front door gives me pause and I rip it from the wood, tucking it under my arm so I can unlock the front door. Once I'm inside, I toss my purse to the couch and lean back against the door, pulling the note out from under my arm and tearing it open. Finnley sent me a text earlier saying she had a surprise for me and I smile to myself, wondering what she's up to and when she resorted to leaving me notes like we were still in high school.

Inside the envelope is a small card with the words *Thinking of You!* printed amongst a bouquet of pink and purple flowers. I shake my head and laugh to myself as I flip open the card. I choke on the laugh and gasp when I see the words printed inside, the messy block lettering nothing like Finnley's girly script.

My heart starts thundering in my chest and my palms sweat. I read the words over and over until I have them memorized and still, I don't understand. Someone knows. Someone saw. How in the hell could this have happened? Is this some kind of sick joke? For a second, I wonder if DJ did it to try and be funny, but I immediately dismiss that thought. He wouldn't do this. As much as he irritates me, he's not the type of man to sink to this level of cruelty.

The note drops from my hands, fluttering to the floor at my feet. There's a *whooshing* sound in my ears that grows louder and louder until I can't even hear the ticking of the clock hanging on the wall right next to me or the sound of my ragged breaths. My skin itches and I clench my hands into fists at my sides to stop from clawing my fingernails down my arms to give myself some measure of relief. There's only one thing that will help me now, only one thing that will stop the ringing in my ears and the put an end to the tightness in my skin.

I push myself away from the front door and walk blindly through my living room and down the hall to my bedroom. My senses are overwhelmed the minute I walk in the room, the sights and sounds and smells coming back to me with a force that has my hands shaking so hard by the time I pull open the drawer of my nightstand that I drop the lighter and the package of Marlboro Smooths three times before I get them out.

I hold the cigarette between my lips, flick the lighter and stare mesmerized at the flame as I inhale enough drags to make the tip of the cigarette glow bright orange. As I exhale a lungful of smoke, I quickly strip off my hospital scrubs and underwear with one hand and let my body sink to the edge of the bed.

Closing my eyes, I bring the burning tip to my hip and breathe easy for the first time this afternoon.

I want the pain.

I deserve the pain.

I can't breathe without the pain.

4

DJ

THWACK-THWACK-THWACK.

The sound of my fists beating the shit out of the heavy bag is almost louder than the music blaring through the speakers. Nothing like a little Rob Zombie to get me even more fired up than I already am. Sweat drips down my back as I shuffle back and forth on the balls of my feet, delivering one blow after another to the bag until I feel my knuckles start to swell and my arms threaten to fall off my body.

I have no fucking idea why I'm so pissed off, no clue why I've been tossing and turning the last week and snapping at everyone I come in contact with. I thought blowing off some steam in the weight room at the station would get me back on track and calm me the fuck down, but I'm pretty sure it just made things worse. With each upper cut to the bag, I see Phina's neck and chest flushed that gorgeous color of pink after one of her orgasms. I slow down my punches to explore the memory, and then that smug bastard's face pops into my head. I see her resting against his chest, I see his hands touching her body, I hear him whispering in her ear and my fists collide so hard and fast with the bag that I'm surprised I don't break my knuckles.

"Motherfucking piece of shit!" I shout as I circle the bag and pound it with everything I've got. "Fucking asshole touching MY girl!"

That thought just pisses me off even more, and I stop where I'm at and let my arms fly. I alternate my punches with each hand, over and over until I feel the skin of my knuckles tear and still, I don't stop. I picture Dax's face in the middle of the bag and I attack it like a fucking beast, blood smearing all over the bag and my taped-up hands in the process. I shout and curse above the thumping bass and screeching guitar, wishing Dax really *was* standing in front of me right now so I could mess up his pretty fucking face. I'd break his nose, split his lip and knock out a few of those perfect white teeth for putting his hands on her.

I'm a goddamn hypocrite. She asked for something and I happily gave it to her, simply so I could have her. I didn't care about her rules, I didn't care about the consequences…I just wanted to taste her.

I've never been a jealous person. If I'm dating a chick and some guy makes a pass at her, I smile and wrap my arm around her, perfectly fine with the fact that other men find her attractive. She's going home with me and that's all that matters. I'm not even fucking *dating* Phina. One night, that's all we had. One fucking night where she set the rules and the boundaries and I did whatever she asked because I couldn't stand the thought of going one more minute without putting my hands on her. She keeps her underwear on at all times? No problem. It's weird as shit, but whatever she wants is okay by me. She's got a little voyeuristic streak and has always wanted another man in the room to watch? Perfect, I know just the guy. I can give her a shit ton of orgasms but I can't fuck her? Fine, whatever. We never speak of what happened in her bedroom ever again? Well, alrighty then, my lips are sealed.

Except when they were sucking on her clit and devouring every inch of her sweet pussy...while Dax rubbed her shoulders.

"GODDAMMIT!" I shout, throwing one last brutal punch to the middle of the bag. My heart is beating so fast and I'm breathing so hard I almost feel like I'm going to fucking pass out. Bending over at the waist, I rest my hands on my knees and try to catch my breath.

The screaming beat of *Dragula* is immediately cut off and silence fills the room. I blink the burning sweat out of my eyes and turn my head to see Collin standing next to the stereo system.

"Jesus, man. Who the hell pissed YOU off?" he chuckles as he strolls over to the heavy bag and rests his hands on it to get it to stop swaying back and forth.

I probably should've gone for a run around my neighborhood or worked out with the equipment in my garage so I wouldn't have been interrupted. My shift just ended an hour ago, and since the county ambulance transport unit where I'm currently working as a paramedic is connected to the fire station that has a state of the art gym, I figured there was no point in going home to punch my frustrations away. Judging by the look on Collin's face, I should've gotten the fuck out of Dodge. He's got that *we should talk* look written all over him. Now that he and Finnley are shacking up, he's surrounded by estrogen day in and day out and he's all about discussing his feelings and all that other bullshit.

"I'm not pissed off," I tell him. "I'm just out of shape."

Collin shakes his head at me as I push off of my knees and stand up, ripping the tape off of my swollen and bruised hands. "Nice try, asshole. You got blood all over my heavy bag. I hope you're planning on cleaning that shit up."

"Fuck off," I growl, tossing the sweaty, bloody tape into the nearest garbage can, trying not to wince when I flex my fingers.

Shit, this is really going to hurt tomorrow.

"Thanks, but no thanks. I'll stick to fucking the gorgeous woman I have waiting for me at home," he laughs.

I shake my head, walking away from him to my duffel bag I tossed on the floor by the door. Grabbing the towel resting on top, I wipe the sweat off of my face and gently blot at my knuckles. "Stop rubbing it in my face. I don't need to constantly hear about your sex life."

"Speaking of sex life, what happened the other night between you and Phina at the gallery? You ready to talk about that smack across the face she gave you? Sex is always involved when a woman is pissed enough to smack a guy," Collin says casually. He's digging for information without coming right out and asking me if I fucked her. He's a good guy like that, but I'm not about to discuss what happened with him, even if he is my best friend. He's engaged to *Phina's* best friend. If she finds out I was gossiping like a girl about what went down with us the other night, she'll have my balls.

With a sigh, I lean my back against the wall and slide down to the floor, giving my legs a break before they give out.

"That woman is fucking insane," I complain.

"And you were a perfect gentleman, I'm sure."

All right, so I might have called her a slut right before she cracked me across the face, but give me a break. One minute she was moaning and shouting my name and the next, she was pretending like she barely knew me. I had my fingers buried inside of her, my head rested between her thighs for over an hour and I could still taste her on my tongue. Phina could pretend all she wanted to, but I wasn't about to put up with that shit. I am man enough to admit that it stung a little when it was all over and she ushered me out of her house like I was a vacuum salesman and she had no use for what I was selling. I can even admit to checking my phone every hour for the next couple of days after that night, wondering why she hadn't called or sent a text. What I couldn't stand was her aloof and bitchy attitude at the gallery the other night. She looked at me like I was the dirt on her shoe and didn't even want to acknowledge what happened.

Did she even give that night a second thought, or did she just blow out the candles, toss the sheets in the washing machine and pretend like it had never happened? And if she *did* do all of that shit, why the hell couldn't I do the same? Why couldn't I just forget the sound of her voice shouting my name? She shouted MY fucking name, not Dax's. She stared at ME the entire time I made her come, not him. He was just another piece of furniture in the room and I feel like a piece of shit for letting it get to me. He was a place for her to rest her head while I licked her pussy and gave her multiple screaming orgasms. That was one of her rules that I actually didn't even question. That night wasn't about crazy, DP porn. She only wanted ME to give her pleasure and Dax to watch.

Fucking Dax.

I hate that he got to see the look on her face when she came, the way her skin flushed after each orgasm and the way her thighs started shaking right before she let go. I clench my sore fists and have to fight the urge to get my ass up off the floor and do some more damage to the fucking heavy bag.

"I feel like it's necessary that I give you a little piece of advice," Collin tells me, pulling my gaze away from the heavy bag calling my name. "Finnley will kick my ass AND your ass if you piss Phina off again. So, just be careful."

I scoff and shake my head. "I have no intentions of going anywhere near Phina again, so tell the little missus she can retract her claws."

The lie easily rolls off my tongue. Who the fuck am I kidding? One taste of Phina only made the craving worse. I thought I could get her out of my system once and for all. The girl I had a crush on in high school, the one who starred in every fantasy I beat off to during my teenage years, had turned into the hottest woman I have ever seen. Nothing like running into your high school crush years later, only to find out time had made her more beautiful than I ever remembered. Absence makes the dick grow fonder, isn't that what they say? She wanted nothing to do with me until I got a few drinks into her and she dropped her guard a little. I wanted to know why she had such an attitude, why she looked at me like she hated me, even though we'd barely said two words to each other in high school and hadn't seen each other in over fifteen years. What better way to break the ice than to play a drinking game called *What's Your Biggest Fantasy?* I was more than a little surprised that the sweet Seraphina Giordano from high school had turned into a kinky little shit who wanted one man to pleasure her while the other watched. Every man's fucking fantasy. Well, aside from having two chicks at once, but I've been there, done that and it's not as much fun as everyone thinks. One pussy at a time is more than enough, thank you very much. It took me a few months to get everything in order after the bullshit that happened between Collin, Finnley and her fucked up ex, Jordan, but I still made it happen and now she wants to ignore it.

The only thing keeping my pride from withering away and dying right now is that she treated Dax with the same indifference once it was all said and done. She told us to see ourselves out and then locked herself in the bathroom. Maybe that's why I'm feeling so on edge. I'm the one who gave her all those fucking orgasms. I'm the one who made her fantasy come true. Is a simple thank you too much to ask? Jesus Christ...

"How's it going being back on the job?" I ask, changing the subject.

Collin raises an eyebrow and stares me down. I'm a little afraid he's not going to let this shit go, but thankfully he realizes I'm in no mood to hash it out right now.

"Good. Busy as fuck. You did a great job taking over as Captain while I was on medical leave, so at least I don't have a mess to clean up. You sure you don't want to come back? I don't know if the new guy filling in for you has what it takes. He threw up in the bushes yesterday after he carried that kid out of the house with the grease fire," he explains with a roll of his eyes.

As a paramedic, I responded to the same call and was there when Eric came out of the house with the girl in his arms. I guess I missed the puking excitement while I was busy giving her oxygen and calming her crying mother down.

"Sorry, dude, you're on your own with that guy. I'm sure he'll get the hang of things with you training him. At least he didn't puke in his own fucking helmet like the transfer I had to deal with while you were out," I tell him with a laugh.

"Jesus, what the fuck is wrong with these newbies? They're going to give me an ulcer," Collin complains. "Still, you know your job is always waiting for you when you're ready."

I nod, reaching into my bag to grab the first-aid kit I always carry with me. Grabbing some disinfectant wipes from the small box, I head over to the heavy bag and start cleaning up the bloody mess I made while I talk to Collin.

"I know, and thanks for that. I just need to do something different for a while. I can't always be there to rescue your ass when you're falling out of a building."

I smile, trying to lighten the conversation, even though just thinking about it makes me want to throw up like one of the newbies. Whenever I close my eyes, I can still see Collin falling to the ground after I yanked him out of that burning house. Even though pulling him out of that second story window saved his life, I was scared as fuck that he'd never walk again after the way he landed. It's better for everyone around me right now if I take some time away from the fire station and stick with the county ambulance squad for a while. I still get to hang with Collin and the rest of the guys from my squad since our buildings are connected and we usually go out on the same calls together, depending on their seriousness. I got the best of both worlds without having a panic attack every fucking time I threw on my turnout gear.

The calls I respond to are mainly routine stuff like shortness of breath, back or leg pain, lift assists and seizures. We also get the crazies, like drunks going through withdrawal who think you'll drive them to a bar or cracked-out drug addicts who think they see a dead baby hidden under their couch cushions. You just can't make this shit up. Maybe someday I'll go back to being a fireman, but for right now, this is about all I can handle.

"All right, well I need to get the boys outside for a few training drills. Sure you don't want to join us?" Collin asks.

Tossing the dirty wipes into the trashcan, I shake my head at him. "No fucking way. I can honestly say that's one thing I don't miss about the department. You have fun carrying a hundred and fifty pound test dummy up and down a few flights of stairs. I'm going home and passing out."

We make our way out into the hallway, Collin heading for the fire truck bay and me heading for the parking lot in the back. My hand is on the door when Collin yells to me.

"Don't forget, the annual FD versus PD Fight Club is next Saturday night. From the way you were beating the shit out of that heavy bag, I'd say we're going to kick the PD's ass this year."

I shake my head as I open the door. "I told you, I'm not fighting in that thing. Let the newbies get their asses kicked. I've done my duty."

Every year, our department puts on a charity event to raise money for the local children's hospital. The city's fire department puts up their best men to go head to head in a few boxing rounds with some of the city's police department guys. Since Collin and I just moved back to this area a few months ago, it will be our first year attending the event. According to the guys at the station, the police department has kicked the shit out of the fire department every year since they started the event about ten years ago. They are certain we're going to take the title this year and even set up a little side wager with some of the cops. If we win, they have to wash all of the fire trucks. If they win, we have to do the same with their cruisers. People from the community place bets on the matches and all the money collected at the end of the night goes to the charity. It's bound to be a good time, and I was looking forward to going as a spectator, not a contender, which I've told Collin multiple times.

"Whatever. You're going to change your mind!" Collin shouts as I exit through the door and head towards my car.

There's no way I'm changing my mind. The only ass I want to beat right now belongs to Dax. Since he's some hotshot detective with the department, I'm sure it's beneath him to get his hands dirty in the boxing ring.

Once I'm home, I grab a cold pack from the freezer and kick back on the couch, resting the ice on my aching knuckles. I stare at my cell phone on the coffee table and contemplate calling Phina and apologizing for what I said to her at the gallery the other night. After a few minutes, I decide against it. The workout did nothing to take the edge off of my jealousy and anger at her attitude. If I call her now, I'll either say some other stupid shit that will piss her off even more, or I'll become the biggest pussy in the world and beg her to come over so I can finally fuck her.

It's best for my sanity if I stay as far away from Seraphina Giordano as possible right now, even if my dick disagrees.

5

Phina

"DON'T GIVE ME that look, Phina," Dax warns as he leans back against the wall in his office and crosses his arms over his chest.

For a moment, I wonder why I feel absolutely nothing when I look at this man, aside from a twinge of irritation. He's a six foot five, well-muscled, gorgeous specimen with his perfectly styled, short black hair, hazel eyes and clean-shaven face. He looks like a goddamn GQ model in his Brooks Brothers charcoal suit and matching striped tie.

Shouldn't I feel, I don't know, some embarrassment that this man has seen me partially naked and watched me have more orgasms than I can count? I take a moment to reach deep down in my subconscious and try to feel something other than a weird sort of brotherly kinship with him. That thought immediately makes me feel dirty and slightly nauseous, but there it is. He feels more like a brother to me than a potential lover. I first met Dax in high school and we hung out a few times at parties and such. Being from the same town, we ran into each other every once in a while and shared small talk. I was actually a little relieved to see DJ bring *him* to my house that night. I felt safer having another man I knew in the room instead of a stranger who would judge me. Even so, I barely said two words to him that night and after no contact for almost a week, here I am in his office at the police station, wondering why I'm not attracted to him. Even though he's getting on my last nerve with his flippant attitude about my problem, I can see us becoming real friends instead of just acquaintances. You know, friends who've seen each other partially naked.

Dax sighs, dropping his arms from his chest and shoving his hands in his pockets. The cheap florescent lighting in the room catches the detective badge attached to his belt and I stare at it for a moment before moving my eyes to the stacks of case files on his desk and the boxes on the floor filled with more files and a few knickknacks.

"Did you get fired, is that why you won't look into this?" I ask petulantly, gesturing to the boxes on the floor.

He shakes his head at me and sighs, pushing himself away from the wall. I watch as he stalks around to the front of his desk and stands a foot away from me. Why don't I feel any butterflies having him this close to me? I can smell his cologne and it's pretty nice, a little more powerful than the subtle, earthy scent DJ wears…

Dammit! Stop thinking about DJ!

"For the last time, Phina, I didn't say I *won't* look into this. I said I can't right now."

I roll my eyes, digging the fingers of my right hand a little deeper into the fresh burn on my hip, letting the sting of pain calm my racing heart. I stand toe-to-toe with Dax with my hands on my hips, studying his eyes to see if I can sense that he's lying.

"I was just assigned as lead detective on a very high profile case in the next county over. I still need to go over all of my current case files with the guy taking my place AND get up to speed on the new case before I hit the ground running tomorrow. I understand why you're upset, but really, this could be about anything," he states, reaching behind him to grab the note I threw on his desk when walked into his office.

He brings the notecard in front of him and flips it open, scanning the words one more time before extending it for me to take.

I take a step back, shaking my head from side-to-side. "I am not touching that thing again. And don't tell me that note could be about anything. You know damn well it's not."

Three's a crowd, don't you think?
Whores always get what's coming to them.

I can see the bold words printed on the card like they're flashing in neon lights, still riddled with the anxiety that's plagued me since I found it taped to my door last night. Dax was a little offended when I first walked in here and threw the note at him. I might have implied that he had something to do with it, even though I didn't really believe it. I *wanted* to believe it, because the alternative didn't leave me feeling warm and fuzzy.

"Look, I think you just need to take a breath and calm down."

My face heats with anger and I rethink the notion that I could be friends with him. Has man really not evolved enough over the years to learn that you never, ever tell a woman to calm down?

"Don't tell me to calm down, Dax. Someone left a note on my door talking about a threesome that only you, me and one other person had any knowledge of. You don't find that the least bit concerning?" I argue.

"Answer me this," Dax speaks softly, cocking his head to the side. "Did you go charging into DJ's place of employment with the same accusations?"

My mouth opens and closes and I stutter a few unintelligible words. I told myself on the way over here that going to Dax was the obvious solution because he's a detective. It's his job to find answers to things.

When I'm unable to come up with a satisfactory response to Dax's question, I realize the real reason I didn't go to DJ first is because I fear what will happen when we're in the same room together. After the other night at the gallery, it's clear what DJ thinks of me. It's exactly what I wanted him to believe…and I hate it. I hate *myself* even more because of it. I'm not a confused person by nature. I know what I want and I go for it. If things don't turn out exactly how I planned, fuck it, there's always another day to plot and plan. Thoughts of DJ and the way my body responds to his touch and the craving I feel deep down in the pit of my stomach have turned me into a bigger bitch than normal. I want to see him again. I want to touch him again. And I fucking hate that I want all of these things that I have no business craving.

This is the conundrum my life has become in the span of a few weeks, and it's seriously pissing me off.

"That's what I thought," Dax responds to my non-answer with a chuckle.

He moves back around behind his desk and flops down in his chair, clasping his hands behind his head casually. "Did you ever think it might have just been a neighbor's kid playing a prank?"

I roll my eyes. "My neighbor's son is six. I highly doubt they've covered the word 'whore' in his weekly spelling tests just yet."

There's a knock on the door and I glance over my shoulder to see the dispatch officer who showed me to Dax's office stick her head inside.

"Captain wanted me to make sure you're still coming to McCallahan's tonight, Dax."

She says his name all soft and breathy and I watch her lick her lips as she blatantly stares wide-eyed at the man behind me.

"Dollar drafts and he's already started a pool that he's going to kick your ass at darts," she says with a giggle.

Dax laughs right along with her and I turn back around to watch him lean forward to rest his elbows on his desk, giving her a wink.

"Wouldn't miss it, Marcie. Seven o'clock?"

Her cheeks blush a deep shade of red, and it takes everything in me not to roll my eyes at what's happening right in front of me. A strong, confident woman in uniform who probably had to bust her ass twice as hard as every guy around her turned into a tittering twit the moment Dax showed her a little attention.

"Yep, seven. First round is on me," she states with a smile and another pathetic giggle before pulling her head back through the opening and closing the door behind her.

I turn back to face Dax and raise an irritated eyebrow at him. "Drafts and darts, huh? Yes, you sound completely SWAMPED with the new job. Also, if you keep banging the women you work with, one of these days you're going to get your balls shot off."

Dax just laughs.

"First of all, the department is throwing a going-away party for me. It's not like the guest of honor can just be a no-show. And second, I'll have you know Marcie was very understanding about our one night together after I explained I was just under too much pressure at work to concentrate seriously on a wonderful woman such as herself. The same with Stacey, Amber, Johanna and Diane," he counts on his fingers, naming all of the women I passed as I made my way through the department to his office.

"Jesus, maybe that note *isn't* about me. It's someone from your harem come to collect some payback," I mutter.

"Hey, I make my intentions perfectly clear before any clothing is shed and orgasms are exchanged. You might want to try doing that sometime," he chastises.

"I have no idea what you're talking about," I scoff.

"Riiiight and DJ, a pretty good friend of mine, or so I thought, didn't threaten to rip off all of my appendages one by one if I so much as *looked* at you again while he and I walked out to our cars the other night.

Someone in this situation doesn't seem to be on the same page, and it sure as hell isn't me."

The fact that DJ actually said something to Dax when they left my house comes as a surprise. I mean, I could see a touch of jealousy in his eyes and in some of his mannerisms the other night, but I just chalked it up to being a new experience for everyone. I thought maybe he wasn't as comfortable with the situation as he initially indicated, but DJ does strike me as someone who doesn't share his toys very well. It should bolster my spirits that he didn't like what happened between us. He didn't appreciate being made to feel like he wasn't special and it was a shot to his ego that he couldn't have me all to himself. I should be on cloud nine right now, gleeful that he got the payback he so richly deserved after leaving my heart shattered in a thousand pieces in high school.

Knowing he was jealous and fought with his friend doesn't make me feel vindicated, however; it makes me feel like the slut he accused me of being. Fifteen years ago, I dreamed of him looking at me the way he did the other night – like I was his entire world and nothing else mattered but pleasing me, nothing else existed but the two of us. A part of me is glad that he hadn't behaved that way all those years ago or I wouldn't have survived the aftermath of what he did to me. Knowing he never loved me, never cared for me, never even remembered what the fuck happened the next morning fueled the anger instead of the depression. It gave me a goal: to one day teach him a lesson, to make him pay for the shit he pulled on me back then. The plan was to give him a taste of his own medicine so that I'd be the one walking away this time.

I should be happy that he thinks I'm a slut and a bitch. I should be able to just hold my head high and walk away, confident that he finally got what he deserved.

Unfortunately, my head is filled with the knowledge that not only is he jealous that another man had his hands on me, he's stable and hard working and fucking saves people's lives for a living. I should have never allowed him back into my life. I poison everything I touch and I know he'll be no different. Why can't I just be happy that I could potentially fuck up his life the way he did mine?

I need to stay away from him and he needs to stay away from me. No man will ever be able to understand what goes on in my head or why I do the things I do, certainly never someone like DJ. Why the hell couldn't I just be attracted to Dax? He's a manwhore who's just in it for the sex. We could have spent a few weeks scratching mutual itches and then went our separate ways without any ruins left behind. Life would be so much easier if I wanted the bad guy instead of the good one.

"Look, if it will make you feel any better, before I leave I'll make some inquiries, find out if anyone else got any fun little notes on their front porches lately. While I'm doing that, you might want to make a list of all the people you've pissed off recently. Take your time, I'm sure it won't be easy to remember all of those names," he jokes.

"Oh, kiss my ass," I fire back as I turn towards the door.

"Not on your life, sweetheart. I like my appendages right where they are, thank you very much. If DJ happens to catch wind that you were here, please do me the favor of calling me so I can at least get a head start."

"Stop being so dramatic. DJ couldn't care less about what I do or who I talk to," I tell him as I pull open the door.

"Uh-huh, sure. And I'm not planning on getting laid tonight," he laughs.

Without turning around, I raise my hand and shoot him the middle finger as the door closes behind me. His laughter follows me all the way down the hall as I make my way out of the building.

6

DJ

LEANING AGAINST THE kitchen counter at the station, I calmly bring my coffee cup up to my mouth, listening to the familiar, ear-piercing page from dispatch that echoes through the building. Glancing down at my watch, I count down the seconds to myself.

Five, four, three, two...

The pounding of footsteps bangs through the sleeping quarters and I take another drink of my hot coffee as our newest paramedic comes racing into the kitchen with a frantic look on his face. His hair is all askew from being woken up so early, his white uniform shirt is partially untucked and buttoned wrong and he's hopping up and down on one foot as he hurriedly tries to tie the laces of his black work boots.

"What's the emergency? Where are we going? Is the truck stocked? Shit! Did I remember to stock everything last night and charge the equipment? FUCK! Why are you so calm?!" Brad shouts at me.

I shake my head at the newbie, setting my cup down on the counter. "Brad, that was the test page from dispatch. They send it out every morning at 7 am to wake us up. How many times do we have to listen to the different sounds the paging system makes before you remember what an actual emergency sounds like?"

I probably could have warned the guy last night before he went to bed since it was his first time sleeping here at the station, but it's much more fun to wake up before everyone else and watch the newbie freak the fuck out.

I send Brad out to the ambulance bay to have him get started checking into what supplies and equipment were used during the last shift so he can restock and make sure all the equipment is charged and in working order. Going through the mental checklist in my head while I finish my coffee, I figure I have about forty-five minutes before our captain shows up. I need to meet with him and find out if we're doing any special activities or training today and then take possession of the controlled substances carried by the ambulance from the last shift, inspect the narcotics and sign the narcotics log. I head down the hall past the sleeping quarters, listening to the men from last night's shift go through their morning routines, joking and laughing about how they encouraged Brad to move his ass because the morning alarm page clearly meant a full-scale emergency.

Taking a seat in the common room at the desk, I check my email and print off a few updates to SOPs and guidelines that will require some meetings with the staff. Hopefully, today is a quiet day in the county so I can get all this shit done. An email at the bottom of my inbox from an address I don't recognize catches my eye. The subject line simply states 'Emergency.' I click on the email and huff in confusion and disbelief at what I'm reading.

Did you have fun passing that whore around with your friend? Enjoy it while you can. Your time is almost up.

I read the email three more times before I whip my head around and search the room, expecting to find some of the guys standing there, laughing their asses off at the prank they pulled on me. Obviously, that's an asinine thought since I never breathed a word about what happened between me, Phina and Dax to anyone. Who in the fuck would send an email like this to me? Did Phina tell someone? Did Dax?

Slamming my fist down on the desk, I pay no attention to the cup of pens that spills or the stack of papers on the edge that flutter to the floor. I'm so pissed off I want to pick something up and throw it across the room, but I don't need the guys coming in here asking me what the hell is wrong. *"Oh, no big deal. I had sort of a threesome the other night and now it seems like someone found out about it and sent me a fucked up email. So, who wants to make breakfast?"*

"Jesus, you're a hard man to get ahold of."

Turning in my chair, I see Dax lounging casually against the door-frame. Fuck. First Collin sneaks up on me in the gym and now Dax. Why is everyone insisting on getting on my last fucking nerve lately?

"Not if I actually *want* someone to get ahold of me. Go away. I've got work to do," I tell him, turning back around to the computer to see if I can figure out who the email came from.

"You don't call, you don't write...are you breaking up with me?" Dax asks.

"Fuck off, dickhead," I mutter, clicking angrily at the keys on the computer.

I hear him move into the room and I growl deep in my throat.

"Now, now, don't be like that. I will have you know that I've taken your threat from the other night very seriously. I haven't touched Phina at all," he tells me, flopping down into the chair next to the desk.

I glare at him, and then the door, hoping he'll get the hint and leave.

"It's not my fault she came to see me and I had to talk to her. And look at her. It would have been rude to close my eyes and pretend I was mute," Dax explains, picking up a piece of paper from the floor and reading it over.

I snatch it out of his hand and slam it on top of the desk with a little more force than I meant to.

She went to see him? She talked to him? Goddammit all to hell!

Dax picks up a pen to examine and I grab that out of his hand, as well. "Stop touching my shit!"

He laughs and shakes his head at me. "Yeah, I already got that message, buddy. Loud and clear."

Pushing myself away from the desk, I get up out of the chair and stalk to the other side of the room. If I don't move away from Dax and his smirk I'm going to shove my fist through his face. This is an ambulance transport unit, though. Any damage I inflict could be easily fixed. While I think about the merits of messing up his pretty face and whether we have enough gauze in the supply room to clean up the mess, I hear the squeak of Dax's chair as he swivels it around to face me.

"She found a note taped to her front door yesterday. You wouldn't by any chance know anything about that, would you?" he questions with a raise of his eyebrows.

"I'm pretty sure she isn't the flowers and love notes type of girl, and I'm smart enough to realize that. So no, I didn't leave any notes on her doorstep."

Dax shakes his head, clasping his hands together on top of his stomach. "Not a love note, man. This one pretty much hinted that they knew about what happened at Phina's place the other night. The word 'whore' might have been used, as well."

My hands shake and my blood boils thinking about Phina coming home alone to find a note like that on her door, not to mention the fact that she went running to Dax about it. Fucking Dax with his three-piece suits and fucking product in his hair to make sure not one piece is out of place. When I got Phina to admit that her number one fantasy was being with one man while another watched, I immediately thought of

Dax. We'd met in high school and ran in the same crowd back then. As adults, we kept in touch over the years and when I moved back to town, we hung out every once in a while when our schedules permitted. He was a decent guy, definitely not the type to settle down or stick with one woman for more than a night. He got more pussy on a weekly basis than a damn whorehouse. He appeared to be the perfect choice for the third wheel in Phina's fantasy, especially since she knew him and it wouldn't be like I was letting a total stranger walk into her house to watch her have a few mind-blowing orgasms. I could finally get a taste of the woman I'd wanted for longer than I could remember and I didn't have to worry about the guy getting attached or taking her focus off of me. I never anticipated feeling so much rage and jealousy at having to share her. I hated seeing his hands on her and listening to him whispering words of encouragement in her ear. It didn't matter that I was the one to feel her come against my mouth every time, it didn't matter that she called *my* name over and over. All that mattered was someone else getting to witness all of that when it should have just been me.

Bringing my thoughts back to the matter at hand, I have a thousand questions I want to ask Dax about the note Phina received, but I keep my mouth shut. I'm finished sharing shit with this asshole. I don't like the fact that I just received an email with similar wording in it from someone I didn't know. Someone knows about what went down the other night, and I'm going to find out who the fuck it is. I don't give a shit if Dax is a detective and makes his living getting to the bottom of mysteries. I can and will handle this on my own and he can just go fuck himself. If anything, it will give me a reason to see Phina again, to try to get on her good side after fucking things up at the gallery.

The piercing sound of the emergency alarm on the paging system rings through the building. A few seconds later, the static voice of dispatch comes through the speakers, giving the details of a car accident on the outskirts of town with two individuals in critical condition.

I don't bother saying a word to Dax, I just turn and head for the door.

"Tell Phina I said hello!" Dax shouts in a chipper voice as I make my way out into the hallway.

I refrain from giving him the finger and calling him every damn name I can think of since my co-workers are currently rushing down the hall with me towards the ambulance bay.

Fucking Dax.

AFTER TRANSPORTING THE two injured parties from the car accident to the emergency room and then explaining several times to the doctor on call why we did certain things out at the scene, I'm exhausted and irritated as I make my way down the hall of the hospital. You would think being at the scene of an accident with life-threatening injuries would be the most stressful part of my job, but it isn't. Explaining yourself to a medical resident with a stick up his ass and arguing about the procedures we conducted that he doesn't agree with when he wasn't even fucking there is the most stressful.

I walk quickly with my head down, making notes on my clipboard for Brad to transfer to our computer system as soon as we get back to the station. I'm not looking where I'm going and so preoccupied that my shoulder slams into someone. I turn around and glance up to throw out a quick apology and stop in my tracks.

Phina stands in front of me in pale blue scrubs with her hands on her hips. Her long red hair is pulled up into a ponytail and her green eyes bore into me with annoyance.

"Next time, watch where you're going," she mutters, turning away from me.

I lunge forward, wrapping my hand around her arm and pulling her back towards me. Her body slams into mine, her hands pressing against my chest to hold herself steady. My nose is instantly assaulted with the smell of her shampoo and the spicy perfume that is distinctly Phina. I couldn't stop my dick from hardening if my life depended on it. I'm still pissed she went to Dax about the note instead of me, and I don't know whether to argue with her or shove her into the nearest empty room and beg her to let me fuck her. I'm pissed that I want this woman so much when she clearly wants nothing to do with me. The disgust is evident on her face and I briefly wonder if she looked at Dax the same way when she went to see him. I'm sure she didn't. She probably flirted with him and turned on the charm, giving him one of those rare smiles that I would kill to have aimed at me. My anger multiplies when I think about her laughing at something he said or being as close to him as she is to me right now. I should be asking her about the damn note she received, but all I want to do is make her pay for the jealousy roaring through me.

"Get your hands off me," she mutters through clenched teeth.

I didn't even realize I'd wrapped my arm around her and pulled her closer to me. I clench my fist into her scrub top at her lower back and hold onto her tighter.

"What's wrong, Fireball? I'm sure you let Dax put his hands on you when you went to see him today. I'm not good enough to get the same benefits?" I ask softly, trying to keep my anger in check.

Her eyes widen when I mention her little visit with Dax. I'm guessing she didn't want me to know she saw him today. I wonder why that is? Because she's guilty of doing exactly what I suggested and letting him touch her?

"What I do or who I see is none of your fucking business," she growls, trying to pull out of my arms.

Bringing my free hand up, I rest my palm on her collarbone before sliding it up and around the side of her neck, pulling her face close to mine. I run my lips along her cheek until I get to her ear, holding my mouth against her earlobe while I speak softly.

"It's my fucking business when I've had my face buried between your thighs and can still taste you on my tongue."

I feel her shiver in my arms and I smile against her ear, happy about the fact that at least I have *some* affect on her.

"Next time you have a problem, you come to ME," I continue.

She instantly starts struggling again and I loosen my hold, letting her push back from me so I can see her face.

"The only problem I have right now is *you*," she complains angrily.

I smile down at her. "That makes two of us, Fireball."

Forgetting about how pissed I am at my reaction to her and the fact that we're in the hallway of a crowded hospital, I quickly dip my head and crush my lips to hers.

7

Phina

MY MOUTH OPENS on a gasp as soon as DJ's lips press against mine and he takes full advantage, his tongue connecting with mine and sliding slowly against it. I hear a foreign sound in the back of my mind and realize it's me, moaning into this kiss. He uses his hand against the side of my neck to hold me in place, his lips pressing firmer and tongue sliding deeper as he prolongs the kiss. My hands clutch to his navy blue uniform shirt instead of pushing him away. Why the fuck am I not pushing him away? We haven't kissed since the night at the bar over four months ago when I told him about my fantasy. He wanted to seal the deal and the tequila I'd consumed deluded me into believing that was a stellar idea. The kiss that night is fuzzy in my brain; I recall the taste of whiskey on his tongue and not much else. Now I remember why I wouldn't let him kiss me that night in my bedroom. Even though I was drunk the last time we'd kissed, a part of me realized what would happen if I allowed it to happen again – I would lose all ability to think rationally.

It was hard enough to keep up the bitch façade when he slammed into me and I got my first good look at him in days. His muscles filled out his short-sleeved button-down shirt better than any man I'd ever seen, his biceps flexing as he stared me down with those crystal clear blue eyes. With my height, most men aren't that much taller than me, but in my tennis shoes, DJ towers over me and makes me feel small and delicate. The way his arm tightens around me, keeping me firmly restrained against his chest, proves that at least he doesn't *think* I'm a delicate fucking flower.

Without thinking, I suck his tongue into my mouth and feel the vibrations of his own moan against my lips. My sex pulses and I feel myself getting wet, remembering what it was like to feel these same soft lips and talented tongue sliding through my folds and licking my clit.

The busy sounds of the hospital fade into the distance as DJ's arm pulls me up and against him so tightly that my feet almost leave the ground. The position puts me on my tiptoes and I immediately feel his erection pressing into me. The rhythm of his tongue repeatedly rubbing against my own lulls me into a haze of desire so strong that I completely forget about the patient whose blood I was supposed to draw and the hospital staff running back and forth about fifty yards away at the intersection of the hallway we're standing in. Any one of them could look this way and see what I'm doing and I can't bring myself to care. I want him to push me against the wall behind me so hard that it bruises my back. I want him to rip my scrubs from my body so roughly that they shred into a hundred pieces. I want to pull his hard cock out of his pants and run my hands up and down his length until he has no choice but to bury himself inside me, pounding between my thighs until I ache from the force of his thrusts. For once in my life, I think I could breathe easily with the pain he could give me instead of the kind I give myself.

His arm is so long and it's wrapped so tightly around my waist that his fingertips skim my hip all the way on the other side. I moan again into his mouth, this time from pain instead of pleasure. His fingertips dig into the fresh burn on my hip and instead of bringing me a sense of relief like it normally does, I feel a shiver of apprehension run through me, like someone dumped a bucket of ice water all over my body. Not only are we in a very public location *and* my place of employment, if I allow myself to continue down this path, he'll feel my scars...he'll *see* my scars. No one is allowed to see the damage I inflict on myself. It's why I wouldn't allow DJ to remove my underwear the other night, no matter how much he protested. He'll never be able to adhere to my demands a second time, so sex with this man cannot happen. He'll question me and he'll argue and push until there's nothing left for me to do but show him what I've truly become.

I smack my hands against his hard chest, pushing with every ounce of strength I have in my arms. He tears his mouth away from mine as I stumble backwards, pressing my fingers to my swollen lips.

"Phina," he whispers, moving towards me.

I hold my palm up in front of him and take a few steps back, putting some more distance between us.

"Don't *ever* do that again," I threaten as I slow my breathing and lift my chin in show of defiance that I don't feel.

I feel like a puppy that's been kicked; like I'm standing outside of my body, watching myself curl up into a ball waiting for another blow. I hate feeling so weak. I hate that this man makes me ashamed of who I am and what I've become. He was one of the catalysts that set me on this path to destruction, pushing me deeper into my addiction after what happened between us in high school, but I will never allow him to see how much his actions affected me. I will not give him that power.

"We had our fun, and now it's over. If you're expecting tit for tat and think you deserve an orgasm because you went home with blue balls the other night, that's not my problem. Go home and jerk off," I tell him angrily as I turn and walk away.

Once again, he grabs onto my arm and pulls me back against him.

"Oh, don't even try to pull that bullshit with me now," he mutters lowly as he stares down at my lips. "You want me. It may not be as obvious as my cock pressing into your stomach right now, but it's there. If I slid my hand inside those scrubs, I'll find your pussy wet and ready for me. Nice try, Fireball."

I scoff at his words and feign indignation, even though hearing him speak like that intensifies the throbbing between my legs. I push away from him again, crossing my arms in front of me to stop myself from grabbing onto him and refusing to let go until he makes good on his threat and slides his fingers inside me.

"Fine, have it your way," he chuckles. "We'll pretend like you don't want me and I'll pretend like you going to fucking Dax about the note someone left you on your porch instead of me doesn't make me want to punch my fist through the wall."

I roll my eyes at the idea of him doing something so childish. "In case you forgot, Dax is a detective. Obviously, I would take something like this to him instead of you. It doesn't concern you, anyway."

Dax and I will most definitely be having a few words about him letting the cat out of the bag to DJ. And to think, I actually let him make me believe he was afraid of DJ kicking his ass. Stupid man and his stupid smirk turning me into an idiot.

"The fuck it doesn't!" he argues loudly, glancing around us quickly before lowering his voice. "You're not the only one who got a strange note about our night together."

My mouth drops open in shock and fear ripples through me. It was stupid of me to go to Dax when I knew damn well who was most likely responsible for that fucking note. There is only one person in my life that would stoop to something so disgusting and pathetic. The fact that he's been behind bars for the last fifteen years doesn't even matter. He had plenty of loser friends back then, lowlife scum I'm sure he's kept in contact with and would still jump to do his bidding. All these years of declining his collect calls and putting his letters right into the shredder without opening them or responding must have finally pushed him over the edge. Even from prison, he's still trying to tell me I'm worthless and don't deserve anything good in my life. Staring up at DJ now, knowing that his association with me put him on that man's radar, makes me feel sick.

The past doesn't matter. Getting revenge doesn't matter. Nothing matters but putting a stop to this before it escalates and DJ is caught in the crossfire.

"This is because of *me*. It's my problem and I'll handle it," I tell him, biting down on my tongue hard enough to make it bleed so that I don't throw myself in his arms and allow someone else to take care of me for once.

"You know who's doing this, don't you?"

I refuse to answer and he wraps his hands around my upper arms, bending his knees to bring himself eye level with me.

"Answer me, Phina. If you know who did this, tell me. I'll take care of the sick son of a bitch."

I shake my head back and forth and jerk out of his grasp. "You have no idea what you're talking about or who you're dealing with. Just leave it alone and go away. I got what I wanted from you, and now I'm finished. Fuck. Off."

He finally lets me go as I turn away and rush down the hall.

"This isn't finished, Fireball!" DJ yells to my back.

I ignore him and the urge to run back into his arms as I turn the corner, pulling my cell phone out of my pocket as I go. Dialing the number to the county corrections unit that I have saved in my contacts under *Never Fucking Answer*, I ask to be put through to the warden immediately as soon as someone picks up.

While I wait, I cross my fingers, silently praying that he hasn't been released. There's no way they could release him without notifying me first. After all, it was my testimony that sent my father to prison fifteen years ago. They would have to tell me if that monster made parole. I would be the first person on his list to visit, demanding retribution for ruining his life yet again.

8

DJ

"TELL ME EVERYTHING you know about Phina's life since high school."

Collin freezes, his bottle of beer hovering right by his mouth. He quickly brings it down and looks over his shoulder before glaring at me.

"Will you keep it down? Finnley is right in the next room. If she hears that you're trying to get me to give you the scoop on her best friend, she'll castrate both of us."

I sigh, leaning back into the couch cushions and shake my head at him. "Quit being so fucking pussy whipped for five seconds and tell me what you know about her."

Collin huffs. "Why the sudden interest in her? I thought you said she was crazy and you didn't want anything to do with her."

He leans forward and glares even harder at me. "DJ, what did you do?"

"Of, fuck off. I didn't do anything." *Much.* "You know, running into her again just made me wonder what she's been up to."

Jesus, the lies roll right off my tongue these days.

"She's a phlebotomist manager at the hospital. Works a lot of overtime, that's about all I know," Collin finally tells me, still looking at me with a suspicious stare.

"Yeah, I bumped into her at the hospital the other night when I had a patient transport. That's not what I meant, though. I mean, like, does she have any family? Is she seeing anyone?"

Collin laughs, bringing the bottle of beer back up to his mouth and finishing it off. "She'll never date you."

I lean forward, resting my elbows on my knees. "Excuse me, asshole. You just got done telling me you don't know that much about her and now you're the expert on her love life?"

"Phina doesn't have a love life, she has a sex life. From what little Finnley's told me, it's pretty active and doesn't have anything to do with love. You know, now that I think about it, you two would be perfect together. You both have an aversion to settling down."

I shake my head at him in irritation. You make one comment about how it's unnatural for someone to settle down with one person for the rest of his life, and suddenly you have a permanent label.

"Who knows, maybe I'm changing my mind in my old age. It worked for you. Maybe I just haven't meant the right woman," I tell him with a nonchalant shrug.

Or maybe I've met the woman and she's hell bent on denying that there's something between us.

"You are the worst fucking liar in the world. I think we should change Fight Night to Poker Night. I could take all of your money with that shitty poker face of yours," Collin laughs.

"Dinner's almost ready," Finnley announces as she walks into the living room and sits down on the couch next to Collin, curling up against his side. "What are you guys talking about?"

Collin raises his eyebrow at me and I try to subtly shake my head so he'll keep his mouth shut. Finnley looks back and forth between us, not missing a thing.

"Alright, what's going on with you two?"

Collin wraps his arm around her shoulder and pulls her closer. "Our friend here was just asking about Phina."

"She won't date you," Finnley states flatly.

"Jesus Christ, what is it with you two?" I grumble. "I never said anything about dating her. I just wanted to know more about her. I haven't seen her in fifteen years, I just wondered what her deal is."

Finnley narrows her eyes at me and for a minute I seriously consider covering my balls. She's one of the sweetest women I've ever met and I'm glad my best friend found her again. She also went through some tough shit with her estranged husband and, with the help of Collin, she was able to find her backbone and turn into quite the little firecracker.

"Maybe if you didn't have selective memory loss you might remember what her *deal* is," Finnley says sarcastically.

"What the hell does that even mean?"

She huffs and leans forward, mirroring my pose with her elbows on her knees. "If you can't remember, then I'm not going to tell you. Besides, it's not my story to tell."

"What the hell is she talking about?" I ask Collin.

He shrugs. "I have no idea. Finn, what are you talking about?"

She rolls her eyes, but doesn't take them off of me when she speaks. "I swear, the two of you must have shared a brain back in high school."

I rack my mind, trying to think of what I could have possibly done to her all those years ago to justify her animosity, but I'm drawing a blank. Anyway, who the fuck holds onto something that happened when they were teenagers? Jesus, get over it already. I remember having a stupid ass crush on Phina and her barely acknowledging me, and then we graduated and I never saw her again.

"Ask me a different question. One I might be able to answer," she adds.

I think about the email I got and the note Phina received and how she seemed to know who it might have come from but shut down when I tried to get more information out of her.

"Okay, here's a question. Has she pissed anyone off in the last fifteen years? Someone who might want to fuck with her?"

I watch as Finnley's expression goes from irritation to worry as she bites her bottom lip. "What are you talking about? Did something happen?"

I didn't come here with the intention of freaking Finnley out or telling her about what happened with Phina, but obviously Phina isn't even confiding in her best friend about it and I don't like that one bit.

"Someone left a note on her door the other night. It wasn't signed and let's just say it didn't have the nicest words written on it. She went to a mutual detective friend of ours to have him look into it and he let me know about it," I explain, trying not to growl the word *friend*. "I got a similar email from an anonymous person and when I confronted her about it at the hospital the other night, I could tell that she knew who it might be, but she wouldn't admit it."

Finnley looks back at Collin. "It can't be him, can it? I mean, she'd know if they let him out, right?"

Collin rubs her shoulder comfortingly and nods his head. "Yeah, they would be obligated to send her a letter informing her of his parole since she testified. She hasn't said anything to you about it?"

Finnley shakes her head.

"What is going on? Who are you talking about?" I ask, my worry growing tenfold at the mention of parole.

Finnley turns back to me and I watch her throat constrict as she swallows nervously a few times. "Why would both of you get similar notes? You guys have only seen each other that one night at the bar a few months ago and then at the gallery."

Deciding now isn't really the best time to inform Phina's best friend about her proclivity to threesomes and how I practically fucked her in the middle of the hospital, I change the subject.

"Not important. The fact is, someone isn't happy with her and now I've been pulled into it. Tell me what you know."

Finnley runs her hand through her hair and takes a deep breath before letting it out slowly. "She didn't have the best childhood. Her mother left when she was little and her father blamed Phina for it. I don't know everything, she's not exactly forthcoming with that information, but I know it was bad. There were times in high school when she would just shut down for days at a time. She wouldn't eat, she wouldn't speak, she just…existed. And then, she'd snap out of it and pretend like nothing was wrong. Her dad owned his own garage in town, but towards the middle of our senior year, it was starting to go under. He was drinking a lot, not showing up for work, arguing with customers, that sort of thing. All of a sudden, right before graduation, he came into a bunch of money. He flaunted it in front of Phina and told her she'd never see a dime of it."

Finnley pauses to collect herself and I take the time to try once again and think back to high school. Phina was smart, beautiful and had just enough of an attitude that no one ever fucked with her. She was in the same popular, jock group that Collin and I hung around with and I never once witnessed the kind of sadness or shutting down that Finnley spoke of. Maybe I just didn't notice. I was a hormonal teenager. My small head was so occupied with trying to get in her pants that nothing else mattered at the time.

"Phina left that big party at Tony Calloway's house around seven in the morning the day after graduation," Finnley continues, pausing to shoot a glare at me when she mentions Tony's party. Before I can question it, she continues.

"She snuck into the house and as soon as the door closed behind her, she heard a gunshot from her father's bedroom. She ran back there and found him standing over a body with a gun in his hand. When he saw her standing there, he chased after her. Thank God she was on the track team. She made it to the neighbor's house and called the police. Turns out, he borrowed money from a loan shark. When he didn't pay it back on time, the guy came to the house. Her dad walked him back to the bedroom telling him he had to get the money out of his dresser and then shot him in the head instead. Phina testified against him in court and he got twenty-five years to life with a possibility of parole in fifteen."

Finnley stops talking and the room is dead silent.

"Jesus Christ," I mutter. "That means he's up for parole this year."

Finnley nods. "Why the hell didn't she tell me about the note?"

"She probably just didn't want to worry you for nothing," Collin reassures her. "There's no way that bastard is out of prison. It has to be someone else."

It could be, but the possibility of that is slim to none. As much as I hate having to go to him, I know I need to share this information with Dax. If her father is out on parole and Phina doesn't know, this could get really ugly, really fast.

"I'm going to call Phina," Finnley announces, pushing herself up from the couch. "I can't believe she didn't tell me about this."

Speaking of getting ugly really fast...

9

Phina

MOST PEOPLE CAN close their eyes and pinpoint a certain memory from their childhood where they felt safe and loved. With the melody of an old song or a particular smell that reminds them of being young and cared for, they can picture it perfectly in their mind. The soft press of their mother's lips on their forehead as she kissed them goodnight after a bedtime story or the scratch of their father's beard as he blew raspberries on their stomach to make them laugh. I stole these specific memories from Finnley when we were in college and had a night of bonding. I told her about the time my mother brought home a Happy Meal from McDonald's as a way to apologize for not being around that much recently and how my father picked up the red and yellow cardboard box, tossed it into the sink and then lit it on fire with his Zippo. Finnley wrapped her arms around me and told me I could keep any of her memories I wanted and use them as my own, so that's what I do from time to time when I'm feeling unusually sorry for myself.

Everywhere I look today I see smiling, happy families wandering through the park. I volunteer to spearhead the blood drive booth for every function the hospital sponsors and I tell myself that it's all for the cause, but I do it for entirely selfish reasons. I like to torture myself by staring at all the families meandering about and wonder why I wasn't blessed enough to have something like that. Why couldn't I have a mother who ran her fingers through my hair and kissed the top of my head as I looked at a craft table? Why didn't my father ever tickle me until I screamed with joy and then lift me up onto his shoulders so I could get a better view of the activities?

Why the hell wasn't I good enough for a life like that?

Today is the annual town festival to benefit the children's wing of the hospital. During the day, there is a fair set up in the park with tons of booths, including blood and platelet donation mobiles, and tonight is the fireman versus policeman Fight Night. It's a great event that always brings in crowds of people and it's the one part of my job I actually look forward to doing. Today, however, I feel like there is a black cloud of doom hovering over me. My calls to the warden at the prison were never returned, but after a few days, it didn't even matter. A certified letter came to my house yesterday informing me that inmate number 45089 qualified for parole and if I have any questions, I should contact his parole officer.

The anticipation of waiting for my father to show up in my life has put me on edge. The cloak and dagger bullshit with the notes is bad enough. He needs to just show his face already so I can tell him to go to hell where he belongs. I'm not the same little girl he pushed around and threatened. I knew he wouldn't stay behind bars forever. The random reports I received from the prison told me he was a model prisoner, never getting into fights and even offering to mentor new men. He put on a great show, I'll give him that. He might have been able to fool the guards and the parole board into thinking he's changed, but he'll never fool me.

At least working the blood drive keeps me from putting any more marks on my body for the time being. The searing pain in my heart while I stand here wishing for something I never had hurts more than any burn on my skin.

"We're good here if you want to take a break," Suzy informs me as she finishes with a donor, placing a Band-Aid on their arm and pointing them outside towards the juice and cookie table.

"I think I'm going to head over to the platelet donation truck. It's been about a year since I last donated," I tell her, grabbing my cell phone from one of the upper cabinets in the donation truck. "I should only be about an hour. If you need me, just give me a call."

The donation trucks are parked right next to each other by the curb with a couple tables filled with pamphlets and other donation information separating them. A few yards away from the trucks, I see a man squatting down, speaking to a little girl. He leans in to kiss her cheek and I let the pain of seeing the kind of affection I've never experienced wrap around me and fill me with determination: to keep moving, one foot in front of the other, to keep the walls up around my heart so no one has the power to hurt me ever again and to never, ever need someone to take care of me. I won't let myself think of the kiss DJ and I shared at the hospital and how badly I wanted to just confide in him and let him take care of my problems. Too bad he's the root of half of them.

As I continue to stare as I walk, the man looks up and our eyes meet. I stop where I'm at and don't realize I'm smiling until he his face lights up and he quickly stands.

"Phina! I wondered if I'd see you here."

Jackson Castillo was a boy I dated briefly in college who turned out to be quite a nice-looking man. He only had two marks against him – he was entirely too nice and he was Finnley's loser husband's cousin. At the time we dated, the whole cousin thing wasn't really a bad thing. Finnley set us up and I actually let her fantasize for a few months about us marrying cousins, living next to each other and living happily ever after. In the end, I couldn't handle all that nice. No matter what I did or said to him, he kept coming back for more. It was like kicking a fucking puppy. He always apologized even if I was wrong and he was just too...sweet. I couldn't handle all that good in my life. It made me feel twice as horrible about the kind of person I was, and every time he gave me a compliment, I wanted to scream and claw at my face to make him see just how truly ugly I was.

"Jackson, it's been a long time. I didn't realize you were...that you had a..." I pause, nodding in the direction of the little girl.

He looks at her and then back at me before chuckling. "Oh, no. She's not mine. Phina, this is my niece, Andreonna."

I smile down at the girl with long blonde hair and big blue eyes, who looks to be around five years old. She gives me a shy wave before hiding behind Jackson's legs.

"She's beautiful," I tell him.

"And she knows it, when she's not being so bashful," he jokes. "I'm not going to lie, I kind of had my fingers crossed that you'd be here today. I might have had ulterior motives when I asked my brother if I could bring Andy to the park."

I look at him in confusion. "How did you know I might be here?"

He winces, shrugging his shoulders and I immediately see where Andreonna gets her bashfulness.

"Finn used to talk about you all the time when our families got together. She always let me know what you were up to, and I remember her telling me that you volunteer at this thing every year."

Guilt rushes through me when he mentions his family. Even though we dated what seems like eons ago, I still saw him from time to time when I was with Finnley since he was related to her husband. I didn't go to Jordan's funeral out of respect for Finnley. That bastard didn't deserve any type of mourning, but I should have gone for Jackson and the rest of his family. They were good people and, even though one of their own tried to kill my best friend and her now-fiancé, he was still a part of their family. You don't go to funerals for the ones who died, you go to support the ones left behind.

"I'm so sorry about Jordan," I tell him softly, even though I don't really mean it. Jordan is where he belongs. My sympathy is solely for Jackson and his grief.

He shrugs again and gives me a sad smile. "I should be the one apologizing. He was like a brother to me, but I had no idea how fucked up he was."

Jackson reaches behind him and grabs Andreonna's hand. "Well, I should probably get this little munchkin over to the face painting booth before I have to go back to work."

I finally stop staring at his handsome face long enough to realize he's in uniform. I completely forgot that he works for the local police department.

"Finnley told me you took some time off after the funeral. It's good to see that you're back at work."

"Well, not back completely. There are still a few loose ends to tie up with the family, but I volunteered to work security today and tonight at Fight Night up at the firehouse. Are you going?"

Honestly, I hadn't planned on going to see a bunch of Neanderthals beat the snot out of each other, but there's something about the hopeful look on Jackson's face that makes me want to change my mind. I know that no matter how grown up he is now or how good looking he is in his police uniform, he's still off-limits for me, but I wouldn't mind hanging out with him and it couldn't hurt to have another police officer on my side if and when things start to escalate with my father.

"I'm not sure yet. Boxing isn't really my thing," I tell him.

"There will be sweaty men with their shirts off all night. What woman wouldn't jump at the chance to see something like that?" he asks with a laugh.

I laugh along with him and for just a moment, I feel normal. Like a woman who can stand in the middle of a park surrounded by happy families and joke with a sweet man. I need more normal in my damn life. It doesn't matter that I'm purposefully blocking out the kiss of another man or the feel of his hands on my body. It doesn't matter that when I get home later, my life will still be the same ball of shit it always has been or that I spend all day waiting for the man from my nightmares to show up and make good on his threats about giving me what I deserve.

With another wave to Andreonna and a promise to Jackson that I'll try and make it to Fight Night, I walk the rest of the way to the platelet donation truck with a smile on my face. I keep the smile firmly in place when I see the ambulance parked in front of the truck and I even go so far as to smile even wider when I see the very unhappy face of the man who kissed me as he leans against the side of the vehicle with his arms crossed in front of him. DJ's narrowed eyes follow me the entire way as I open the door to the truck and walk up the steps inside. I can see his glare through the front windshield of the truck and curse myself for the stupid goose bumps that pebble my skin from just the force of his stare.

I'm like a fucking teenager all over again, giddy with the thought that I just made him jealous by talking to another man. Rubbing my hands up and down my arms angrily to get rid of the goose bumps, I don a fake smile for the nurse as she gets me situated on a portable bed and begins the process of hooking up my IV line for the platelet donation.

A GENTLE PAT on my arm jerks me awake.

"Sorry, I didn't mean to scare you," the nurse says with a kind smile.

"You're all finished. I'm guessing I don't need to tell you to take it easy and grab some juice and cookies on your way out."

She points to my pale blue scrubs with my hospital ID pinned to it.

"Yeah, I'm pretty familiar with the do's and don'ts," I tell her with an embarrassed laugh. "Sorry I fell asleep there."

She helps me up from the bed and I sway a little, grabbing onto her arm for support.

"Whoa! Maybe I do need to go over the platelet donation checklist with you," she says in a concerned voice.

I shake the cobwebs from my head and extract myself from her grip on my arms. "No, it's fine. I'll make sure to grab as many cookies as I can."

She watches me like a hawk as I walk down the steps of the truck, going so far as to follow me to the bottom step and make sure I go right over to the table of refreshments. I ignore the pounding in my head and the tingling in my hands and arms as I smile and wave at her over my shoulder.

I've always felt a little bit woozy after a platelet donation. It's a little tougher on your body than just giving blood since a small portion of blood is drawn from your arm and is then filtered through a cell-separating machine to take out the platelets. After the platelets are removed, your blood is filtered back into you with a little bit of saline. The whole process takes about an hour and when I've donated in the past, the lightheadedness is gone after a few minutes and I can be on my way. As I brace my hands on top of the refreshment table and squeeze my eyes closed as I start to see black spots, something tells me it's going to take a little bit longer than normal for the wooziness to pass this time. I made sure to eat a huge breakfast before I left the house today since I knew I'd be donating, hoping the extra sugar and carbs would help afterwards, but something isn't right.

When I slowly open my eyes, the black spots are still dancing in my vision and now everything in front of me is blurry. My heart is beating so fast I'm afraid it might explode. I need to calm the fuck down. Freaking out isn't going to make this any better.

The tingling in my hands and arms has gotten worse and when I lift one hand from the table to try and shake the feeling away, I feel my body start to list to the side. I quickly grab the table again, holding onto it for dear life. My hands start shaking so hard against the table that I hear packages of cookies and paper cups filled with juice start to bounce around on top. The black spots at the edge of my vision have turned into bright bursts of light that make my head feel like it's in a vice.

"Ma'am, are you alright?"

I hear a voice speaking next to me, but I can't make any words form to answer whoever it is. This isn't normal and I know immediately that something is seriously wrong with me.

My heart beats faster and faster and I break out in a cold sweat. I can feel every inch of my body shaking and I grit my teeth to try and make it stop. I look around frantically, opening my mouth to try and scream for someone to help, but the blurry shapes in front of me suddenly swirl and the world tilts on its axis. I feel myself falling and then everything around me goes black.

10

DJ

FUCKING WOMAN. SHE'S going to be the goddamn death of me.

Today was supposed to be a nice, carefree day. One where I could wander through the park, try my hand at a few carnival games to win some prizes for my nieces and nephews, maybe give some oxygen to a few old folks who got overheated and avoid thinking about the shit storm brewing around me. I just wanted one day where my dick wasn't fighting with my brain over the maddening woman standing fifty feet in front of me, smiling at some douchebag.

Fucking smiling when all she does is snarl at me like a pit bull.

I don't know who the dude is since all I can see is his back, but I immediately hate the cocksucker for making her laugh. Plus, he's got a kid. I can't compete with a cute motherfucking kid. I didn't even know Phina *liked* kids. Obviously, she saves her hatred just for me. I came here today wanting to take my mind off of this annoying woman who clearly wants to fuck me, but doesn't want to speak to me or even *like* me. I figured it was just a case of lust roaring through my veins and it would

71

go away eventually. It's not like I thought she had any redeeming fucking qualities. She's full of piss and vinegar, won't let anyone close to her aside from Finnley and enjoys pissing me off, going by the extra wide smile she shoots in my direction as she heads towards the truck parked behind my rig when she's finished talking to the dickhead dad.

I just HAD to go and act like a creepy fucking stalker, following her around all morning and watching her work from a safe enough distance that she couldn't see me, but I could see and hear everything she said and did.

Seraphina Giordano is *sweet*. Not just sweet, but kind and thoughtful with a sense of humor. She made funny faces and told silly jokes to every kid who came up to her tent, she charmed every old man who volunteered to give blood and gave hugs to every woman who picked up a pamphlet from her table. When a particularly nervous little boy stood off to the side and watched through the open door of the donation truck as his mother gave blood, Phina pulled him closer, got down to his level and softly explained everything her co-worker was doing to his mother so he wouldn't be afraid of what was happening to her. Ten minutes after they left the area, the little boy came running back with a fistful of dandelions he'd picked from the grass and thrust them into Phina's hands. She made a huge production out of smelling the flowers and telling him they were the most beautiful things she'd ever seen, before bending down and giving him a big kiss on the cheek.

Who the fuck IS this woman?

Thank God Collin and Finnley weren't around to witness my pathetic behavior. As soon as they got here this morning, I sent them on their way to check out the tents and get some food, telling them I had work to do and would meet up with them later. They didn't need to know that my 'work' including figuring out the maddening woman walking towards me.

I continue to glare at her as she puts a little extra sway in her hips while she goes up the steps of the truck and disappears inside. Glancing back to the spot where she stood with that motherfucker and his kid, I see they've disappeared into the crowd and I've lost my chance to find out who he is. Jesus, I really am a fucking stalker. What the hell was I going to do, walk up to him and threaten him in front of his daughter? *"Hey, dick fuck, I don't know you, but you're never allowed to make that woman smile again. That smile is for me, and me alone."*

I've lost my goddamn mind.

My crazy thoughts are interrupted by a little boy with a splinter in his thumb, a man who thought he was having a heart attack, which thankfully turned out to be indigestion from one too many chili dogs, and at least ten people asking me for directions. Before I know it, an hour has gone by and I hear the *swoosh* of the truck door parked behind me opening. I watch as Phina steps down from the truck, smiles and waves at the nurse standing on the bottom step and walks over to the cookie and juice table they have set up right next to the truck. She places her hands on top of the table and drops her head between her shoulders. I've been keeping an eye on everyone giving platelet donations today and, for the most part, everyone reacts the same. They're a little off-kilter for a few minutes and then they're fine. I see Phina lift one hand from the table and can see it shaking erratically from here.

Stupid woman probably forgot to eat breakfast.

I head in her direction with the sole purpose of pissing her off by forcing her to drink some juice when I'm stopped by a woman looking for the french fry stand. By the time I'm finished pointing her in the right direction, I glance over at Phina just in time to see her sway and then collapse like a ton of bricks to the ground right next to the table. My heart plummets straight down to my feet and I stand there in shock for longer than I ever have in an emergency situation. Strong, independent Phina just fucking fainted.

Pulling my head out of my ass, I race to the back of the ambulance, fling open the doors and grab my first responder bag and the portable oxygen tank from the floor, throwing their straps over my shoulder as I sprint over to where she's lying.

"What happened?" I shout to the man hovering over her as I fall to my knees, throw my bag to the ground and flip the switch on the tank.

"I don't know, man. I was just standing here drinking my juice. I asked her if she was okay, but she didn't answer me. Then she just keeled over," the guy replies in a worried voice behind me.

Placing my hands on either side of her face, I turn her head towards me, not liking the clammy feel of her skin at all. Sweat beads on her forehead and she's white as a sheet.

"Phina! Baby, can you hear me? Phina, open your eyes," I tell her softly as I check her pulse on her neck, right behind her jaw. It's fast...way too fast. Letting go of her face, I reach into my bag for my stethoscope, putting the ear tips in and placing the diaphragm against her chest in the V-neck opening of her scrub top. Her heart is thundering out of control and sounds like a herd of elephants in my ears.

"Oh, my God! What the hell happened?"

I recognize Finnley's voice next to me and see her kneel down out of the corner of my eye and grab one of Phina's hands.

"She passed out after donating platelets. Is she diabetic?" I question Finnley as I unwind the oxygen mask from the tank and place it against Phina's mouth and nose, gently wrapping the head strap around her to keep it in place.

"No. No, she's not diabetic. She's given platelets a ton of times before and nothing like this has ever happened," Finnley informs me with worry in her voice.

Grabbing the Accu-Chek glucometer from the bag, I power it on, lift up Phina's hand and prick her finger with the sterilized test needle. After a few tense seconds, the machine beeps and I look at the screen.

"Jesus Christ. Her glucose level is 23. She's hypoglycemic," I mutter, tossing the machine to the side and snatching a Glucagon syringe from the side pocket of the bag.

"What does that mean? What are you doing?" Finnley asks frantically.

"It's alright, babe. It just means her blood sugar is way too low," Collin reassures her from somewhere behind me. I can hear an edge in his voice and know he's thinking the same thing I am, but doesn't want to voice it out loud in front of Finnley. If Phina isn't diabetic, there is no way her blood sugar would have dropped this low without some help. Not even a platelet donation would cause a reaction like this.

"I knew she wasn't feeling well. I should have kept her on the truck longer," the nurse from the vehicle says as she squats across from me, checking Phina's pulse for herself.

I glare at the nurse, but keep my mouth shut. Right now, I just want Phina to open her eyes and look at me.

"Finn, I need you to pull her pants down for me," I tell her as I ready the syringe.

She doesn't question me, just quickly leans over Phina's body, grabs onto the waistband of her scrubs and yanks her pants down to her knees. With a quick stab, I press the needle into Phina's thigh and release the glucose into her system.

Handing the needle over to the nurse for her to dispose of, I press the stethoscope back to Phina's chest and wait. It takes almost twenty minutes for her heart rate to slow to a normal level before Phina slowly opens her eyes and squints at me.

"Hey there, Fireball. Welcome back," I tell her with a smile, trying not to kiss every inch of her face and pull her into my arms.

I've never had to work on someone I know. When I'm on the job, I'm a robot, doing what I need to do to save someone's life. I never think about who they are, what would happen to their family if I couldn't do my job or how me possibly fucking up in a critical situation could end their life. I do what I'm trained to do and then I walk away. Kneeling here next to Phina, I didn't even realize I was praying to God the entire time, begging Him to keep her safe. As much as she pisses me off, she's wormed her way into my life and I can't stand the idea of her not being in it. I want to know everything about her. I want to know why she's so angry and why she won't let me in. I want to know what makes her tick and there is no fucking way I'm going to lose her before I can get to that point.

Phina reaches up and pulls the oxygen mask away from her face before pushing herself up on her elbows. I finally let myself touch her, wrapping my arm around her back to help her sit up. Placing my hand on her back, I rub slow, comforting circles there, the constant touch the reassurance I need that she's really okay.

I watch as she looks down at her bare thighs and then quickly scrambles to pull her pants back up. When they're in place, she holds her hands against her hips at an awkward angle before shooting me a dirty look.

"Why the hell were my pants off? Did you look? What did you see?" she fires at me.

I start to bristle at her attitude towards the man that just saved her fucking life when I see tears forming in her eyes. I have no idea what she's so upset about. It's not like I haven't seen her with her pants off before.

"It's okay, hon. He had to give you a shot of glucose in your thigh," Finnley tells her comfortingly as she pats her leg.

Phina yanks her leg away from Finnley's hand and quickly gets up from the ground. I jump up next to her and try to grab onto her arm, but she swats me away.

"Will you stop being so fucking stubborn? You were out cold for over twenty minutes because your blood sugar plummeted. I'm guessing you forgot to eat this morning?"

She rolls her eyes at me, pulling the oxygen mask strap over her head and tossing it to the ground. "I'm not an idiot. Of course I ate this morning. There's no way my blood sugar dropped that quickly just because of my donation."

She's absolutely right and before I can let that thought fester and turn into outright panic, the nurse comes back outside from the truck after disposing of the glucose injection syringe.

"I don't know how this could have happened. This truck is always monitored. I should have double-checked," she says worriedly as she rushes over to us with a couple of vials of saline in her hand.

"What are you talking about?" I question when she stops in front of us.

"At the end of a platelet donation, we have to inject a little saline to finish off the process and flush out the I.V. We keep them in a line on the table and use them in order for each donor. Someone switched the vial of saline that was supposed to be used for her with insulin."

She holds the vials out to me and I grab them from her. Sure enough, a small vial the exact same size and color as the saline is mixed in with all the rest. The word insulin is printed in small script on the label, but it's been partially scraped off. The donation truck has been a zoo all day with people coming in and out for donations non-stop. The nurse looks like she's ready to burst into tears and as much as I want to shout at her for not checking the label of the vial, I know it was an honest mistake on her part. She grabbed the supply right next to her, not even fathoming that it wouldn't be what it was supposed to.

I look up and see Phina staring at the vials in my hand. The tears from moments ago are completely gone and she's back to looking like she wants to kick someone's ass. I can handle angry Phina. At this point, I'm a fucking pro. I don't know what the hell I would have done if she broke down right in front of me and started crying. That, along with the compassion I saw from her today, would have completely done me in.

"Are you ready to let me fucking help you now?" I ask her in a low voice.

Without answering me, she gives Finnley a quick hug and pecks Collin on the cheek.

"We need to call the police. Clearly he's got someone on the outside trying to get to you," Collin tells her softly before she backs away from him.

Phina doesn't acknowledge the fact that everything is all out in the open now that I know about her scumbag father. She has no reason to push me away and exclude me from this shit because she has something to hide. I put myself in her shoes and think about how I would feel if one of my darkest secrets was out there for everyone to know.

I would hate that kind of vulnerability. I would be pissed at everyone around me and take it out on anyone I could. More than ever, I want to just pull this damn woman in my arms and tell her to let me take care of her, but I know just by the look on her face that she'll never allow it.

She laughs cynically at Collin and takes another step away from him.

"Don't worry, my father doesn't need anyone on the outside, he's been released. All of this twisted shit is being done by his own hands. Stay out of it, Collin."

With that, she turns and walks away. Finnley calls her name and goes running after her.

"I have to call this in. She's going to fucking hate me, but I have to do it," Collin tells me.

I nod and let out a huge sigh. "I have the number of someone you can call. He already knows about the notes and he's been looking into things."

Pulling my phone out of my back pocket, I text the number to Collin before packing up my first responder bag.

I saved her life, but Dax is going to save the day.

Fucking Dax. I really should have beaten his ass when I had the chance.

11

Phina

CHECKING OUT MY reflection in the windows on either side of the door to the firehouse, I briefly wonder if the outfit I chose is a bit much for Fight Night. The A-line, black leather skirt barely covers my ass and crotch and the knee-high black stiletto boots look great paired with it, but could easily be confused for hooker boots. Adjusting my dark green shirt that hangs down off of one shoulder and perfectly compliments my green eyes, I realize I don't give a fuck if the outfit is too much. It makes me feel bold, sexy and in control, something I am in dire need of after this morning's events.

Another note was taped to my front door when I got home from the fair, this time asking me if I enjoyed being the 'damsel in distress.' It was bad enough to faint in front of a park full of strangers, but to have DJ see me so weak and pathetic was just too much for me to handle. I know I should have thanked him for what he did. He saved my life. If he hadn't been there to give me that shot of glucose, who knows what would have happened? I was too busy worrying that he saw my scars and what he would think of me to bother with thanking the man for making sure I didn't die. A part of me wished he saw them, hoped his eyes roamed over the burns on my hips and realized just how incredibly fucked up I am. Maybe then he would leave me the hell alone and I wouldn't have all of these conflicting feelings about him. I wouldn't be afraid that he knew the truth about me and I wouldn't be having second thoughts about paying him back for what he did to me in high school. My father is out of prison, sending me notes and trying to kill me. Clearly I have more important things going on in my life than worrying about what some guy thinks of me. Tonight, I'm going to waltz into this fucking firehouse and be the person I'm comfortable with: bitchy, in control and independent. I don't need anyone to save me and I don't need anyone to protect me from the big bad wolf. If they look close enough, they'll realize *I'm* the one with the sharpest teeth. And I definitely like to bite.

Pulling open the door to the station, I head inside, following the signs through the reception area pointing towards the truck bay where Fight Night is to be held. Halfway down the hall, I hear clapping and cheers, indicating the fights have already started. I step through the open doorway into the bay and I have to say, I'm pretty amazed by what I see. All of the trucks have been removed and the wide-open space has been transformed into a boxing arena. Right in the center of the room is a large, professional looking boxing ring, and there are two men in the middle duking it out. Several rows of chairs are set up all around the ring, currently occupied by people sitting down to watch the fight while a hundred or so other people are content to stand behind them, screaming and giving each other high-fives. Walking over to the cafeteria table next to the door, I pay the twenty-dollar entrance fee and make my way through the crowds of people to the only quiet corner in the place. Pulling a flask out of my purse, I discreetly tip the small, stainless steel container back and swallow a few huge mouthfuls of tequila. I feel a hand tap my shoulder and quickly hide the flask behind me. Being that this is a government building, I don't think they would take too kindly to me having alcohol in here. Turning around, my eyes meet the bare, muscular chest of Dax. Even though the sight of him does nothing for me, I'm woman enough to appreciate the fine specimen that he is. I trail my eyes up his chest to find him smirking down at me.

"Go ahead, say it. I'm the hottest piece of man meat you've ever seen," Dax says with a grin.

The tequila has made it's way into my system, warming my skin and easing the conflict pounding through my brain, turning it just fuzzy enough for me not to care. Tossing my head back, I let out a full belly laugh before shaking my head at him.

"I don't know how you manage to fit through doorways with your giant head," I reply. "And *man meat*? Please tell me that doesn't usually work for you."

"It's a tough job, but somebody has to do it," he tells me with a shrug, holding his hand out in front of me. "Give me that flask you're hiding behind your back."

I raise my eyebrow at him as I bring the flask around and shove it into his waiting hand. "Going by your half-naked body and the gloves tucked under your arm, I'm assuming you're joining in on proving your masculinity in the ring tonight. Should you really be drinking?"

He raises the flask in my direction in a silent toast before tipping it into his mouth.

"I could take any man in here with both arms tied behind my back and a whole bottle of tequila in my belly. Don't worry about me, love."

He hands the flask back to me, leaning closer so he doesn't have to shout over all the yelling and cheering.

"I heard you have quite an eventful morning. I think *I* should be the one asking *you* if you should be drinking."

I look away from his concerned gaze, scanning the crowd. "I'm fine.

Don't worry about me."

He *tsks* me and chuckles. "I'm well aware of the fact that you *think* you can take care of yourself, but this is getting serious. What happened today isn't just about a love note taped to your front door. He tried to kill you, Phina. If DJ hadn't been there to save you-"

"Don't," I stop him. "Don't even finish that sentence."

I'm pissed that Collin took it upon himself to call Dax and tell him about my father. It's bad enough he had to tell DJ. I don't need someone else in my life feeling sorry for me.

"We don't even know for sure if it was him. It could have been an accident."

Now it's Dax's turn to raise his eyebrow at me. "If you believe that, you're not as smart as you look. I called his PO today after I got off the phone with Collin. Your father has yet to check in with him since he's been paroled. He's off the grid and no one knows where he is. I'm putting a cop on you twenty-four-seven and if you argue with me, I'll have DJ spank your ass. I'm sure he'd enjoy it."

I really wish they would let women participate in this fucking Fight Night. I'd grab a pair of gloves and beat the snot out of Dax.

What he's saying makes perfect sense. I'm not an idiot, but that doesn't mean I have to like it. I don't need someone following me around, getting into my business. I like my privacy and the thought of some overweight, donut-eating annoyance trailing me like a puppy everywhere I go pisses me off.

"I swear to God, this guy better stay as far away from me as possible," I concede with a frown.

Dax smiles before wrapping his arms around me, pulling me in for a tight bear hug.

"I'll be nice this time and I won't force you to tell me I'm right, even though it would be so nice to hear."

Untangling myself from his arms, I shove him away and can't help but laugh. Dax makes it easy to follow his directions when he can't be serious for one second. I'll never tell him that, though.

"Get away from me. You smell like sweat and testosterone. Go up there and kick some ass. If I'm feeling generous, maybe I'll even place my bet on you," I tell him with a laugh.

Pulling his gloves out from under his arms, he slides them on his hands, punching his fists together a few times while bouncing back and forth on the balls of his feet.

"Float like a butterfly, sting like a bee, motherfucker!"

The gong of a bell echoes through the room along with a deafening cheer and I watch as a few guys jump up into the ring to help their fallen comrade, practically dragging him out from under the ropes and down to the ground.

The announcer flips on the microphone and attempts to calm the crowd down as he begins introducing the next pair of fighters. He starts listing Dax's stats and how long he's been with the police department, while his brothers in blue scream and clap so loud I almost feel the need to cover my ears. Dax raises his arms above his head, pumping his fists in the air as he gives me one last smirk before jogging through the crowd and up to the ring.

"Ladies and gentleman, we've had a slight change in the lineup tonight. I'm proud to announce that we have a new opponent set to fight against Dax Trevino."

Half of the crowd boos while the other cheers. I crane my neck to try and see through the crowd, wondering who will be the poor sap that has to go up against Dax.

"Hey there, hot stuff," Finnley says with a smile as she steps around a few guys and bumps shoulders with me.

"Aren't you supposed to be working the food table?" I ask, still trying to see through the crowd.

"I took a break. This is definitely a fight I don't want to miss," she laughs.

Before I can ask her why, the announcer's voice booms through the microphone again.

"From the fire department, let's give a big round of applause to DJ Taylor!"

Everyone from the fire department starts jumping up and down like kangaroos on crack, smacking each other on the back and chanting DJ's name.

"You have got to be kidding me," I mutter.

Finnley laughs, sliding her hand around my arm. "Collin almost shit himself when DJ agreed to fight a few minutes ago. We had a last minute cancellation from the guy in our department who was scheduled to fight Dax. He came down with the flu or something. Collin's been begging DJ to fight for weeks and he kept turning him down. He barely had to say two words to DJ tonight and he jumped at the chance to fight Dax. So weird."

Yeah, not that weird, my friend.

I watch as DJ easily bends down to slip under the ropes. He stands up to his full height and walks into the middle of the ring and my brain immediately drops right into my vagina. I've seen him without a shirt. I've felt his bare chest against the inside of my thighs, for Christ's sake. There's just something different about seeing him shirtless in the middle of a boxing ring with his dark blue work pants hung low on his hips and pure, unadulterated rage on his face as he circles Dax. The muscles in his chest and arms ripple as he smacks his gloved fists together. Just seconds ago, I watched Dax do the exact same thing and I rolled my eyes at his attempt to look macho. Watching DJ do it makes me want to drag him out of the ring and fuck his brains out.

Dax and DJ are matched for height, but DJ definitely has a few more pounds of muscle on Dax's lean body. Where before I was worried about the man who had to go up against Dax in the ring, now I'm worried *for* Dax. Judging by the look on DJ's face, this isn't going to be a fun fight just for show to raise money for charity. This is a pissing contest and DJ just whipped his dick out.

"This is not going to end well," I mumble, unable to take my eyes off of DJ as he stretches, twisting his torso from side to side.

I want to lick the indents in his hips so badly that my mouth waters, and I hate him for that. I shouldn't want him, but I can't help myself. He looks angry, mean and full of fury. Sex with him right this moment would be hard and powerful. The lace boy shorts I'm wearing under my leather skirt are so wet I could probably wring them out. I can practically feel him pounding into me so hard that I wouldn't be able to walk for a week.

I want that man's anger. I want to feel it like a living, breathing thing, slamming into me, want to take it away from him and into myself.

I fucking hate him for making me feel like this.

12

DJ

"FOR THE LAST time, I'm not fighting in this fucking thing. I'm not even *working* with the fire department anymore," I complain to Collin as I scan the crowd, looking for Phina. Collin said he saw her come in a few minutes ago, and I want to find her so I can kick her ass. She should be at home, in bed, recuperating after what happened this morning.

I see a flash of red hair on the other side of the room and I take a step away from Collin. He grabs onto my arm and yanks me back.

"Come on, don't let me down, man. Douglas has the damn flu and I'm short a guy."

I barely hear what Collin is saying. The crowd has parted enough that I can see Phina standing entirely too close to a shirtless Dax. I watch as she throws her head back and laughs and a growl rips from my throat. The skirt she's wearing barely covers her ass and the green shirt she has on is hanging down off of her shoulder, giving me a perfect view of her creamy, smooth skin.

"It's one round of fighting, that's all I need from you. Ten minutes, tops," Collin continues to plead.

My hands clench into fists at my side as I watch Dax lean in close to Phina while she stares up at him.

"You know the guy you'll be fighting, so it doesn't even have to be a *real* fight. You can just throw a few punches to make it look good for the crowd and then you guys can hug it out and have a few drinks," Collin continues.

Dax wraps his arms around Phina's body and pulls her against his chest. Her cheek rests right against his pecs and a ball of rage slams into my body so hard that it feels like my skin is on fire.

"Seriously, you and Dax are perfectly matched in size. It will be a quick fight."

My head whips around to stare at Collin, processing what he just said. That motherfucking cocksucker is holding Phina on the other side of the room. I saved her fucking life today and I get the silent treatment while she lets *him* put his hands all over her.

"I'm in. Find me a fucking pair of gloves," I bark, reaching over my shoulder and grabbing a fistful of shirt, yanking it up and over my head.

"Holy fuck, are you serious?" Collin asks in surprise as I chuck my shirt at his face.

"Get me a goddamn pair of gloves before I fight him with my bare hands," I order.

Collin races off without another word, shouting to Finnley at the food table and telling all the guys in the department the good news as he goes in search of a pair of gloves.

Motherfucking piece of shit is going to wish he never laid eyes on Phina when I'm finished with him.

THE RUSHING OF blood in my ears as I circle Dax drowns out the sounds of the crowd screaming all around the ring out.

"Oh, come on. Do you really want to do this?" Dax asks.

I smirk, stopping in front of him to stretch my arms and waist. "You have no idea how much I want to do this."

Dax shakes his head at me, putting his gloved fists on his hips.

"I'm not fighting you, man."

The bell on the side of the ring dings, signaling the start of the round.

"You better put your fucking fists up, because I'm sure as hell fighting *you*," I threaten as I advance on him.

He doesn't even have time to lift his arms. I put all my weight on my front foot and let my arm fly, my fist connecting with his cheek. His head jerks to the side with the force of my blow and I stand there with my fists up in front of my own face, waiting for him to get back into stance.

"Are you fucking kidding me?!" he yells, holding his glove against his cheek. "This is a charity fight, asshole. You're supposed to take it easy!"

I shake my head at him as I bounce on the balls of my feet.

"Fuck you! You better throw a fucking punch or you're just going to look like a big pussy," I argue, jabbing my fist quickly into his ribs.

This hit does the trick and immediately pisses Dax off. He charges towards me, but I refuse to take a step back. He gets right up in my face and I should probably take advantage of the situation and knock his ass out, but something in the look on his face makes me keep my hands stationary in front of my face.

"YOU'RE the one being a pussy! I know this is about Phina, you stubborn fuck! How about you just *talk* to her instead of trying to prove something by beating my ass?" he shouts.

"STOP TALKING AND FUCKING FIGHT!" I yell back.

I take another swing at his face, but he easily blocks me.

"I am NOT going to fight you! There is nothing going on between us, dickhead!" Dax yells, taking a step away from me.

I follow him, throwing more punches that he smacks away with his gloves.

"Really? Could have fooled me!" I argue, punching him as hard as I can in the chest.

He stumbles backwards, groaning and coughing as he rubs his glove over his chest. Once again, he stalks towards me and gets right in my face. "She doesn't want ME, you clueless bastard! She's been looking at you like she wants to fuck you into next week ever since you stepped into this ring."

That throws me for a loop and I make the mistake of dropping my guard. Dax takes the opening and slams his fist into my eye and I go down like a ton of bricks. The dinging of the bell clamors over the cheers and shouts from the crowd as Dax puts his feet on either side of my body and leans down over me.

"Get your head out of your fucking ass and go get your girl. I don't want her, she doesn't want me. The next time you and I get in a ring together, I won't take it this easy on you, you dumb fuck!"

He storms off and I let my head fall back onto the floor of the ring and stare up at the lights in the ceiling, calling myself every kind of asshole.

Collin's face leans over me a few seconds later, covering up one of the lights. "Well, that was a pretty pathetic display of prowess, Nancy. What the hell *was* that?"

Lifting up one of my arms, he wraps his hand around my forearm and yanks me to my feet.

"That was just me, being an asshole," I grumble as we bend down to exit the ring.

MY EYES ARE closed as I sit on the bench in the small locker room on the other side of the station, far away from the noise. With my back and head leaning against one of the lockers, I think about just how big of an idiot I was and it pisses me off even more. Dax has been working overtime to try and figure out what the hell is going on with Phina and I act like a jealous dick because he makes her laugh and gets to hold her. I have no right to any part of Phina and that thought just makes me even angrier. If my face didn't feel like someone smacked it with a two-by-four, I'd probably get up off this bench and apologize to Dax. I'm lucky he didn't kick me when I was down and turn my face into hamburger meat after the way I acted.

I hear the click of the door opening and closing, but I keep my eyes sealed shut, knowing it's probably just Collin coming in here to fuck with me some more. If I open my eyes right now, the stabbing pain in my cheek and eye will get even worse.

"If you came in here to call me Nancy again…ah, fuck it. I can't even threaten you. My face hurts too much."

My nose immediately fills with the smell of spicy perfume and though I know it's going to hurt like a motherfucker, my eyes open wide and my jaw drops when I feel a soft hand press against the bruise on my cheek.

Phina has pushed her legs in between mine and she stands in front of me like a fucking goddess, a light from the ceiling surrounding her head and making her red hair glow like the sun as she stares down at me.

Without a word, she drops her hand from my cheek, pressing both of her palms to her thighs. She slowly slides them up under her skirt, grabbing onto her panties and sliding them down. The black lace drops from around her knees and pools at her feet. She steps out of them, using the toe of one of her boots to kick them away.

I swallow thickly and try not to moan, my dick hardening as she reaches up to the scooping neckline of her shirt, pulling it down to expose her tits.

Fuck me. She's not wearing a bra. Or panties now.

"I hate you," she whispers, trailing the tips of her fingers over one pebbled nipple.

I want to tell her I don't care if she hates me, I don't care if I'm the last person on earth she wants to be with, but I can't make my mouth form any words as she places her knees on the bench on either side of my hips and straddles me.

My hands go to her hips, clutching the leather of her skirt as I pull her down on top of me, the heat from her bare pussy burning right through the crotch of my pants to my dick.

She uses both of her hands to grab her tits, kneading them and running her thumbs over her nipples.

"I really fucking hate you," she whispers again.

Letting go of her hip with one hand, I run my fingertips over her lips to get her to stop fucking saying those words to me. Her tongue darts out, licking the tips of my fingers before sucking them into her mouth. She grinds herself against my dick as she hollows out her cheeks while she sucks my fingers all the way inside her warm, wet mouth. I quickly pull my fingers away, trailing them down over her chin, her throat and her collarbone before circling her nipple with their wet tips.

"Goddammit, I hate you," she mumbles as she lifts her hips, reaching between us to unzip my pants.

Her hand dives inside the opening, wrapping around my cock. She strokes the length from root to tip, letting her thumb slide around the pre-cum leaking out, spreading it all around the head of my cock.

I continue circling her nipple with the tips of my fingers, rolling it between my thumb and forefinger and pinching it gently. She drops her forehead to mine and closes her eyes, humming her approval as I add more pressure with my fingers. Bringing my free hand up behind her head, I grab a fistful of her long, red hair, yanking her head back so I can look into her eyes.

"I don't give a shit if you hate me. I need to fuck you," I tell her with a growl, thrusting my hips in time with her strokes on my cock.

The lie flies right off my tongue. I don't want her to fucking hate me. I want her to need me, I want her to come to me when she has a problem and I want her to *know* me. Right now, though, I just fucking want her.

Reaching into her boot, she pulls out a condom and quickly rips the package open. I watch with rapt interest as she places the rubber over the head of my dick and then slowly slides it down my length, squeezing me as she goes.

She raises her hips just enough to line the tip of my cock up with her wet pussy. She takes her time, sliding the sensitive tip back and forth, dragging it through her wetness until I'm completed coated with her.

Taking my fingers away from her nipple, I clutch onto her hip again and tighten my hold on her hair, pulling her down on top of me.

Her hands fly to my shoulders and she fights against my pull, holding herself completely still with just the tip of my cock inside of her. I'm breaking out in a sweat and panting against her mouth. It's killing me not to move, but if she's having second thoughts, I will drop her onto the floor, tuck my dick back into my pants and walk away. Nicely, of course.

I hold my breath as she sinks down on my cock another centimeter.

"If you want to fuck me, then do it," she whispers angrily. "Fuck me hard, and make it hurt. I'm not going to break."

I should probably question her need for pain when all I want to do is wrap my arms around her and make love to her like a pansy-ass, but my dick is doing all of my thinking for me right now.

She practically purrs when I tighten my grip on her hair, so I clench her hip even tighter and thrust upwards, slamming myself all the way inside of her tight pussy. Phina lets out a yelp and an apology is on the tip of my tongue until she lifts her hips, my cock sliding almost all the way out of her before she drops right back down, impaling herself on my dick.

Clutching onto her hair, I jerk her head back and expose her throat while I begin roughly fucking up into her, pushing and pulling her hips as hard as I can, moving her up and down on my cock. I lean forward, wrapping my lips around the smooth skin of her throat and bite down while I fuck her.

"I fucking hate you, I fucking hate you," she chants in between moans as the bench beneath us creaks and rocks with the force of my thrusts.

Her thighs tighten around my legs as she helps me move her. She bounces up and down on my cock, slamming our groins together so hard I swear I'm going to have bruises. Everything about this moment is going to be forever seared in my brain. The sound of her moans of pleasure ringing through my ears, the way her pussy clenches around me and how her skin tastes as I continue to bite and nip at her neck. She's so wet that she easily slides up and down my cock, no matter how hard I fuck her. She's so tight I feel like a fist is squeezing my cock. Something about this moment, about the feel of her wrapped around me, the smell of her arousal and the taste of her skin is so goddamn familiar that it's like a punch to the gut. She *feels* familiar. She feels like home and like I've been waiting years to come back to this exact place, waiting for this exact moment when I could be inside of her again.

My balls tighten with the need to come and I push those thoughts aside because they have no business here. I've never fucked Phina before, but I've dreamt of it so many times that the familiarity is probably only natural.

"Harder!" she shouts as she slides her fingers through my hair and squeezes so hard I feel some of it being pulled out by the roots. I'm so glad she didn't tell me she hates me again that I'll do whatever the fuck she asks.

My hips move like pistons, my cock driving into her so hard and fast that my thighs start to ache, but I don't let up. I keep pounding into her over and over, slamming her down on top of me so hard I'm surprised I don't break her in half.

"Fuck, I'm coming! Fuck, I fucking hate you!" she shouts as she grinds herself on top of my dick and her pussy clenches around me.

So much for stopping that whole hate thing.

My dick is surrounded by wet heat and the pulsing of her release and it feels so fucking good that it pushes me right over the edge. With a roar, I bite down even harder on her neck as I come, tasting blood on my tongue as she bounces up and down on top of me, prolonging my orgasm until I feel like I'm going to die from pleasure.

Her pussy milks my cock as she continues to ride me, and I swear to Christ nothing has ever felt better. With a final thrust up into her, I hold myself still for a few seconds before my ass slumps back to the bench. Phina's body follows, her hands dropping from their death grip on my hair as she drapes her arms over my shoulders and collapses against my chest.

With my cock still buried inside of her, I wrap my arms around her and hold her against me until my heartbeat returns to normal and I feel like I can finally breathe without passing out.

"I hate you so much," she whispers softly, her face pressed against the side of my neck. There isn't any anger or conviction in her voice this time, just a tinge of sadness and exhaustion.

"I hate you too, Fireball," I lie with a smile, tightening my hold on her.

13

Phina

"I SHUCKING FATE him," I slur, after my sixth shot of tequila. Or was that seven?

After removing myself from DJ's lap in the locker room, I watched him scoop up my underwear and shove them in his pants pocket before I stormed out of there and away from the comfort of his arms. Fight Night had officially ended by the time I got back out to the truck bay, and a bunch of people were heading to McCallahan's to celebrate the police department's victory over the fire station. I figured it would be a good place to hide and drink away my troubles without having to worry about DJ showing his face. He basically lost Fight Night for the station because of his jealous pissing match with Dax, and I figured his ego wouldn't allow him anywhere near the place. Stupid me for thinking for one second that DJ wasn't a stand-up guy and wouldn't want to celebrate even though he lost. Five minutes after I got here, he came strolling in, congratulating the victors and easily taking all the good-natured ribbing from everyone. I ordered as many shots of tequila as the bartender would allow, slammed my ass down on a barstool and haven't moved since. It didn't help that every time I fidgeted on the wooden seat, I winced at the tenderness in my fucking vagina and thighs and immediately remembered every second of what it felt like to have DJ pounding away inside of me.

Every. Fucking. Glorious. Second.

Finnley grabs the refilled shot glass I started to reach for and moves it out of my way. "Yep, you're cut off. When you can't even properly explain how much you hate someone, you've had enough to drink."

I close my eyes and the room starts to spin, so I immediately open them. "You don't understand, Finn."

She rubs her hand on my back and nods. "You had sex with DJ. Now you're drowning your sorrows because, instead of fucking the guy over for what he did when he was young and dumb, you just fucked him. And you liked it."

She wags her eyebrows and laughs while I sit on the barstool, staring at her in shock. There's no way she knows I had sex with DJ. I tried not to hobble when I walked in here and I grit my teeth whenever I cross my legs instead of moaning in a mixture of pleasure and pain. I asked him to give it to me hard and that man sure did deliver, Jesus Christ.

"Close your mouth, you're catching flies," Finnley giggles. "Did you honestly think you could hide something like that from your best friend? Besides, I saw you disappear into the locker room after DJ went in there and when you came out, your skirt was twisted around backwards and you had messy sex hair."

I try to smack her in the arm, but the liquor running through my body makes the appendage feel like a wet noodle and I just sloppily paw at her.

"I hate him for what he did to me back then," I tell her.

"I think you hated him back *then*. I KNOW you hated him back then, but he's a different person now, Phee. I think you've seen just how different he is and you just hate the fact that you DON'T really hate him."

What she's saying would make sense if I were sober, but all I hear are words, words, words and none of them make me happy.

"I see the way you look at him when you think no one is watching and I also see how protective he is of you, especially after we told him about your dad. I know you're pissed we told him, but he had every right to know since he got a note, too. Why is it so hard for you to just let him in?" She asks softly.

I glare at her. "You know exactly why."

Well, not exactly, but she knows enough.

"Hon, you were both kids when that shit happened. It's not like he did it on purpose just to fuck with you. He was so drunk that, if I remember correctly, you were even having second thoughts about going into that bedroom with him. It's been fifteen years, Phee. You can't keep hating someone for something they don't even know they did."

"I thought you were on my side?" I argue.

"I AM on your side, but when you're acting like an idiot, I'm going to call you on your shit. Be honest with *yourself* at least. You don't hate him and that's what's pissing you off most right now. I know the shit with your dad is making you crazy and I get it, even though you've been keeping secrets from me. I know you didn't have a good life growing up, but you've made something of yourself. You're a strong, independent woman, but that doesn't mean you can't lean on someone every once in a while. Especially a hot guy who looks at you like you're the sun in his sky."

Oh Jesus, now she's becoming a poet.

Reaching around her, I grab the shot glass she stole from me and down it quickly, letting the burn of the tequila numb me so I don't have to think about my shitty childhood or being the fucking sun in anyone's sky. I'm not a bright shining light, I'm a cloud of doom and gloom that rains on everyone's parade.

"DJ took my virginity and didn't even remember it the morning after. I'm sorry, how is it possible NOT to hate someone for that shit?"

Finnley opens her mouth to reply and then quickly covers it with her hand as she looks over my shoulder. I don't need to turn around to know DJ is standing right behind me. Even if Finnley didn't look like a ghost just magically appeared behind me, I can smell him. He took a shower after that whole locker room incident and I can smell his soap and shampoo. He smells clean and fresh and like the most delicious man in the world. Obviously, he felt dirty after our little rendezvous and needed to rid his body of the uncleanliness that is me.

"What. In. The. Fuck?" DJ shouts over the blare of a rock song from the jukebox.

Twisting around on the chair, I try not to let the sight of DJ with hair still damp from the shower and his smell turn me into a pile of mush.

"You. Suck," I tell him, punctuating each word with my finger in his chest.

He quickly grabs my finger and pulls my body towards him. I slide right off of the stool, my feet slamming to the ground and my chest colliding with his.

"I repeat, what in the fuck?" he asks angrily as I glare up at him.

"Oh, please! You have no right to be all indignant with me, mister wham-bam-I-don't-remember-anything-ma'am!" I yell at him, the alcohol rushing right to my head, making me sway against him. "You got what you wanted earlier and now it's MY turn to walk the fuck away."

I attempt to pull my hand out of his grip, but he wraps his arms around me.

"Let me go so I can walk away," I growl angrily, squinting my eyes so I stop seeing three of him standing in front of me. Three DJ's, all sharing the same pissed-off look on their face, is three too many.

"I honestly have no idea what you're talking about," he tells me firmly, reaching up to smooth the hair out of my eyes.

I swat his hand away and jab my elbow into his arm so he'll drop his hold on me.

"Clearly. You've been a complete idiot for fifteen years. Jesus, how stupid was I back then to think I actually had a chance with you? Mr. Star Quarterback, most popular guy in high school. Why the hell would you even look twice at me? But hey, I got my wish, all right. One drunken night, I got what I'd always wanted and you STILL don't fucking remember!" I shout.

Punching my fist into his chest, he finally lets go of me and I stumble backwards. Finnley grabs onto my shoulders to steady me while DJ stands in front of me, looking like someone just shot his favorite dog.

"Everything okay over here?" Collin asks, walking up to our group.

"Just fucking peachy!" I say in a cheerful voice while I try my hardest not to throw up on everyone's shoes. The room is full-on spinning right now and I'm sorely regretting that last shot of tequila.

"Collin, can you give me a ride home? I don't feel very well," I mumble as I turn away from DJ and start walking towards the door in what I hope is a straight line.

"I fucking HATE you!" I shout over my shoulder, slamming my hands into the door to swing it open as I step out into the night air.

Leaning forward, I place my hands on my knees and take a few deep breaths, wondering why the fuck my eyes sting and I feel like crying. I fucked DJ in the locker room for all the wrong reasons. Sure, I wanted him. The sight of him up in that boxing ring turned me on something fierce, and watching him take that hit from Dax and hit the mat made me feel protective. I wanted to run my hands over his face and make sure he was okay, kiss away the pain and give him comfort. But a part of me did it in the hopes that a fucking light bulb would turn on in his head. I thought he'd feel me around him, look into my eyes and *remember*.

I just wanted to be good enough for him to remember.

14

DJ

I'VE STOOD HERE in the corner of the bar watching Phina down shot after shot and I can't help but feel shitty about it. Is she drinking to try and forget what happened in the locker room?

FUCK!

Every time I think I take a step forward with this woman, I wind up taking fifty steps back. It's been a blow to my ego, listening to people from the force and the fire department giving me shit for my sad boxing skills, but at least I had the memory of *finally* fucking Phina to get me through the night. I caught sight of her as soon as I walked in the door and my dick hardened in my pants. I wanted her again, immediately. I wanted a chance to take my time, undress her and stare at every beautiful inch of her body. I wanted to hear her shout my name this time instead of telling me how much she hated me over and over. Even from across the room, I could see the mark I left on her neck when she turned her head to the side and I wanted to beat my chest like a fucking caveman and start chanting 'Woman, mine!' for the entire bar to hear.

Taking Dax's words in the ring to heart, I decide to go get my fucking girl. She's not going to just walk away this time and ignore me like she did the night I made her damn fantasy come true. She's going to acknowledge me, she's going to *see* me and I will make sure she finally fucking admits she doesn't hate me.

Slamming my bottle down on the nearest table, I make my way through the crowd until I'm standing right behind her. The smell of her perfume makes my cock pulse and I curse myself for taking that fucking shower after she walked out of the locker room. I wanted to keep the smell of sex and her skin all over me and never wash it off, but my muscles and black eye were screaming in pain, and I knew a hot shower would be the only thing to make me feel better.

I stop subtly sniffing her hair when I hear Phina speak to Finnley.

"DJ took my virginity and didn't even remember it the morning after. I'm sorry, how is it possible NOT to hate someone for that shit?"

A flash of memory flies through my head and I close my eyes, trying to grab onto it.

"I'm sorry! I'm so sorry, am I hurting you?" I asked, looking down into Phina's face, still not able to fully grasp that this was happening.

Her red hair was spread out on the pillow behind her head and she stared up at me with a smile, running her fingers down my cheek.

"I'm fine, it's okay. You can keep going," she told me softly.

I moved my hips the tiniest bit, my heart practically breaking in half when I saw her wince in pain. I was so fucking drunk that I didn't even know how I was able to keep my dick hard, aside from the fact that being inside of the girl of my dreams was the best damn feeling in the fucking world. I wanted to make this good for her. It was killing me that I couldn't make it good.

"Just go slow, okay?" she whispered, wrapping her arms around my shoulders.

I buried my face into the side of her neck and tried counting backwards from a hundred to keep myself from moving too fast. I really hoped she didn't fucking hate me after this. Her first time shouldn't be with a drunk idiot like me, but how in the hell was I supposed to say no to her?

As I moved slowly in and out of her, I swear I heard her whisper that she loved me, but I knew my drunk brain must have been playing tricks on me. There's no way this beautiful, amazing girl loved an asshole like me.

"What. In. The. Fuck?" I shout, my eyes flying open as I glare back and forth between Finnley's shocked face and the back of Phina's head.

That memory can't be real. There's no fucking way it's real.

I think about fucking her in the locker room and how familiar she felt and how I just *knew* I'd been inside of her before, but I thought I was just out of my mind wanting her so much.

Jesus Christ, what the fuck have I done?

Phina whirls around on her stool and jams her finger into my chest and tells me I suck. I have to agree with her at this point, but all I can do is yank her towards me and ask the same question again because none of this makes any fucking sense.

"I repeat, what in the fuck?"

I really, really want her or Finnley to just start laughing, telling me they had too much to drink and they're talking out of their asses, but that never happens. Finnley continues to stare at me in shock and Phina proceeds to bitch at me. I hate what she's saying, and it makes my fucking chest hurt hearing that she thought I wouldn't even look twice at her back in high school. Doesn't she have any fucking idea that I ALWAYS looked at her? I saw her everywhere I went, in everything I did and in everything I fucking dreamed. The memory from that night back in high school comes rushing back with perfect clarity and I want to scream and put my fist through a wall. I'd been celebrating with my friends the whole damn night, drinking way too much beer and vodka, and then Phina walked into the party looking so fucking gorgeous that I couldn't think straight. All that booze finally gave me enough liquid courage to approach her and tell her that I was in love with her. Instead of speaking, I just grabbed her and kissed her right in front of everyone. After the kiss ended, she slid her hand into mine and pulled me down the hall to the nearest bedroom. It wasn't my first time, but when she told me it was hers, I almost walked away. Then she started removing her clothes and my feet felt like cement blocks. I couldn't move even if someone came in and tried to drag me out of there. She was so gorgeous and I felt like the luckiest fucker in the whole world. I can't remember anything after we fell asleep in that bedroom. I don't remember waking up the next morning, I don't remember talking to her or even leaving the damn house. All this time, I thought it was a dream. I thought there was no way Phina would have ever given something like that to me, and that my feelings were just one-sided. I went off to college and I didn't see her again until a few months ago. Now all of her anger and hatred towards me makes perfect sense and I wish Dax had finished me off in that ring. The pain of his punches would have felt like cuddling a pillow compared to how I feel right now.

Phina asks Collin for a ride home before stumbling out of the bar and into the parking lot. Collin starts to go after her, but I put my hand on his shoulder.

"Nope, I'll make sure she gets home safely," I tell him.

"You sure that's a good idea?" Finnley asks.

"Fuck no, but I'm still going to do it. I'm not fucking letting her down ever again," I tell her before heading towards the door.

PULLING INTO PHINA'S driveway fifteen minutes later, I glance over at her asleep in the front seat. When I got out to the parking lot, I found her slumped over the hood of someone's car. As soon as I lifted her into my arms, her head curled into my neck and she passed out. Good thing for me since I'm sure she would have punched me in the face if she knew I was the one who was taking her home instead of Collin.

I take a few seconds to stare at her beautiful face before getting out of the car, rounding the front end and opening her door to scoop her back up into my arms. As I make my way up her front walk, I hear footsteps behind me and pause, holding her body tightly to me and wondering what the fuck I'm going to do if her father chose this moment to make his move. Turning around, I see a guy in a police uniform making his way up to us. He looks familiar as he smiles at me and nods in Phina's direction.

"Everything okay here?"

I nod, looking at him questioningly.

"Oh, sorry! My name's Jackson. Dax Travino asked me to keep an eye on Phina and her house for a few weeks. I was parked across the street when I saw you pull up," he explains, pointing to the cruiser on the other side of the street.

"Yeah, I forgot about that. Thanks for keeping an eye on things. She just had a little too much to drink tonight," I tell him as Phina starts to stir in my arms. I really don't need her waking up right now and making a scene in front of this poor guy.

"No problem, just doing my job. If you need anything, just let me know. Here's my card with my cell number on it."

He reaches into the pocket by his chest and hands his card to me. I shift Phina in my arms to take it from him, scanning the information, including the guy's last name.

"Holy shit, Castillo? That's…"

"Yeah, Jordan was my cousin," he tells me with a sad smile.

I start to apologize, but what the fuck can I say? Sorry I let your cousin burn to death so I could save my best friend instead? There's no apology in the world that can make up for that, even though I did what I had to do at the time.

"Anyway," he continues, "the street's been pretty quiet tonight, but like I said, if you need anything, just flip the lights in one of the front rooms a few times or call me on my cell."

Pocketing his card, I nod, wrapping my arm back around Phina. She starts to groan against my neck, so I thank Jackson one more time before turning and making my way up to her front porch.

When I glance back towards Jackson as he crosses the street, he gives me a friendly wave and I give him another nod. I shift Phina higher up in my arms so I can reach into my pocket and grab her keys that Collin gave me when I left the bar. Unlocking her front door, I walk inside and kick the door closed behind me before running my hands along the wall to flip the light switch.

The sight in front of me makes me loosen my hold on Phina and she slowly slips down my body. Thankfully, she's fully awake at this point, even though she's still completely trashed, and plants her feet on the ground. We're both staring at the disaster in her living room when she starts laughing.

She laughs so hard that tears stream down her cheeks, and I have a feeling those tears are a mixture of too much booze and being complete-ly freaked out, even though she'll never admit it.

Every piece of furniture has been tipped over, picture frames have been smashed and her carpet looks like someone set it on fire in several different places before putting it out. The plush, cream carpet has large sections that are black and charred, and my nose finally recognizes the nauseating smell of burnt fibers that hit me as soon as I walked in the door.

"Oh, Daddy, you've been a bad, bad boy," Phina says through her laughter as she looks around at the mess.

She sways on her feet while she continues laughing like a crazy person and I scoop her back up into my arms.

"You're going to be in sooooooo much trouble for this," she laughs again before wrapping her arms around me and dropping her head to my shoulder.

"You're not staying here tonight. I'm taking you back to my place," I tell her as I turn and head back out the door.

"Okey dokey, smokey!" she giggles against the skin of my throat.

I pause when I see the note taped right under the light switch that I missed when we entered. I lean forward and use the hand tucked under Phina's knees to rip it off the wall and flip open the folded piece of paper.

Why can't you stop being a whore? Hope you enjoyed your time in the locker room. I'm coming for you. Be ready.

I crumple the note in my fist and leave the house, stomping down the steps so hard I'm surprised my feet don't break right through the wood. I see Jackson in his car across the street, looking at me questioningly through his side window as I load Phina back into my car and secure the seatbelt around her. My tires screech as I pull away from the curb, grabbing my cell from the cup holder and calling the number on Jackson's business card.

"Someone's been in her house and it's a fucking mess," I tell him, not bothering with a hello. I don't want to be pissed at the guy, but he's been watching her house the entire night and her fucking father *still* managed to sneak in right under his nose.

"Jesus Christ," Jackson mutters through the line. "He must have come in through the backyard. I'll get some people in there to take fingerprints and clean the place up. Anything missing?"

"I don't fucking know!" I shout into the phone. "He left another goddamn note. I didn't feel like sticking around to check the place out. I just wanted to get her out of there."

"Do you want me to follow you guys and let someone else take care of the house?" he asks.

"No. I've got it under control tonight. Just find this motherfucker."

I end the call, tossing my cell back into the cup holder.

THE SIGHT OF Phina lying in the middle of my bed does things to me. Girly things. Pussy things. Definitely not *manly* things. She's curled up on her side with her hands under her cheek and my heart fucking melts as I sit on the edge of the bed staring at her. When I got her to my place, she woke up long enough to let me force a glass of water and a couple of aspirin into her before she passed out again and I carried her to my room.

Leaning over her, I smooth her hair off of her face and press my lips to her temple, closing my eyes and breathing her in.

I move my lips away, replacing them with my forehead.

"I'm so sorry," I whisper.

She sighs and I lean back a little to look at her face, but she doesn't open her eyes.

"I loved you. I really, really loved you," she mumbles in her sleep.

I smile sadly down at her, wishing more than anything that I could go back fifteen years and not drink one drop of alcohol that night at the party.

"You have no idea how in love with you I was back then," I whisper back, running my hands softly through her hair.

"I just wanted to be good enough for you. He always said I wasn't good enough for anyone before he'd push his cigarette into my skin. I wanted to be good enough for you to remember," she mumbles, burrowing herself deeper into my pillow.

That motherfucking piece of shit.

I want to take all of her clothes off right this minute and find the scars that pathetic piece of shit left on her body. I want to kiss each and every one of them and tell her she's better than anyone I've ever met and that shit should have *never* been done to her. I think about how she refused to let me take her underwear off that night with Dax and the idea that her own father left marks on her on any part of that covered area fills me with rage. I remember how panicked she was this morning in the park when she woke up to find her pants pulled down and now the words she said to me make complete sense. She was afraid I'd seen what he did to her. She's so strong and fierce and I know it would have killed her for me to see something like that – the one time in her life when she couldn't fight back and a permanent reminder of what she went through.

I take a few deep breaths, pushing my anger aside for the time being.

"Oh, Fireball, I always remembered. I was just too stupid to see it. How in the fuck could I ever forget? And you are *more* than good enough, dammit."

She smiles in her half-asleep state.

"I hate that I still love you," she murmurs.

My hand pauses with my fingers tangled in her hair. I want to shake her awake. I want her to open her eyes and look at me when she fucking says something like that. Jesus Christ, she probably won't even remember she said this shit to me tomorrow, and it's exactly what I deserve.

Placing another kiss on the top of her head, I pull my shirt off as I get up from the bed and toss it over into the dirty clothesbasket. I do the same with my pants before turning off the lamp on the bedside table and walking around the bed to climb in under the covers behind her. Sliding one arm under her neck and wrapping the other around her waist, I pull her back against me and let every inch of her body mold against mine. I bury my face into her hair and close my eyes.

"I love you, and I won't let anything happen to you," I promise her quietly in the dark room.

15

Phina

THE SMELL OF bacon and eggs makes my stomach growl, but I'm so warm and comfortable in bed that I pull the covers tighter around me and keep my eyes closed. I hear humming coming from somewhere outside of the bedroom and my eyes fly open. I bolt up in bed, looking around the room frantically.

This is not my bedroom and this is definitely not my bed. The sheets smell like DJ and I groan, dropping my head and cursing myself.

What in the hell did I do last night? I remember going to McCalla-han's and drinking myself silly, but everything after that is fuzzy. Shit, I think I might have yelled at DJ and told him about what happened in high school.

Fuck, I am never drinking again.

Pulling the covers up, I glance down at myself nervously, hoping to God DJ didn't undress me. There are only so many truths that need to come out in one night, thank you very much. Thankfully, I'm still wearing clothes. The only thing missing are my boots.

Sliding out of bed, I pad across the carpet and let my nose lead me to the kitchen. My traitorous stomach growls again at the smell. I don't even remember the last time I ate, but all I want to do right now is get the hell out of here. I don't like feeling embarrassed and I know as soon as I look at DJ's face, I'm going to regret the truth serum I drank last night. Jesus, did I tell him anything aside from the fact that he drunkenly took my virginity?

Rounding the corner into the kitchen, I see DJ standing in front of the stove, his chest bare and a pair of drawstring pants hanging low on his hips. He happily hums as he stirs whatever he's cooking and my mouth twitches with the need to smile. My hands also start tingling with the need to run them down his muscular back and possibly around the front to dip into the waistband of his pants and palm his cock.

A scoff flies out of my mouth at my errant thoughts, the sound making DJ turn his head and smile at me over his shoulder.

"Breakfast is almost ready. How's your head this morning?" he asks.

I try not to feel mortified as I think about all the things I might have said under the influence last night.

"Fine, my head is fine," I tell him, clearing my throat when my voice comes out rough and scratchy.

DJ turns back around to face the stove, removing the pan from the burner before walking across the kitchen to stand in front of me.

"Do you want some more aspirin?" he asks gently.

I roll my eyes. "Stop being so fucking nice to me."

He just laughs and shakes his head at me. "Shut up and grab a plate before it gets cold."

I grab onto his arm when he starts to walk away and pull him back to me. "Why in the hell am I at your house and where are my damn boots?"

I really just want to get out of here before DJ brings up things I may or may not have said last night. Also, the sight of him standing in front of me shirtless makes me want to strip off my clothes and beg him to fuck me again.

"You're here because your place was trashed last night, and so were you. You don't remember going home?"

I try to recall the events that occurred after I walked out of the bar, but all I can remember is laughing like an idiot and being in DJ's arms. Fuck, I definitely remember how good it felt to have him hold me.

"Yeah, I can tell by the confused look on your face that you don't remember," he tells me with a smile. "It's probably better that way. Your father broke into your house while you were gone. Made a mess of your living room and left another note. The cop that was supposed to be watching your house must have been taking a donut break or some fucking shit. The place is being cleaned and fingerprinted, so you're going to have to wait before you can go back there. And before you even try to argue, if you *do* go back there, I'm not leaving your side. Say hello to your new roommate."

The smirk on his face pisses me off. I don't like being told what to do and I especially don't like the idea that he feels the need to stick to me like glue. I smack my hand against his chest.

"You're not living with me," I growl.

"The fuck I'm not," he argues back.

I smack his chest again, harder this time. "There is no fucking way I'm living with YOU!"

"Give me one good reason why?"

I huff, pulling forth every bit of anger and hatred I've held onto towards him for years, ever since that fucking night of the graduation party.

"BECAUSE YOU TOOK MY VIRGINITY AND DIDN'T EVEN REMEMBER IT, YOU ASSHOLE!"

He loses a bit of the fight in him, but that doesn't stop me.

"I finally got the damn courage to give up the V, to someone who I truly liked and probably even loved a little, and you didn't even remember it the next morning!" I shout.

"Phina," he whispers softly, pain laced through his voice.

"NO! You don't get to be all sweet and sorry now. Do you have any idea what my childhood was like? To never know what it was like to be loved and touched with something other than hatred? I found that in you for one fucking night. One fucking night I was able to forget everything and think that maybe I had a chance at a normal life with a normal guy who could love me back and you shit all over it!" I yell, feeling the sting of tears behind my eyes.

I will not cry, I will not cry. I don't fucking cry!

"I woke up in that bed alone. You fucking left me alone, but I still couldn't stay away from you. I got dressed and came out to the living room to find you and do you know what you said?"

He shakes his head back and forth and I don't know if it's him answering my question or telling me not to keep going.

"You took one look at my tangled hair, my smudged eye make-up and my wrinkled clothes and said, 'Rough night, sweetheart? Who was the lucky guy?'"

I feel a tear slip down my cheek and I brush it away angrily. I hate that I'm crying over him. I hate him for making me feel all of this stupid emotion about something that happened years ago.

"So, you want to know why I won't live with you? Why I won't do THIS with you?" I ask, motioning between us. "Because you broke my fucking heart, DJ Taylor. You broke my fucking heart and you're a DICK!"

Turning away from him, I storm out of the kitchen, grab my boots when I see them sitting by the front door and head outside.

16

DJ

I AM DIRT. Lower than dirt. I am the worms *beneath* the dirt. Every good argument I had for having her stay with me flew out the window when she started to cry. I can handle a lot of things, but I can't handle a woman who cries. Talk about breaking someone's heart. I should have told her that I *did* remember. It took me fifteen years, but I remembered. Instead of chasing after her, I pulled out my cell phone and made a few really quick calls while she stood on the front porch and angrily pulled her boots on.

This is probably going to be the opposite of getting back on her good side, but I can't let her leave until she hears me out.

Stepping out onto the front porch, I see her arguing with Jackson, who is parked in my driveway. She gestures wildly at the house and I watch him shake his head at her. She points at him and then turns her angry eyes on me, stomping back up the walkway and pounding up the stairs.

"You called him and told him not to let me leave? Have you lost your fucking mind?" she shouts.

She stands two steps below me and I can still see the tear tracks on her face, even though her cheeks are flushed with anger.

"Right now, you're safer here," I tell here. "What's the real problem?"

I want to add that I'm sorry I made her cry, I'm sorry I hurt her and I will do anything to make up for it. I wisely keep my mouth shut for now. My balls are entirely too close to her knee.

"BULLSHIT! You just want to torture me! And the real problem is that I used to DATE HIM! I don't want him following me around, that's just embarrassing!"

She turns and goes back down the steps, flopping her ass down on the grass in the front yard.

I let the dating comment go for now because I'm trying really hard NOT to fight with her, but Jesus Christ! Someone could have filled me in on that shit ahead of time.

"What are you doing?" I ask as I walk down to stand next to her.

"I'm not going back inside that house. Go away," she tells me stubbornly.

I hear the rumble of a fire truck and smile to myself as it pulls up to the curb right in front of my house. Ah, the cavalry is here.

Walking past Phina, I meet Collin by the side of the truck and shake his hand. "Thanks for doing this. I promise it will only take a minute."

He opens the front passenger door and reaches inside for the radio, pulling the cord taut as he hands it to me.

"Are you kidding me, I wouldn't miss this shit for the world!" Collin says with a laugh. "Cord should reach all the way to the top. Just stomp on the roof when you're ready."

Collin jumps back inside the truck on the passenger side and I put the cord to the radio in my mouth and climb up the side of the truck until I'm at the top. I stomp twice on the roof and Collin pounds back from the inside. From up here, I have a clear view of Phina still sitting on the lawn looking pissed off, but a little curious. I clear my throat nervously and press the talk button on the radio.

"My name is DJ Taylor and I'm a dick."

My voice echoes through the neighborhood since Collin turned on the switch to the external speaker and I hear him laugh from inside the truck.

I stomp my foot again to get him to stop cackling at my expense.

I point towards Phina and continue. "That beautiful woman right there gave me the most amazing gift in the world and I shit all over it."

Her mouth drops open as she stares at me. I hear dogs start to bark and see a few neighbors walking out on their front porch to see what all the commotion is about.

"I just want you to know, in front of God and all of my neighbors, that I DO remember. I remember it all. It took me fifteen fucking years to remember and that doesn't make it okay, but I remember. I'm sorry for hurting you, I'm sorry that I broke your heart and I'm sorry that you don't trust me because of it. Did I forget anything?"

She pushes herself up from the grass and glares at me.

"You're an asshole!" she shouts.

"Right, also, I am a complete and total asshole," I announce into the radio.

She turns around and stomps back up my stairs and into the house, slamming the door behind her. With a smile, I climb back down off of the rig and hand Collin the radio through the open passenger window.

A few of the neighbors clap and I wave my hand at them.

"Got it all on video. Can't wait to show it to the guys," Collin laughs as he slides over behind the wheel.

"Fuck you."

He continues to laugh as he starts up the truck. "Good luck in there, buddy."

I turn away from the truck as he pulls away and head inside the house. I find Phina back in the kitchen, pacing across the tile, still fuming. She stops moving when I walk up to her.

"Why in the hell did you do that?"

"I just wanted you to know how sorry I am. And I wasn't lying when I said I remember. I remember you asking me to go slow, I remember how I felt like the luckiest fucker in the entire world and I remember thinking that it must be a dream because the girl I had been in love with for years would never give something like that to an idiot like me," I explain. "I had A LOT to drink that night, and I know it doesn't excuse anything, but it's the only excuse I have. And do you know why I said that shit to you the next morning? Because my hung-over ass really thought you'd slept with someone else and I was pissed. I'd wanted you for as long as I could remember and I wanted to kick the ass of whoever got to have you. If I could, I would kick my own ass right now."

I hold my breath as she walks closer to me.

"You drive me crazy," she says.

"The feeling is mutual. When do you want to go to your place and pack a bag?"

She rolls her eyes and shakes her head at me.

"That is non-negotiable. I am still not going to live with you."

I let myself touch her, wrapping my hands around her arms.

"I need to make sure your safe. I don't want to worry about you when you're not here."

She shrugs out of my grasp angrily and takes a step back.

"I am not your fucking responsibility!" she shouts, smacking her hands into my chest.

I move towards her, refusing to let her move away from me. "I love you! That makes you my fucking responsibility!"

17

Phina

"I LOVE YOU! That makes you my fucking responsibility!"

Oh, Jesus, why did he have to go and say THAT?

I hear the conviction in his voice, see the pure honesty in his eyes and it's like someone punched their fist right through the walls of my chest, wrapped their hand around my heart and squeezed the life out of it. I've never felt more unworthy than I do right at this moment. How can he love me? How can he possibly love someone with so much baggage and who is so clearly fucked up? I'm standing here hitting him again when all I want to do is latch onto him and never let go. His words mean more to me than he could ever know. No man has ever loved me. No man has ever looked at me and saw something more, something deeper, something other than the façade. DJ *sees* me. He sees what I could be, he recognizes that there's more to me than the bitch who pushes everyone away, and it scares the shit out of me. His words have branded my soul and have cracked that last piece of armor I've firmly held in place for so long. I want to fall apart in his arms and beg him to give me more, which just makes me lash out.

I clench my hand into a fist and punch his fucking chest because anger is the only emotion I know how to handle.

"You don't love me! You fucked me, there's a huge difference!"

He shakes his head. "Nice try, Fireball, but I happen to know you love me, too, so quit being so goddamn stubborn!"

I pull my fist back again and let it fly towards his chest, but he grabs onto my wrist and hauls me against him.

"Stop fucking hitting me! What is it with you and pain?!"

"Stop fucking talking about love!" I fire back, choosing to ignore the pain remark. "You're just saying that because you feel guilty about what happened in high school."

"It has nothing to do with guilt. I LOVE YOU! I FUCKING LOVE THE SHIT OUT OF YOU!" He screams into my face.

I stomp my foot like a two-year-old and try to hold back the words that are on the tip of my tongue, but I can't stop them. I can't stop the truth from flying out of my mouth.

"GODDAMMIT, I HATE THAT I LOVE YOU, TOO!"

His face immediately loses every ounce of anger and his jaw drops.

I want to laugh. It's right there, bubbling around in my belly and I want so badly to just throw my head back and let it out, but I can't do that. I just told him I loved him right back, and now I'm even more pissed than I was before. This irritating man made me fall in love with him all over again, dammit!

"Let me tell you something," I shout angrily.

He doesn't even let me finish my sentence. His mouth crashes to mine and I immediately part my lips and let him in. I groan as soon as I feel his tongue against mine. I don't remember what the hell I was going to say to complete that last sentence and right now I don't care. His tongue sliding against mine has turned me stupid.

Pressing my hands against his chest, I push him backwards without stopping the kiss. His feet move and his arms wrap around me as he pulls me with him. I push harder when we get to the other side of the room and slam his back against the wall so roughly that it knocks a picture loose and I hear it crash to the floor.

He quickly turns both of us, pulling his mouth away from mine to spin me around, placing his hands on my back and shoving the front of my body against the wall. I slam my hands against it to hold me up while I feel him push his pants down behind me and hear the crinkle of a condom wrapper being opened.

Jesus, does he keep those things in his pajamas? Should I be offended that he assumed we'd fuck this morning and grabbed one for the road or just thankful that he's resourceful?

Pressing my cheek against the cool wall, I sigh in relief and forget about the magically appearing condom when he roughly pushes my skirt up over my ass, bends his knees and drives his cock up inside of me in one hard thrust. We both groan when he pauses, and I feel my pussy clench around him.

"Fuck, you drive me crazy," he mutters against the back of my neck as he starts moving, slamming his hips against my ass, his cock filling me and making me beg for more.

"Harder, fucking harder!" I shout.

He does as I ask even though it seems to piss him off, fucking me so hard that the front of my body slams against the wall over and over.

"I wanted to do it slow this time," he growls as he pumps into me faster and faster. "Jesus Christ, you feel so fucking good taking my cock."

One of his hands slides around to the front of my body and his fingers immediately dive under my skirt and find my clit.

I moan loudly as he uses the tips of his fingers to circle the wet, swollen bud. His fingers move slowly, even though he's fucking me like a machine, and I feel myself pulsing against them as he continues sliding them around and around with just the right amount of pressure. He doesn't stop, he doesn't switch up his movements, he just rubs my clit like an expert until I'm panting against the wall, jerking my hips against his hand to help him make me come. I need this relief like I need air to breathe. I'm so fucked up inside and my heart is swelling with so much emotion that I need DJ to wash it all away. I need him to make me feel worthy of everything he's given me.

My movements are erratic as I race closer and closer to my orgasm, but that doesn't disturb DJ's rhythm as he fucks in and out of me. His cock almost slips out every time I jerk my hips against his hand, but that just makes him pound into me even harder the next time.

"Oh, fuck! Oh, my God!" I shout as the pleasure grows and grows between my thighs while he adds pressure to his fingers as they continue to slide around my clit.

"Say my fucking name when you come," he tells me through clenched teeth right by my ear as his fingers swirl faster around my clit, rubbing it like he fucking owns it.

Goddamn him with the orders again! Too bad I'm so far gone in ecstasy that I don't even care. My thighs start to shake with the effort of holding myself up and the tireless bucking of my hips against his fingers. My orgasm uncoils low in my belly and I feel my pussy pulse with the start of my release, every inch of my body tingling in anticipation.

"Fuck, I can feel you coming. That's it, baby, come on my cock. Say my fucking name."

His words make my orgasm even more intense and a scream rips from my throat as I come.

"DJ!" I scream. "Fuck, fuck, DJ! Fuck, I'm coming!"

He stops fucking me long enough to hold himself inside of me and let me ride out my release against his fingers. My hips rock against his hand as he continues the maddening brush of his finger tips against my clit, prolonging my orgasm until I'm chanting his name for so long that my voice grows hoarse. He keeps his fingers against my pussy as he starts slamming into me again. It only takes a few thrusts before it's his turn to shout my name. I feel his warm breath against the back of my neck as he pants and presses his upper body harder against my own while his hips jerk and pound against my ass and his cock pulses as he spills his come into the condom.

He finishes with one last shout, slumping against my back and pushing me harder against the wall. His fingers are still pressed gently against my clit and I feel his cock continue to pulse inside me with the aftershocks of his release. Aside from our heavy breathing, the only other sound in the room is the ticking of the clock hanging above the sink.

Did we really admit that we loved each other and then have angry sex against the wall?

He slowly pulls himself out of me and quickly turns me to face him.

"Don't even think about taking back that whole 'I love you' thing," he warns as he pulls the condom off, tosses it into the trashcan and yanks his pants up.

Yep, that totally happened.

"Fine, but you're still not going to live with me," I argue, moving away from him, smoothing my skirt down and heading over to the now-cold pan of scrambled eggs and bacon.

He walks up behind me, wraps his arms around my waist and kisses the back of my head.

"We'll discuss it later. After we have dinner with my parents."

Oh, hell no!

18

DJ

I HAVEN'T STOPPED staring at Phina since we got to my parents house, partly because I can't believe how fucking beautiful she is, but mostly because she was entirely too agreeable about having dinner with my family. Finding a note on my front porch when I took out the garbage after breakfast asking me if I'd had my fill of the whore yet might have had something to do with it. I immediately called Jackson and told him I'd changed my mind. I wanted him on Phina at all times, even when she was with me. Just because I *want* to protect her and *think* I'd be good at protecting her doesn't mean I *can,* and I'm man enough to admit that. I'm a trained fireman and paramedic and I'm useful in emergency situations, I'm a hell of a fighter (when I'm not blinded by jealous rage) and I know my way around firearms, but I'm not going to pretend that I would know exactly what to do if that crazy fuck finally showed his face one night while Phina and I were cozied up on the couch watching a movie or some shit. He's obviously keeping a close eye on Phina, he's trashed her house and he's tried to kill her with an overdose of insulin, even if the PD has officially ruled it an accident due to the lack of fingerprints or any kind of solid evidence to the contrary.

Our conversation was tense on the car ride over and I wasn't sure she'd even get out of the car when we got here.

"It's just my parents and my sisters, no big deal."

Phina glared at me from the passenger seat. "No big deal, my ass. I don't do family gatherings. These people are huggers, aren't they? Oh, Jesus, I think I'm starting to get hives."

As I passed a slow moving truck, I watched out of the corner of my eye as she started scratching the skin of her arms.

She could pretend all she wanted, but I'd seen the way she acted around families at the charity fair. She thrived on being around happy people, especially children. I knew my sisters would be bringing their kids to our weekly Sunday dinner and I was looking forward to making Phina eat her words, as well as my mom's pot roast.

"I love you, and my family is going to love you. Just relax," I reminded her as I pulled onto my parent's street.

"I hate you so much for this right now," she muttered.

Luckily, I've become a master at Phina-speak. I've learned that every time she says she hates me, it really means she loves me, so I'm not as bothered by it anymore. She can *hate* me over and over, all night long.

After breakfast, I got a call from Jackson, letting us know Phina's house was all clear. They weren't able to obtain any fingerprints, but at least the mess was contained to just the living room. He called in a cleaning service and when we stopped by for her to take a shower and get a change of clothes, you couldn't even tell that anything had happened the previous night. The crew even threw a couple of rugs down in the living room until the singed carpet could be replaced.

I thought for sure she would fight me when it came time to leave her place to head to my parent's house, but she was anxious to leave. I could tell she no longer felt safe there by how she refused to stay in the living room for more than a few seconds and wouldn't touch or look at one thing in that room as she walked through it. I hated that she couldn't feel comfortable in her own home, but at least I could sleep easier at night knowing she would be curled up next to me in bed without us having to argue for hours about it. She packed a bag as soon as she got out of the shower, and I didn't even have to beg her. We're definitely making progress.

"Your mother has hugged me seven times in the last thirty minutes. SEVEN," Phina whispers, walking up next to me to stand in front of the fireplace.

Wrapping my arm around her shoulder, I hug her to my side and kiss the top of her head. "Don't let her fool you. She's been begging me for another grandchild for years. She was probably trying to feel up your ovaries when she hugged you to make sure they are in working order."

Phina elbowed me in the ribs and we both laughed.

A few seconds later, the front door opens and the house erupts into chaos and noise. Men, women and children pile through the door, tossing coats and shoes in the general vicinity of the entryway, their voices growing louder as they tell stories, argue and shout greetings to my parents.

"Oh, my God. You said it was just your parents and sisters, not an entire fucking zoo," Phina grumbles with a worried look on her face.

"Uncle DJ! Uncle DJ!" my six nieces and nephews shout all at once when they see me standing in the living room.

I remove my arm from Phina's shoulder and brace myself for the herd that is running full speed across the living room to me. Six heads slam into my knees, thighs and stomach and six sets of arms grab onto me as they each continue to shout my name, vying for attention.

Groaning in mock pain, I take my time kissing each of their heads and telling them to stop growing or they're going to be taller than me before Christmas.

"Alright, monkeys! Everyone back away from Uncle DJ and let him breathe!"

I look up and smile at my oldest sister, Dannica, as the kids extract themselves from my legs and scurry off to find their grandparents.

Dannica gives me a kiss on the cheek before turning towards Phina.

"You must be Phina," she tells her, holding her hand out. "Sorry about the noise level."

The shrieks and screams coming from the kitchen must mean that the kids found my father and he's currently tickling each of them.

While Phina shakes Dannica's hand, I look at her questioningly.

"Oh, please. Did you really think mom wouldn't call each of us as soon as you brought a woman home? I knew her height, weight, hair and eye color and what she was wearing five seconds after you got here," Dannica informs me.

The squealing and shouting all of a sudden gets louder, but this time it's from my other two sisters as they come running into the living room, wrapping their arms around Phina and jumping up and down.

"These two overeager idiots are Delaney and Devon," I shout over the noise as Phina catches my eye above Delaney's head.

The girls let go of Phina and each take their turn smacking me in the arm.

"Oh, shut up!" Devon scolds me as she beams at Phina. "It's not every day you find out your brother isn't gay."

"Heeeeey!" I protest.

"Please, he was never gay," Dannica states.

"Thank you," I tell her in appreciation.

"He was a manwhore who never stuck with one woman long enough to bring her to dinner," she finishes.

I groan while Phina laughs.

"I'm so glad you're enjoying yourself," I tell her.

Her face lights up in one of those rare smiles that I've been dying to have aimed at me for weeks.

"Seriously, this is the best day EVER!" she laughs again.

Turning to face Dannica, she leans in and whispers loudly. "Tell me you have baby photos somewhere. Particularly awkward ones of him in tighty-whiteys or wearing your mother's make-up."

Dannica laughs. "Oh, I've got something even better. How about him dressed up as a pretty princess? Little brother especially liked the tiara and high heels."

Delaney and Devon start laughing at my expense and head off to the hall closet to grab every embarrassing photo they can find.

"You are going to pay for this," I whisper in Phina's ear when Dannica heads off to help find photos.

"Whatever you say, pretty princess," she laughs before leaning up on her tip toes to kiss my cheek.

"DRAKE JEFFERSON TAYLOR, GET IN HERE AND HELP ME SET THE TABLE!" my mother screams from the dining room.

I groan and drop my head into my hands.

"Drake Jefferson?" Phina questions.

She pulls my hands away from my face and I roll my eyes. "My mother is the only one who's ever allowed to call me that, so don't get any ideas."

Wrapping her arms around my waist, she looks up into my eyes. "I don't know, I might like shouting that name later tonight instead of DJ."

My dick turns to steel in my jeans.

Phina kisses my chin, then my cheek, and then uses her teeth to tug gently on my earlobe.

"I wonder if Drake can make me come harder than DJ," she whispers against my ear.

Her words make me wonder if it's possible to come in my pants just from the feel of her warm breath alone.

PHINA STARES OUT the window at the passing landscape as we make our way home from my parent's house later that night. I check the rearview mirror and see Jackson's cruiser a few hundred yards behind us. He stayed parked outside my parent's house and Phina insisted on taking him a plate of food when we were finished eating. It didn't take her long to get over her embarrassment that a guy she dated would be the one in charge of keeping her safe. If only *I* could get over my irritation that she dated him in the first place. I didn't want to worry my parents about what's going on, so I kept them busy in the living room while she snuck into the kitchen to grab the food and run it outside.

As I wait at a red light, I glance over at her profile, reflected in the streetlights from the curb. I don't know what she was so worried about tonight. She fit in perfectly with my loud, obnoxious family. She laughed and joked with them, she got down on the floor and played a dozen games of Candy Land with my nieces and nephews and she even initiated the good-bye hugs when it was time to leave. My heart aches for Phina the little girl and how she never knew what it was like to grow up in a loving family like I did. I want to ask her more about her childhood, but I don't want to take the happy, serene look off of her face right now. The little information she did give me when she was practically passed out last night was almost too much to for me to handle. The idea that anyone, especially her own father, would do something as sick and twisted as put his cigarettes out on her skin disgusts me.

I don't want to push her. I know I need to let her talk to me on her own, when she's sober and aware of what she's saying to me. I can't take away her scars and I can't erase her memories from her past, but I can kiss the pain away and promise her a better future. One filled with family and love and happiness. One where she doesn't have to be afraid to trust and lean on other people. I want her to know that not everyone in her life will let her down. I don't know how to even begin helping her when there's still the threat of her father out there somewhere, trying to bring all of that pain back into her life. I want to end that motherfucker, to ruin him for what he did to her as a little girl and I want to make him pay for what he continues to do to her as an adult.

Reaching across the console, I wrap my hand around hers, resting on her thigh. With her face still turned to look out of her window, she threads her fingers through mine and squeezes.

At least we're making progress. She smiled and she laughed just for me today. I'll take that one tiny step forward for now, but soon enough, I'm going to make her give me an entire leap in the right direction.

19

Phina

I DON'T KNOW how long I can keep this up. I'm not this person who is in a loving, committed relationship and who's happy all the time. It feels right, and every day I spend with DJ is better than the one before it, but how much longer will he put up with my strange requests in the bedroom?

Okay, technically not *in* the bedroom, since we never seem to be able to make it further than the front door of his house before he's bending me over some piece of furniture to fuck me, but still. A few times in the last week he's tried to move us down the hall and I've always stopped him. I tell him I just can't wait that long and that I need him inside of me right that minute. While it's true for the most part, I also know that there's a whole shitload of intimacy that comes from having sex in a bedroom that I'm just not ready for yet. Every time he's inside me, he complains that I have too many clothes on and that he wants to see all of me. It doesn't stop him from fucking me like an animal on the kitchen counter, against the wall of the living room or on the hood of his car in the garage, though. I know what we do isn't normal. I know that at some point this carnal fucking is going to slow down and he's going to want to take his time, remove all of my clothes and just stare at me, because it's exactly what I want to do to him. My insides twist with that thought, though, and my hands itch to run to my house, grab the lighter and cigarettes from my bedroom and let the searing pain of burning flesh ease this anxiety. I've transferred that old, familiar need to DJ, letting the slap of his hips against mine and the pounding of his cock inside of me take the edge off my need for pain. My addiction to branding myself has turned into an addiction for a man, one who loves me, takes care of me and makes me laugh. I know it's all going to disappear as soon as he finds out the truth about me. I spend each day thinking how that inevitable conversation will go, imagining the look on his face when he finally sees all of me and realizes what I've done to myself. He'll never understand. He thinks he knows who I am. He believes I'm standoffish and bitchy because of the things my father did to me. What will he do when he finds out I've continued with my father's sick brand of punishment because it's the only way I know how to live? It's all I've ever known and even though his body is enough to calm my nerves for now, it's not going to last forever. Soon enough, I'm going to dream about pressing a cigarette to my hip to slow my rapid heartbeat and stop my cold sweats. Soon enough, feeling him inside of me and letting him bruise my body with rough sex isn't going to cut it. I'm an addict and this insane twelve-step program of DJ Taylor isn't going to cure me, it's just another addiction I'm piling on top of the first one.

"I just don't understand how *no one* has been able to find the fucker yet," DJ complains to Dax on the phone as I load our dishes from dinner into the dishwasher.

One quiet night in front of the television a few days ago, he admitted he was an asshole with Dax and needed to do some groveling. I didn't tell him just how much it excited me to know he was jealous of my friendship with the guy. I grabbed his phone from the coffee table and handed it over, telling him to just apologize. He called Dax right in front of me and, even though the conversion that night was only filled with grunts, stammering and no real apology, at least the two men called a truce and were back to speaking to each other.

"We've got your cop following our asses every damn place we go. How is this piece of shit getting around him to keep leaving these damn notes?" DJ argues.

Eighteen notes in total so far, each one placed in their own individual zip lock bag and handed over to the police as evidence. Just like with the first couple we received, none of them had any fingerprints or any real way to tie them to my father. Every time we left DJ's house, a new one would appear on the front door. After that, we tried staying home, figuring there was no way he'd be able to get by Jackson, but he still managed to do it. Notes showed up tucked inside the mail in the mailbox, they were stuck under the windshield wiper of DJ's car and they were even delivered via certified mail. They all contained some sort of threat, escalating with each one, and Dax believes he's getting angry because I'm never alone and he can't get to me. I don't care about what he says to me, but he's still including DJ in this shit and that pisses me off. All of his damn notes mention something that happened privately between DJ and I, and they almost always call me a whore.

I can hear my father's voice, screaming at me when I was in high school like it was yesterday.

"You're a stupid whore, just like your mother! How many times have you spread your legs this week to get what you want?"

"No good man will ever want a whore like you. Especially with those ugly burns on your back. How about you come over here so I can add another one?"

I close my eyes and shake my head, trying my hardest to get his fucking voice out of my brain.

"Alright, man, keep me posted. No, I'm not letting her out of my sight. She's even going to do a ride-along with me at work tonight."

DJ grins at me with the phone pressed to his ear and I try to look angry, but it's impossible when he smiles at me like that. At Dax's insistence, I took a leave of absence from work. He didn't like the idea of me being so easily accessible in such a busy hospital, and there's no way the administration would let DJ and Jackson follow behind me like a rabid guard dog on my shifts. When DJ was called in on his days off for emergencies, I'd go out to Jackson's cruiser and have coffee with him until DJ came home. I enjoy his friendship and I feel like I'm doing some good by rekindling it again. It's my way of making up for the shit that went down with Jackson's cousin and it's also nice to sit and chat with someone about nothing important. It takes my mind off of what's happening with my father and what I'm going to do about my relation-ship with DJ. It's strange to be friends with men that I have no intention of sleeping with, first Dax and now Jackson. I've made Jackson tell me all about his life since we briefly dated. He's never been married and he likes to joke that he could never find a woman who could live up to my high standards. He's very close to his family and has been spending a lot of time with his aunt and uncle, doing whatever he can to ease the pain of losing their child. He doesn't ask about Finnley and I don't offer any information. Jordan was fucked up in the head from his drug and alcohol addictions, harassing Finnley after she kicked him out of the house and then breaking in one night with the intention of killing her, spreading gasoline all over the first floor of the house before lighting a match. I know it has to be hard for Jackson, wanting to blame *someone* for what happened. Jordan was his best friend and it must be difficult to recognize the bad in someone when you have so many good memories of them. Unfortunately, no one is to blame for Jordan's death aside from

Jordan himself. He made his choices and he had to die with them.

The nice thing about Jackson is that being friends with him is easy. He has a great sense of humor and he never asks about my father, even though he knows most of the gritty details. We talk about mundane things like the weather, television shows we saw or books we read. We talk about nonsense and for a few hours, I can just be a normal woman without a care in the world. Part of me feels like I'm betraying DJ in some way by having these thoughts. I want to be normal with him. I *try* to be normal with him. We laugh, we cuddle, we fuck and we do most of the other regular things a normal couple does. I just won't let him see me naked and he pretends like it isn't an issue.

DJ ends the call with Dax and shoves his phone in his pocket. He walks over to where I'm leaning against the counter, wraps his hands around my hips and easily lifts me up onto the counter. He kisses my lips and then makes his way across my cheek and down to my neck, nipping my skin with his teeth. I wrap my legs around his hips and my arms around his shoulders, pulling him closer.

"We've got about twenty minutes before I need to leave for work. How about an orgasm or two before we hit the road?" he asks with a laugh against my neck.

The bright light from the ceiling fan hanging in the middle of the room and the fact that I'm wearing jeans instead of a skirt make that idea less exciting than it should be.

I place my hands flat on his chest and push him away, sliding down off the counter. Making quick work of his belt buckle, zipper and button, I shove his pants down to his knees, kneeling in front of him as I go.

"I think I can handle that," I tell him with a smirk as I wrap my hand around his cock and lean forward.

"I meant you, not me," DJ starts to complain.

He moans loudly in the small kitchen as I take him fully into my mouth. His hands slide through my hair and he clutches it tightly in his fists. I love that he doesn't push me, he just holds on tight and lets me do all of the work.

I suck his cock as hard as I can, sliding my hand up and down the length as I go, increasing my speed when he starts thrusting his hips. With my hand still pumping him, I pull back to tease him, swirling my tongue around the tip before taking him all the way back into my mouth.

He chants my name in time with the thrusting of his hips. I increase my speed and the pressure of my hand, sliding him so far into my mouth that I feel the head of his cock touch the back of my throat.

"Jesus Christ, Phina," DJ groans each time I take him that deep.

Bobbing my head up and down his cock, I start twisting my hand each time I slide it up and down his length.

"Fuck, your mouth should be illegal," DJ moans as his hips start moving faster and faster.

I hum my approval, knowing the vibrations from my voice wrap around his cock and push him right to the edge.

"Baby, I'm going to come. SHIT! FUCK!" he shouts.

He tries to pull back, but I wrap my free hand around him, clutching onto his ass to pull him deeper inside my mouth. I want to taste him on my tongue.

He comes in my mouth with a roar, tossing his head back and squeezing his eyes closed. I pull him into my mouth harder, letting each spurt of come slide down my throat until I've sucked him dry. His hands drop from my hair to smack down on the counter behind me as his body sags.

Pulling my mouth away from his cock, I get up from my knees to stand between the cage of his arms and he finally opens one of his eyes to look at me.

"I'm never going to be able to work tonight. Every time I look at you, I'm going to think about my cock in your mouth. Take your pants off, it's my turn now," he mutters.

I've been tagging along with DJ while he works the last week, but he's been staying back at the station doing paperwork and training instead of going out on calls. Tonight I'll actually get to see him in action.

I smile and pat his cheek. "We don't have time. You now have ten minutes to get to work and I still need to change."

Leaning up on my tiptoes, I slide my cheek against his and then run the tip of my tongue across the edge of his ear. "I've always wanted to have sex in an ambulance. You can pay me back later."

Sliding out from under his arms, he smacks my ass as I head upstairs to change out of my jeans. I let the sound of his laughter follow me as I go, warming the chill in my soul so I don't have to think about what's going to happen to me when all this normalcy disappears.

20

DJ

"No, Mrs. Ortiz, we can't give you a ride to the hospital to see your nephew," I tell the old woman for the third time tonight.

Mrs. Ortiz is in her eighties and her nephew is a junkie who winds up hospitalized from an overdose at least every other month. Each time he's admitted, we get a call that Mrs. Ortiz is having chest pains. Even though we know it's not true, we still have to drive out here, assess the situation and scold her for making a false emergency call to the station.

"They took away my license!" she complains. "You drive through the lobby of one Red Lobster and suddenly you're unfit to be behind the wheel of a vehicle."

I try to stifle a laugh as Brad packs up the first responder bag, grumbling under his breath. Even though I knew fully well that Mrs. Ortiz wasn't in any dire situation, I still made Brad go through the normal routine of checking her vitals. He can bitch all he wants, but the newbie needs the practice. I'd much rather have him practice on this old woman with an attitude than on an actual emergency.

"I know damn well you're still driving, so don't give me that non-sense," I tell her. "Your car was still warm and the engine was still ticking when we pulled in."

I raise my eyebrow at her and try to keep a stern look on my face.

She harrumphs, crossing her arms over her chest. "The Quick Mart was having a sale on TV dinners. A woman's got to eat, you know."

Following Brad out of the kitchen, I remind her that we're not a taxi service before joining Phina in the open doorway of the living room. Giving her a wink, I grab her hand as we make our way down the front porch and out to the ambulance. Phina gives a wave to Jackson, who's parked right behind the rig while I hold open the passenger door and take my time putting my hands on her ass to help push her up into her seat.

Brad jumps into the back of the ambulance while I round the front end and get behind the wheel.

While I start up the vehicle, Brad reaches through the seats to hand me the patient report card he filled out so I can call the information in to dispatch and inform them that once again, there was no medical emergency at Mrs. Ortiz's house.

As soon as I end my call to dispatch on the radio system and finish entering the information into the computer attached to the dashboard, Phina starts laughing. "Boy, your job is full of so much excitement, I almost can't handle it."

Pulling away from the curb, I can't help but laugh with her. Her happiness and laughter is almost as addicting as her attitude. "Shut your yap. I know you got hot standing there in the doorway listening to me use my 'adult voice' on Mrs. Ortiz."

She continues to laugh, asking me about other calls I've been on in my career. As much as I don't want someone to get hurt, I can't help but be a little salty that our call-outs tonight involved someone who fell and couldn't get up, a woman whose son had food poisoning and a drunk going through withdrawal who assumed he was dying. Is it too much to ask for a little gunshot wound or stabbing?

After we get back to the station, I let Brad and a few other guys disinfect the back of the ambulance, restock the supplies we used tonight and start charging all of the equipment for the next shift while I finish up some paperwork. Phina sits on the edge of my desk, crossing and uncrossing her legs while she flips through a magazine.

It's bad enough I've had thoughts of that stellar blow job in my head all night long, now I have to try and concentrate on filling out these fucking performance evaluations for Brad with a clear view of Phina's long, smooth legs that I can still feel wrapped around my waist.

A throat clears from the doorway and I guiltily look away from her legs to glare at Brad.

"Ambulance has been cleaned and stocked. I gave the outside a good scrubbing, so it's still sitting out in the driveway drying off. The guys and I are all heading to bed. Anything you need before we turn in?"

I check my watch and realize it's already after midnight.

"No, go ahead and turn in. As long as we don't get any calls during the night, I'll just see you in the morning and we can go over your review," I tell him.

I catch him giving Phina's bare legs an appreciative glance and it's my turn to clear my throat in irritation.

He still doesn't stop staring and Phina chuckles.

"Brad, go to bed before I shove my fist up your ass," I warn him.

He finally looks away in embarrassment before scurrying off down the hall.

"Awww, go easy on the kid. He's kind of cute," she tells me with a laugh, pushing herself off my desk to slide easily onto my lap.

My hand runs up the inside of her thigh and I graze my fingertips over the lace of her underwear that covers her sex.

"If he's cute, what am I?" I ask quietly, letting my fingers gently play between her legs.

"You're poking into my ass," she smirks, wrapping her arms around my neck.

Sliding one arm under her knees and the other around her back, I quickly stand, lifting her up with me. She lets out a surprised yelp, holding onto me tighter as I head towards the door.

"I'm going to poke you somewhere else and make you take back that cute remark," I warn her, heading down the hall and out the front door to the privacy of the now-clean ambulance.

"LIGHTS. OFF," SHE growls for the second time as I slide her red lace underwear down her thighs and off her legs, shoving them into the front pocket of my pants.

I've got the upper half of her body strapped to the gurney in the back of the ambulance and technically, I don't have to listen to anything she says. She's under my control right now and there isn't a damn thing she can do about it. Unfortunately, the florescent lights in the back of the ambulance are a bit too bright even for my liking. Leaving her side, I lean in between the two front seats and flip the switch on the dashboard, bathing the ambulance in shadowed darkness. Luckily, there's a street lamp on the edge of the driveway shining enough light through the front windshield that I can see where I'm going.

"Thank you," she whispers, when I crawl back on the gurney with her and straddle her thighs.

"I'll concede to letting you have that one thing, but your time for demands ends right now," I warn her.

Leaning forward, I run my hand over the straps holding her in place, reaching to the side of the bed to tighten them just a little bit more.

Resting my lips against her ear, I whisper softly. "I've let you dictate every time we've fucked, and while it's been great, it's *my* turn to be in control. Close your eyes and hold on, Fireball."

I move away from her, letting my body slide down hers until I'm lying on my stomach in between her legs.

Running my hands up the inside of her thighs, I push them wide apart as I get myself settled.

She moans as I slide my thumbs up the lips of her pussy, spreading it open as I go. I really want to turn the fucking lights back on so I can see her, but tasting her and listening to her cries of pleasure are going to have to do for now.

"Do you want me to lick your pussy, baby?" I ask softly, letting my breath skate over her.

Her hips jerk towards me and if her arms were free, I'm sure she'd be digging them into my scalp right about now, yanking my face right where she wants it.

I put my middle finger in my mouth and get it wet with my tongue before bringing it to her clit to circle it slowly. My fingertip touches her like a whisper, just barely grazing the swollen, stiff bud. Her body shakes with need and the clacking and creaking sound of her pushing against the restraints on the bed tell me she's had enough of the teasing.

"Let me hear your voice. Tell me to lick your pussy," I whisper in the shadows, adding some pressure to my finger.

I glance up her body and I can just make out the shape of her in the darkness. Her head is thrown back and her chest is heaving. Resting my cheek against the inside of her thigh, I slide my finger down through the lips of her pussy, gathering her wetness before trailing my finger back up to circle her clit with her own liquid heat.

"Fuck, fuck, fuck!" she shouts.

I smile against her thigh, continuing to torture her with my finger.

"All you have to do is say the words, Fireball," I tell her softly, swiping against her clit with the tip of my finger like I'm flipping the page of a book on a Kindle.

"Jesus, fuck! Lick my pussy, fucking lick it already!" she shouts in irritation, jerking her hips against my finger, trying to get me to move faster.

I'd laugh at her frustration if I weren't dying to put my mouth on her.

Using my elbows to give me leverage, I dive my head forward and wrap my lips around her clit, sucking it into my mouth.

Phina shouts in relief as I flatten my tongue and lick the hell out of her pussy, quickly pushing two of my fingers inside of her. She's so wet and ready that my fingers easily slide inside. I pump them in and out of her slowly and flick the tip of my tongue over her clit in a maddening pace.

The gurney rocks and squeaks as she thrusts her hips up to meet my mouth and the motion pushes my fingers even deeper.

I pull my mouth away long enough to speak while I continue the motions of my fingers in and out of her. This fucking woman needs to be praised.

"I could eat your pussy every day and never get tired. Fuck, you taste like sugar."

She whimpers as I go back to work, fucking into her with my fingers. I feel her clit pulsing against my lips and tongue and I push my fingers into her all the way to the knuckles. Bringing my other hand up, I flatten my palm on her lower abdomen and gently push down, curling my fingers forward at the same time to brush against her swollen g-spot.

Phina screams in pleasure, as I slowly brush my tongue back and forth over her clit. As much as I don't want to stop, there's just one more thing I need to hear from her, one thing I need her to promise me.

"From now on, I'm the only man who gets to watch you come. No more third wheel in the bedroom and no other hands on your body but mine. This pussy," I whisper, flicking my tongue over her clit, "is

MINE."

She whimpers in protest when I pull my mouth away.

"Say it," I growl, my mouth hovering right above her as I push my middle finger against her g-spot.

"JESUS, IT'S YOURS! FUCK! ONLY YOURS!" she screams as I smile to myself before burying my face back in her pussy.

"DRAKE! Fuck, Drake!"

He hips buck against me erratically as she comes while I lick and suck the juices from her pussy and continue to lightly rub her g-spot.

I chuckle against her pussy as her lower body slumps back down to the gurney and listen to her whimper every few seconds while she tries to catch her breath.

Pulling my fingers out of her, I make my way back up her body and rest my hands on either side of her head to stare down at the shadow of her face.

The faint light from outside allows me to see when she opens her eyes to look up at me.

"You win. You can have control during sex ANYTIME," she mumbles in a sleepy voice.

I laugh, leaning down to press my lips to hers before backing away.

"And you, Fireball, also win. You can call me Drake anytime. Especially when you're coming and giving me complete ownership of your pussy."

21

Phina

THE RUSHING PANIC that filled me when DJ first strapped me to the gurney disappeared as soon as he turned off the lights to the ambulance. I know I'm behaving like a fool, I know I need to just come clean with him, but I can't. I want to keep up this illusion for as long as I can. I need to pretend like everything is fine or I'll go insane.

I tried not to let the fear come out in my voice when I demanded that he turn off the lights. I forced myself to make it sound like I was just a controlling bitch and to keep the quiver in my throat from sneaking out.

I concentrated on how hot it was to be strapped down, unable to move my arms or slide my fingers through DJ's hair. I closed my eyes and pushed everything out of my mind except for the feel of his mouth on me, bringing me to orgasm. Jesus, that man is talented. I've never come that fast in my life, not even with my own hand.

DJ unhooks the straps over my chest and arms and I shake out the soreness in them before wrapping them around his neck and pulling him down on top of me.

"Your fingers and tongue should come with a warning," I tell him, running my hands through his hair and placing soft kisses on his lips and chin.

"You could always get me a t-shirt that says *Champion Muff Diver*," he says with a laugh.

I squeeze chunks of his hair in my hands until he laughs and shouts in mercy.

"You are impossible," I laugh right along with him.

DJ leans forward to kiss me, but I quickly turn my head to the side, breathing deeply.

"Do you smell that?"

He holds himself still, sniffing the air. "Is that smoke?"

I hear confusion in his voice as he pushes himself off me to look out the front windshield. I crane my neck back and we both see the source of the smell at the same time.

"WHAT THE FUCK?" he shouts, jumping off of the gurney to race up between the two front seats.

I scramble off the bed and look beyond him, my eyes widening in shock and fear.

Orange flames flicker through the front windshield of the ambulance, growing higher and higher with each second that passes.

"*DJ! PHINA!*"

We hear muffled shouts coming from outside and I move out of DJ's way as he charges to the back of the ambulance and throws the door open. He immediately backs away when he sees more flames behind the truck, billowing towards the opening.

"GET AWAY FROM THE DOOR! IT'S ALL AROUND THE TRUCK!" Jackson shouts frantically from the other side of the wall of flames.

Climbing between the front seats, I look out the driver's side window and sure enough, there is a circle of fire about six feet high surrounding us. I watch as the front doors of the fire house burst open and ten men come running outside, dragging a hose between them.

Making my way towards DJ, he wraps his arms around me and holds me close while we watch through the flickering flames as their blurry shapes shout orders and begin trying to contain the fire.

I can feel the heat from the fire coming in through the door and sweat drips down my neck and back. How long does it take for a fire like this to get to the gas tank and blow this entire thing with us inside?

"It's going to be fine. They're going to put out the fire and get us the fuck out of this thing," DJ promises, rubbing his hands up and down my arms.

No sooner than those words leave his mouth, something that sounds like a shotgun going off thunders through the vehicle, making me jump and scream. The ambulance suddenly jerks to one side, causing DJ and I to lose our footing and topple sideways, slamming into the wall.

Men outside are shouting even louder now and I don't realize I'm still screaming until DJ gathers me close, holding his hand against the back of my head and pressing my face into his shoulder.

"Shhh, it's okay, baby, it's okay. It was just one of the tires blowing," he tells me in a soothing voice.

The smell of burning rubber, gas and fire surrounds us and I squeeze my eyes closed and hold onto DJ for dear life, listening to the sound of the water from the hose spray against the outside of the vehicle. Hitting the steel body of the ambulance, I can almost make myself believe it's just a soft, soothing rain that's coming down outside instead of the only thing standing between us and death.

DJ and I stay wrapped in each other's arms for the five longest minutes of my life before Jackson sticks his head into the back of the vehicle.

"Fire's out. You guys okay?"

Pulling myself away from DJ, I nod my head as DJ storms out the doors, grabs a fistful of Jackson's shirt, twists him around and slams him against the back of the wet ambulance.

"WHAT IN THE FUCK HAPPENED? YOU'RE SUPPOSED TO BE MAKING SURE NOTHING HAPPENS TO HER, YOU INCOMPE-TENT FUCK!" DJ shouts into Jackson's face.

I jump down from the back of the ambulance and grab onto DJ's shoulders, using all of my strength to pull him off of Jackson.

"DJ! Let go!" I order. "Let him go!"

DJ gives him one last rough shove before releasing his shirt and holding his hands in the air.

"I'm fine! No one got hurt, calm down."

DJ whirls on me and stares at my face like I've grown two heads. "Are you fucking kidding me? He had one job to do. ONE!"

Jackson takes a step towards us and lifts his hand to rest it on DJ's shoulder. I give him a warning look and pray he's not that stupid. If he touches DJ right now, he's going to get his ass beat.

He quickly drops his hand.

"I swear to God, I haven't taken my eyes off of this fucking truck ever since I saw you two come out here. It's been quiet and dark all night long. Not one person has come or gone from this entire block since you guys got here two hours ago," Jackson explains.

DJ keeps his eyes glued to mine and I can tell by all the deep breaths he's taking that he's trying to calm himself down. I grab onto both of his hands and squeeze them tight.

"The fire marshal will have to come out here and give an official ruling, but it's pretty obvious by the circular shape the fire took around the truck that an accelerant was used," one of the guys from the fire station informs us.

"We could smell gas from inside," DJ finally speaks.

"He must have come from the opposite side of the ambulance, out of my line of sight, and used some sort of sprayer from underneath the vehicle to get it everywhere. I swear to you, I didn't see anything until the flames exploded all around it," Jackson tells us. "I flew out of my car, yelled inside to the station and then ran over here and started screaming at you guys inside."

DJ takes another deep breath and then hangs his head. I can tell he's feeling guilty and it kills me. This wasn't his fault. It has nothing to do with him. He just had the unfortunate luck of being with me.

"I'm sorry, I'm so sorry," I whisper, fighting back tears.

His head jerks up and he lets go of my hands, bringing them up to cup my face.

"Don't you dare. Don't you *dare* blame yourself for what happened! This is NOT your fault, Phina. Do you hear me?"

I nod, even though I don't believe him. If I were alone, if I was as far away from DJ as possible, he never would have gotten caught up in this mess.

DJ hugs me to him, exchanging a few more tense words with Jackson and then thanking the guys from the firehouse. With one arm still around me, he pulls his cell out of his front pocket and calls Dax.

"ALRIGHT, I THINK that's everything we need," Dax tells us as he finishes clacking away at his computer, taking our statement. "You sure you guys don't want to go to the hospital? Get checked out for smoke inhalation?"

DJ turns to look at me and I shake my head. I just want to go home. I want to curl up in bed and stop thinking about how I'm fucking up DJ's life by being with him.

The door to Dax's office opens and a tall brunette walks in with a cup of coffee in her hands. He smiles at her, giving her the full-on Dax double dimples and I shake my head, knowing this poor woman doesn't stand a chance.

"Harley, these are my friends, DJ and Phina," he introduces, giving her a wink as she pauses next to us.

"Nice to meet you. I apologize in advance for my behavior," she tells us.

Before I can ask her what the hell she's talking about, she walks right behind Dax's desk and dumps the cup of hot coffee right in his lap.

"MOTHERFUCKER!" Dax shouts, jumping up from the chair while he glares at her.

"Your coffee, *sir*," she tells him in a sickeningly sweet voice.

She immediately turns on her heels and I give her a huge smile as she walks by.

"Oh, I really, really like you," I tell her with a laugh.

She nods in my direction before exiting his office, slamming the door behind her so hard the walls rattle.

DJ lets out a low whistle from the chair next to me while Dax tries to hold the soaked crotch of his pants away from his junk.

"What did I tell you about banging the women you work with? She didn't shoot off your balls, but she sure did a nice job with the third degree burns," I laugh.

Dax continues muttering and cursing about pig-headed women while DJ and I get up from our chairs and leave him to deal with his burning balls.

"Who would have thought filling out a police report could be so much fun?" DJ asks with a smile as we head out of the building and across the parking lot to his truck.

I hear my cell phone ringing in my purse so I stop and dig for it. When I pull it out, I see that it's from an unknown number. DJ looks at the screen questioningly and I just shrug my shoulders, hitting the answer button and bringing the phone up to my ear.

I hear nothing but silence for a few seconds and I start to pull the phone away when I hear someone clear his throat.

"You sure are a hard woman to get ahold of."

My stomach plummets all the way to my feet and vomit makes it's way up into my throat. It's the voice from my childhood, the same one I hear in my nightmares every night calling me a whore and telling me I'm not good enough.

"Baby, are you there?" he asks.

"Don't you *dare* call me baby," I whisper angrily into the phone.

DJ wraps his hand around my arm, but I barely feel it. He asks me who's on the phone, but I can't speak.

"I got out, but I'm sure you already know that," he laughs.

My hands shake and I can barely hold onto the phone anymore. Why can't I just hang up the fucking phone? Why can't I just tell him to go to hell and leave me alone?

"I had a lot of thinking to do while I was behind bars, baby. A lot of years to become an old man and think about all the things I've done. I'm supposed to make amends to the people I've wronged, so I figure I should start with you."

His voice through the line is like nails on a chalkboard and my arms pebble with goose bumps.

"Did you get any of my notes?"

I whimper and squeeze my eyes closed.

"Give me the fucking phone," DJ curses right next to me.

I turn away from him and wrap my arm around my waist, trying to hold myself together. It feels like my insides are going to spill out of my stomach and splatter all over the ground at my feet. I don't want DJ to see me like this. I don't want him to know how weak just the sound of this man's voice makes me.

"I'm comin' clean now, baby, it's time. Your momma, she didn't run away. She talked about it all the time, but she never had the guts to do it until that last day. I came home from work and found all her shit packed. She told me she was done and she was leavin' both of us. I just couldn't have that, baby. I couldn't have her leavin' me with a kid to take care of all by myself. I took care of it, though. I wouldn't let her leave unless I was the one makin' it happen."

A sob works its way up my throat, but I force it back. I don't want to hear the next words out of his mouth. I don't want to know that he's even more of a monster than I ever thought.

"I killed her, baby. I'm sorry, but I killed your momma. She was a whore and a worthless mother, but I'm still sorry about it. I just didn't want you to turn out like her. You didn't turn out like her, did you baby? You didn't turn into a liar and a whore and a cheat, did you? People burn in hell for something like that."

The phone falls from my hand and clatters to the ground. DJ snatches it up and screams into it, but I know he's not there any more. He said what he needed to say, he messed with my mind and my heart and there was no reason for him to stay on the line for another second. Somehow, he killed my mother and made me believe she left because she didn't love me, that she went away to start a new family because I wasn't good enough. He tried to burn me tonight to send me to hell where he thinks I belong.

I finally turn around and look up into DJ's angry face and I realize he's probably right. I *do* belong in hell. I deserve to burn for dragging DJ into my life and putting him on my father's radar. How could I ever think that I was deserving of a good future, when the sins of my past would never let me go?

22

DJ

PHINA HASN'T SAID more than two words to me the last few days. It scares me more than thinking about everything that could have gone wrong the other night if we hadn't been parked right out front of a fire station. What if Brad hadn't been with us all night and I just pulled over on the side of the road? We would have been trapped. Not only could the gas tank have exploded, the back of the ambulance is filled with compressed air oxygen tanks. If it had gotten any hotter inside of that thing, we would have been blown to bits. Once again, I was fucking helpless with Phina. I couldn't do anything but stand inside that fucking tin box on wheels and wait for someone else to save us. This shit has GOT to stop.

Dax got a court order to pull Phina's phone records and the call that she got right outside the PD came from a payphone on the other side of town, only a few blocks from the fire station. An APB has been put out for Phina's father, but so far, there's been no trace of him. It's like he just keeps disappearing into the fucking wind.

I glance at Phina on the opposite end of the couch, watching her stare blindly at a movie I put in after dinner. I want to reach over and pull her against me. I want to hold her and tell her everything will be okay, but I can't make that fucking promise. I can't make her any kind of promise when her father is still out there. I have no idea what he said to her on the phone and after I questioned her a few times on the ride home that night, she completely shut down and told me it didn't matter. She's quickly retreating back to the person she was just a few months ago: cold, aloof and pretending like everything that happened between us isn't real. I hate that she won't trust me. She'll give me her body and she'll give me the words, but they mean absolutely nothing when she doesn't really believe them. She doesn't believe that she's good enough to be loved and nothing I do will change her mind.

The doorbell rings and when Phina looks at me with curiosity, I don't say a word as I get up from the couch to greet my guests. The only thing I have left is emotional manipulation. Hopefully, it works.

As soon as I open the door, my small townhouse is filled with so much noise you'd think I invited a hundred people over. I hold the door open as my sisters and my mother file inside, each one wrangling a child or two and helping them remove their coats and shoes. Kids yell, women argue, shoes are thrown around the entryway like landmines and I couldn't be happier.

"Whoever is quiet the longest will get a cookie from Uncle DJ!" Dannica announces.

A hush falls across the room and I'm the first one to speak.

"Uh, cookies? Was I supposed to make cookies?"

I hear a quiet laugh from behind me and turn to see Phina standing in the doorway with her arms crossed. "We don't need you burning the house down. Who wants to help me make cookies?"

The kids immediately forget about the quiet rule and start screaming and bouncing up and down. I wink at Phina and she gives me a small smile, holding her hands out for two of my nieces to grab as she leads everyone down the hall and into the kitchen. My sisters each give me a kiss on the cheek before following behind her, filing out of the room until I'm left alone by the front door with my mother. She gives me a hug and pats my cheek, holding her hand against the side of my face as she searches my eyes.

Not knowing what else to do to bring *my* Phina back around, I called my mom and told her as much as I could without worrying her too much. She immediately suggested bringing my sisters and the kids over so Phina could have some extra company to take her mind off of things. I knew she would have probably preferred the company of her best friend, but Collin and Finnley were out of town for the weekend and I didn't want to tell them about what happened over the phone and freak them out.

"You're a good man," she tells me quietly.

I look away from her, not sure I agree with her right at this moment.

"Do you remember that time I was mugged when you were back in high school?"

I nod my head quietly, thinking about that night when I was fifteen and my mom was late getting home from work. We got a phone call from the police saying she'd been walking out to her car and had been attacked from behind. The scumbag beat the hell out of her face and broke her arm just to take her purse with all of twenty dollars inside.

"Your father was beside himself. He was angry that he hadn't been there to help me and he blamed himself for being laid off from his job those couple of months, forcing me to take a part-time one at night," she explained.

I remember my father coming home from the hospital that night, going out into the garage and trashing the place. He threw a hammer through a wall and cracked his workbench in half by pounding it over and over with his fists.

"I ignored him for a week after I got out of the hospital, but not because I blamed *him*. I could never have blamed him for a freak accident like that, but I did blame myself. I knew better than to walk out to that dark parking lot alone. I knew I should have asked the security guard to walk out there with me or even call your father to come and pick me up, but I was stubborn back then."

I cock my head to the side and smirk. "Just back then?"

With her hand still on my cheek, she smacks it a little harder this time.

"Watch it, smartass," she laughs.

Properly chastised, I wipe the smile from my face while she continues. "My point is, there's nothing you can do to fix her right now. You aren't responsible for the things that have happened any more than she is. All you can do is be there for her when she's ready. Give her time and if she needs space, give it to her. If she loves you as much as you love her, she'll come back when she's ready. She'll talk to you when she's ready and she'll lean on you when she needs it. Your Phina is a very strong woman. When someone like her falls, they fall hard and they need a soft place to land."

She leans up and kisses my cheek one last time before turning to head into the kitchen, where I hear the clanging of bowls and laughter.

Wise woman, that mother of mine. I just hope I have the ability to be soft enough for Phina when she comes crashing down.

THE HOUSE IS finally quiet and the heavenly smell of fresh baked cookies still fills the air. My family stayed just long enough to bake and eat a couple dozen cookies and tell Phina embarrassing stories about my childhood that made her laugh so hard she cried before they helped clean up the mess and went home.

I've been lying on my back in the dark, the covers pulled up to my waist with my hands tucked under the back of my head, listening to the sound of the shower in the bathroom connected to my bedroom. My dick hardens at the thought of Phina standing in there with water sluicing down her body, but I force myself to stay right where I'm at. My dick hates me and calls me all sorts of trashy names, but thankfully, I hear the shower shut off and I give my dick the middle finger.

A few minutes later, the bathroom door opens, bringing steam and the smell of Phina's shampoo billowing out into the room. I hold perfectly still, staring at her silhouette from the glow of the bathroom light before she flips the switch and throws the room into total darkness. I hear her walk around to the other side of the bed, lift the covers and slide in with her back to me. She's taken to wearing just her panties and one of my old FD t-shirts to bed every night, and even though it's pitch black in here, I can picture how the worn cotton molds to her body and how soft it would feel if I wrapped my arms around her right now and pulled her back against me.

I stay where I'm at, taking my mother's advice, even though it goes against everything I believe. She needs to come to me; I can't force her.

After a few minutes, my eyes grow heavy with sleep. I let them close and right when I start to nod off, I hear Phina speak so softly that I almost think I imagined it. I wait a few seconds when she speaks again, a little louder this time, but still in a soft, barely there whisper.

"The first time he did it, I was eight years old. I spilled a glass of milk on the kitchen table. He held me down and pushed his cigarette into me, laughing the entire time."

My throat gets thick with emotion, but I don't say a word. I turn gently onto my side and stare at the back of her head while she continues to speak in a low, monotone voice like a robot.

"I never did anything right. I ruined his life and I paid for it over and over. The first time he called me a whore I was nine. I didn't even know what that word meant, but I knew it was horrible by the way he practically spit it at me."

I close my eyes and want more than anything to beg her to stop. Stop speaking, stop the world from spinning so I can go back in time and make sure no one ever hurt her, but I keep my mouth shut. She needs to tell me this and I need to hear it. I need to know how to take it all away.

"Day after day, year after year, it never stopped. He kept holding me down to punish me for being just like my mother and I let him do it. I let him turn me into this person who can't even be happy for two weeks. I push people away because I can't stand the thought of them finding out that I'm not worth their love. I hate who I've become. I hate that just the sound of his voice turns me into that weak little girl who couldn't fight back."

I feel a tear run down my cheek and I don't even care that it's the most un-fucking-manly thing in the world. I would cry a thousand tears for this woman just to prove to her that she's worth EVERYTHING.

After a few minutes of silence, she whispers again. "Turn on the light."

Even though I'm confused by her words, I lean back and flip the switch to the small bedside lamp, quickly turning back to face her. The tiny bulb barely lights up the bed area, but it's bright enough for me to see her reach down to her waist and pull the t-shirt up her body and over her head. She tosses it to the foot of the bed and I hold my breath as she slowly pushes the covers down to her waist.

I take in every inch of her smooth, naked back, shoving my fist against my mouth when I get to the area right above her underwear. With a shaking hand, I reach out, running my fingertips over the scarred flesh. My fingers trace over about fifty tiny circles that are the exact same size as the butt of a cigarette. They are faded and white, but clearly visible on her beautiful skin. The fact that she's showing me these scars and trusts me with the secrets of her past is equal parts amazing and horrifying. I don't want her to have these marks on her skin, I don't want her to wear a permanent reminder on her body for the rest of her life that some piece of shit thought she wasn't good enough. I don't know how to take away her pain, to make her believe she's better than anyone I've ever known. There's nothing I can do but show her.

Scooting down on the bed, I lean forward and take my time kissing each and every scar. I tell her I love her after each kiss. I tell her she's beautiful after each kiss. I tell her she's strong after each kiss.

She turns suddenly, rolling onto her back and I see that her cheeks are wet with tears. She puts her hands on either side of my face and pulls me up her body, pressing her lips to mine. I can taste the salt from her tears on her lips as she wraps her arms around my back and pulls me on top of her under the covers. Her hands slide down the skin of my back and her fingers hook into the waistband of my boxers, pushing them down my hips. I keep my lips attached to hers as I lean on one arm and use my hand to push them down far enough to wiggle out of them and kick them under the covers somewhere while she does the same with her own underwear.

She spreads her legs when I roll back on top of her until I'm cradled between her thighs, my cock pressing right against her. She tilts her hips and rubs her wet pussy against my cock, coating the entire length. With my elbows on either side of her head, I pull my head back so I can look into her eyes. I move my ass back and I don't take my eyes off of her as I slide inside of her, so easy and so perfectly. Another tear falls down her cheek and I kiss it away as I slowly rock my hips.

Each slow push and pull of my cock inside of her sets off shock waves through my entire body. I'll never get tired of being inside her, of feeling her wrapped around my cock and knowing that for this one moment, we are perfectly connected in every way.

Her hands slide down to my ass, urging me deeper, but this time, there are no shouts of "harder" or "faster." We take it slow and she finally, FINALLY lets me love her the way she deserves.

23

Phina

EVEN THOUGH I haven't felt any sensation in the numb, deadened skin of my lower back in years, every kiss DJ places over my scars is like a lightning bolt right to my heart. He shocks me back to life with the press of his lips against my skin and his words of love, strength and beauty overwhelm me. The tears fall steadily from my eyes and I don't bother to hold them back or hide them. I roll over and let him see that his actions and words have touched a place in my heart and soul that no one has reached before.

He stares into my eyes when he pushes slowly inside of me and it's the most beautiful, heartbreaking feeling I've ever known.

"I *see* you," he whispers against my lips as he rocks inside of me, his cock moving slow and deep.

I shudder beneath him, my hips churning up to meet him.

"I see you, and I love *all* of you," he whispers again.

He moves his hands down the bed next to my body, sliding them under me to cup my ass and pull me against him. I bring my feet up and plant them on the bed on either side of his thighs so I can push my ass off the bed and meet each of his thrusts. With his hands clutching my ass, he helps me tilt my pelvis upwards so that each time he slides back inside, his cock pushes deeper than I thought possible.

He stops pushing and pulling his cock out of me, keeping himself buried to the hilt inside my pussy, with the lower half of my body still tilted up to meet him. He moves my hips in slow, tight circles around him, my clit rubbing against his pelvic bone while the head of his cock pushes against something deep inside of me that immediately sends shock waves through my sex. With my arms wrapped around his shoulders, I pull his body closer and push my hips harder and harder against him.

I shake and gibberish flies from my mouth, my body warning me the release that's coming is going to be far more powerful than anything I've ever felt before. He's too deep. He's not deep enough. I'm overwhelmed with sensations and I feel his cock swell inside me when he keeps hitting that same spot.

"Do you feel how deep I am, Seraphina?" he asks in a low, tight voice, the sound of him using my full name sending a wave of pleasure through my pussy. "No one will *ever* feel you like this. No one will *ever* know you like this. Tell me it's just me. Say I'm the only one."

I sob as I grind my body faster against him. "Only you. *Always* you."

His lips capture mine and my mouth opens to feel his tongue. It swirls around my own, making the connection between us that much more erotic. I'm so wet I can feel it dripping down the inside of my thighs as I rock and churn my hips faster against him and still, he holds his cock steady inside of me, letting me take over and grind against him. The upward angle of my hips and the way the head of his cock continues to bump against that spot so far inside of me drives me out of my mind. My hips are moving fast and erratically and I don't know how DJ manages to continue to hold himself so deep. Within seconds, my release is barreling down upon me without any warning. My stomach flips in anticipation and my toes curl as I try to slow it down and stop it from happening so soon. I'm not prepared to feel the magnitude of this pleasure that has already stolen the breath from my lungs and made my pussy clench so tightly around him that I can feel each and every ridge and pulse of his cock inside me.

I try to hold myself back, to make this release build and slowly slip out of me like every other orgasm I've experienced, but it's no use with the way the head of his cock pushes and presses against that glorious spot inside of me each time he pulls me into him and grinds himself against my clit. It's like trying to stop a runaway train from going off the tracks and crashing into a brick wall. I come suddenly and so strongly that I cry out into DJ's mouth. He sucks on my tongue and clutches my ass harder, holding me against him to ride out my release. The combination of his groin rubbing against my clit and his cock hitting my g-spot prolongs my orgasm past the point of what is normal. I feel pleasure from the inside and it flows out, washing over my pussy in wave after wave of intensity. I claw at his shoulders and back while I buck my hips against him, never wanting this feeling to end.

DJ pulls his mouth away from me, resting his forehead against mine as he moans loudly.

"Fuck, you're coming so hard. I can't...fuck! I can't stop, baby."

He tries not to move, to make this last as long as he can, but I feel my pussy continue to clench around him and I know it's driving him crazy.

"Don't stop," I whisper, my body still soaring with the tingles and pleasure of my orgasm as he keeps his movements shallow, barely moving his cock in and out of me. "Fuck me. I need to feel you come."

He curses, burying his face in the side of my neck as my words push him over the edge. I immediately feel him coming and I wrap my legs around him, using my thigh muscles to hold him deep. His body jerks and shudders against me while his cock pulses as he comes inside of me and I swear to God his *come* hits that fucking spot this time, forcing another smaller orgasm out of my body. It's shorter than the first, but no less powerful as it rips through me and I throw my head back, crying out with pleasure.

His hips grind to a halt when he's spent every drop of himself inside me and his body slumps on top of mine. I relish in the heavy feel of him, the way our chests move together to catch our breaths and the way I can feel his heartbeat thundering against my own. I don't even care that we didn't use a condom, I don't care that I can feel his come dripping out of me, mixing with my own wetness on the inside of my thighs. He's absolutely right. No one will ever know me like this. No other man will ever make me feel the things DJ does and I want to carry a part of him inside of me forever so that I never forget how I felt in this exact moment – loved, cherished and worth it all.

"I'M ON THE pill and I'm clean. I get tested every six months working at the hospital."

DJ finishes tucking his work shirt into his pants and sighs audibly as he watches me nervously dig through my bag for something to wear today. I woke up this morning while he was still sound asleep, cursing myself for passing out completely naked as I quickly found my underwear under the covers and slipped them on, along with the t-shirt of his I discarded on the floor the night before. He could have lifted the covers at any moment and seen the marks on my hips, the euphoria from our love making last night going right out the window.

"You've already said that three times this morning. Will you stop trying to freak me out? It's not going to work," DJ says with a laugh as he sits down on the edge of the bed to pull his boots on. He got a page from work that woke him up seconds after I'd finished throwing on my clothes from the night before and he's been scrambling around, trying to get dressed in a hurry. I'd hoped he was too distracted to notice what I was trying to do.

I'm out of my element here. I've never had sex without a condom before and I've never had sex that actually *meant* something. He's right; a part of me is trying to freak him out for some stupid reason. It's like my mind won't even *let* me be happy.

"I just…you know, if you have any regrets, I totally understand."

Lies, lies, lies!

DJ pushes himself up from the bed and walks around to the foot of it, where I'm still digging around in my bag trying not to meet his eyes. His hands grab mine to still my movements and he bends his knees and lowers his head to get me to look at him. When I finally do, I see nothing but happiness and love shining in his eyes.

"No regrets. NEVER any regrets with you," he whispers.

I let out the breath I've been holding and lean forward to kiss him. When I pull back, I can't help but remind him of all the reasons why he should be regretting falling in love with me.

"He's still out there. I don't want anything to happen to you because of me," I tell him softly.

He shakes his head at me, bringing his hands up to cup my face.

"Haven't you learned *anything* from living with me these last few weeks? I am a bad ass motherfucker and you have nothing to worry about."

I glare at him, but he just smiles in return.

"I'm going to carry my gun on me at all times from now on and Dax has added another one of his guys to help Jackson on guard duty. The fact that you think I couldn't take some old fucker who's been in prison for fifteen years is insulting."

He lowers his lips into a pout and I try my hardest not to laugh at him.

"Stop making jokes. This is serious," I scold.

"Yes, it's SERIOUSLY insulting. Have you checked out my guns lately?"

He lets go of my face to flex his arms and this time I do laugh. He lowers his arms after a few seconds and finally gives me a somber look.

"I'm more worried about you. I don't like the idea of you going in to work today when I can't go with you."

Since it's cold and flu season, the phlebotomy department is extremely short staffed. I got an urgent call from my supervisor this morning telling me she hated to cut my time off short, but it's all hands on deck. DJ wanted to go with me, but the page he received notified him of a huge car accident on one of the main highways. As much as he doesn't want to go to work, he needs to be there for Brad's first big emergency or the poor guy will probably puke all over the side of the road.

There's a knock on the front door and DJ leaves me to finish getting dressed for work while he answers it. A few minutes later, when I've donned my scrubs and pulled my hair into a messy bun on top of my head, DJ sticks his head in the bedroom doorway.

"Jackson is here to drive you to work. His partner is outside waiting to follow me to the accident. See? Everything is going to be fine," he tells me with a reassuring smile.

I meet him in the doorway and he grabs my hand to pull me down the hall and into the living room where Jackson is waiting by the front door.

"All set?" he asks as I grab my purse and coat from the couch.

I nod at him before turning to DJ, wrapping my arms around his waist and pulling him into me for a tight hug.

"Everything's going to be fine," he whispers, kissing the top of my head. "I already told him he is to stick to your ass like glue. I'm sure the guy waiting for me outside is chomping at the bit to do the same and piss me off all day."

I pull my head back and stare up into his handsome face. "Your guns are pretty impressive, but don't do anything stupid, do you hear me?"

DJ nods and I paste on a smile so he doesn't see the worry written all over my face. I don't like the idea of us going separate ways today. It's not even *me* I'm worried about. My father has made it perfectly clear that the man holding onto me right now is fair game in his quest for revenge. If anything happens to him, I will never forgive myself.

"I'll be fine, Fireball. The same goes for you, too. That asshole is not worth your life. You let the cops do their jobs. He's going to make a mistake one of these days, and they're going to nail his ass to the wall."

I let DJ's reassuring words flow through me and erase all of my doubt and negativity. As we part ways with one last kiss in the driveway, I watch his truck disappear down the street with an unmarked cop car right on his ass the entire way as I get into the passenger side of Jackson's cruiser.

We make small talk the entire way to the hospital and I rest my head on the back of the seat, thinking about how much my life has changed in the last few months and how happy I am for the first time since I was a teenager.

24

DJ

PARKING MY TRUCK as close to the scene of the accident as I can off to the side of the road, I quickly jump out with my ALS trauma bag in my hand and weave in between the line of cars that are stopped until the accident can be cleared so they can get around it and head to wherever it was they were going.

I pick up the pace, jogging until I reach the first vehicle, where a few of my men are pulling the driver out of the mangled car.

"What do we got, boys?" I ask as I pull a pair of latex gloves out of my back pocket and quickly slide them on.

"Male, mid-fifties, responsive and steady pulse," Brad replies as he helps move the man to the gurney they've set up on the road next to the car. "We stabilized him inside the vehicle with a neck and back brace. Contusions to the head, most likely from the airbag, and superficial cuts and scrapes to the face and arms from glass."

I lean over the man, checking his eyes for dilation and signs of a concussion. "What's your name, sir?"

His eyes are darting around nervously, but they latch onto mine quickly. "Martin Roberts. The car ran right through the red light. I didn't even have time to slam on my breaks. Is she okay? Is the other driver okay?"

"Don't you worry about that right now, Mr. Roberts. My men are going to get you to the hospital and take good care of you."

He nods his head as best he can while Brad finishes strapping him to the head brace and securing the rest of his body to the gurney.

I pat Brad on the back for a job well done and hear the unmistakable motorized sound of the Jaws of Life firing up.

"Are there more ambulances on the way?" I ask, scanning the area and not seeing any more in sight aside from the one right in front of us. I help everyone push the gurney to the back of the ambulance and lift it up inside.

"There were two more in route, but we just cancelled one. We already secured the third driver and determined she didn't need to be transported because of the extent of her injuries," Brad explains. "She already signed a refusal to be transported, so now we're just waiting on the one for the woman in that red car. ETA three minutes."

"Good. Let these guys head off to transport, you can stay here with me and work on the last driver," I inform him.

I close the ambulance doors, pounding twice to let the driver know he's good to go. Brad and I turn and rush over to the car with the worst damage. Whoever was driving what used to be a red SUV obviously took the brunt of the accident. The driver's side door was t-boned so badly it's no wonder the fire department needed to use the Jaws of Life.

"How's it going?" I ask the fireman holding the hydraulic rescue tool as he cuts away at the metal and steel of the roof.

"Driver has been unresponsive since we got here, so it's going to be quicker and safer to take off the roof and get her out this way," he shouts over the sound of the motor. "One of my men crawled through the passenger side window that shattered and is keeping an eye on her vitals. When she was t-boned, it pushed the other side of her car into a light post, so we couldn't even open the passenger door to get to her."

I nod at him and gesture for Brad to follow as I make my way around the back of the car, tapping the fireman who has his ass end sticking out of the passenger window. He quickly slides out and gives me a rundown on the injured woman's stats.

"Female, late twenties, early thirties, thready pulse, no visible eye movement or response to stimuli. Trauma to the head most likely caused by it smashing into her side window upon impact."

I thank him as he moves out of the way for me and I lean inside the window to get my first look at the woman. My stomach drops and my heart almost stops when I see her. Still in her seatbelt with blood coating her face and neck from the wounds on her head and her chest, arms and hands covered in blood from a combination of the laceration on her head and cuts from the glass, is Finnley. Even under all the blood, I can see how pale her skin is. Before I can lean in closer and fully assess the damage, I hear shouting in the distance. I take a deep breath and quickly pull myself back out of the car, rattling off a list of instructions for Brad.

"She's Trauma Alert with that head injury, so start two IV's in case there's internal bleeding and we need to pump her full of fluids. Get a neck brace on her and keep an eye on her pulse and breathing. If it starts to plummet, get a bag valve mask on her immediately."

Without waiting for his response, I take off running away from the vehicle and trust that Brad can keep Finnley stable while I take care of this other problem.

A few cars back, Collin is being held by a cop and two of the men from the fire department as he screams and curses at them, kicking and fighting to get out of their hold and get to his woman.

"GET THE FUCK OFF OF ME, I NEED TO SEE HER! FINNLEY!" he screams as I get right in front of him and put my hands on his chest.

"Collin, we're handling it," I tell him as calmly as I can. "You of all people know you can't be here right now. Go sit your ass down in my truck and let me do my job."

His eyes are wild with unshed tears and fear and it breaks my heart to see him like this. He's already been through enough to get to a happy, normal life with the woman he loves. He doesn't deserve this shit.

"Oh, God! How bad is she?"

I don't answer him right away because I can't say anything good. Finnley is a mess and she's lucky to still be alive at this point.

"FUCKING ANSWER ME!" he screams as he continues to struggle against the arms that are holding him in place.

"She's alive, Collin. That's all you need to think about right now."

The flashing lights of three fire trucks and four cop cars illuminate his face and thankfully, the other ambulance pulls up right then.

"Wait in my truck and I'll keep you posted as soon as we get her out of the car, okay?"

The tears finally fall from his eyes as he nods his head in understanding.

"I'm going back and I promise you, I will take good care of her. Luckily, the hospital is only a few minutes away, so we don't have to worry about Life Flight. We'll follow right behind the ambulance in my truck, got it?"

The fight leaves his body and he slumps into the men's arms as they help him over to where my truck is parked while I toss my keys to one of the cops. I turn and race back to Finnley's car just as the firemen break through the roof and yank the thing off.

Two other paramedics catch up to me with the gurney and thankfully, it's two of my own men. I can work well with any paramedic, but the group of men I've trained and worked side-by-side with run like a well-oiled machine.

"Patrick, get the backboard ready," I tell the one closest to me as I climb up onto the top of the car and carefully ease myself down inside and crouch on the center console, checking her pulse while Brad rattles off her BP from behind me.

Her pulse is weak, but it's there, thank God. There is no fucking way I'm going back to my fucking truck without news that Finnley is alive.

Brad has done everything he was supposed to, her IV lines are in place, oxygen mask is pressed against her nose and mouth and the brace is wrapped firmly around her neck. I use my pocketknife to saw through her seatbelt as Patrick climbs up the rear of the car with the backboard. When the seatbelt comes loose, I hold her body steady so Patrick can slide the backboard down behind her through the open roof of the car. I turn my body so my back is pressed up against the dashboard as Brad slides almost fully inside the vehicle from the passenger side, places Finnley's IV bags on the passenger seat and helps us secure her to the backboard. Patrick calls for assistance and I hear the clamor of feet as a few more people climb onto the car. On the count of three, I hold Finnley's legs and help Brad lift her while Patrick and everyone else pulls her up and out of her seat as gently as possible. Once we've got her resting on the tops of the seats, I help push her body the rest of the way up the backboard so her legs aren't dangling off and secure the straps around them, as well. Brad slides back out of the passenger side window and runs around to help everyone else move her the rest of the way off of the car as I climb out of the top with her IV bags.

Once we get her secured to the gurney, we take off running, me holding the IV bags above her as Patrick and Brad push the bed through the wreckage and other vehicles. Collin is waiting for us by the open back of the ambulance, and I shoot him a dirty look as we stop and flip the latches to collapse the legs of the gurney. I watch as he quickly leans over Finnley, smoothing her bloody hair off her face, full on sobbing when he gets his first good look at her. My anger that he didn't wait in my truck quickly fades when I see how important it was for him to see her. Even though she looks really bad, I know it helps for him to see that she's still breathing.

"You gotta move, man. We need to get her to the hospital STAT," I tell him as we fold the gurney down and lift it inside. Patrick and Brad jump inside and immediately start working on her, taking her blood pressure and checking her vitals.

Slamming the doors closed, I pound on the back end. The siren wails and the ambulance takes off at top speed.

"Come on, let's get to my truck," I tell him as I grab onto his arm and help him walk.

We have to walk back through the accident site as we go, and I try to get Collin to look anywhere but at Finnley's car, but it's no use. His feet come to a halt like they're filled with cement when we get right next to her car.

"Oh, Jesus. Oh, my God," he sobs, running his hands through his hair over and over as he stares at the wreckage.

"It just looks bad because they had to take the roof off," I tell him stupidly. Shit, he's used the Jaws of Life enough times in his life as a fireman and he's seen what an accident that bad does to the people inside.

A cop who is assessing the damage to all the vehicles and checking the road for skid marks walks in front of us and crouches down to look under Finnley's car.

"Any ideas on how this happened?" I ask him as he makes notes on a pad, hoping he can give Collin some peace of mind before we head to the hospital.

"Can't really confirm anything until the vehicles are cleared," he mutters over his shoulder.

"Best estimated guess. My fiancé was in this car," Collin growls angrily.

The cop sighs, standing up to face us. "The driver of this one definitely caused the accident. Based on the noticeably absent skid marks, I'd say she ran right the red light without even tapping the breaks and the blue one over there t-boned her. I already spoke to the woman who was driving the third vehicle. She saw the accident happen, but was too close behind the guy driving this one to stop fast enough. Her car was the only one that left skid marks as she tried to slow down, but she still slammed into his back end."

I thank the guy for the information and pull a zombie-like Collin to my truck as quickly as possible. As we head towards the hospital, I try calling Phina to give her a heads-up, but the call goes right to voicemail. I hope to God she's holed up in her office instead of taking blood today. If she gets called down to the ER when Finnley comes in, she's going to be a complete mess. Flipping the switch on my dashboard to turn on the emergency light bar on top of my work truck, I hit the gas and fly through every red light and intersection to get us to the hospital as fast as I can while Collin keeps his eyes closed and his head in his hands the entire way, most likely praying. If I were a religious man, I'd be doing some praying right about now, too. I try calling Jackson to tell him to keep Phina away from the ER until I can get there, but that call also goes to voicemail. I angrily throw my phone against the dashboard, cursing everyone who has a cell phone but never bothers to answer it.

Too many thoughts are running through my head and I don't like any of them. Finnley is a good driver. How in the hell could she just run a light? Phina and I are being watched like hawks, so her father can't get anywhere near us. What if it pissed him off enough that he decided to transfer his obsession over to someone else she cares about?

25

Phina

"ARE YOU WHISTLING?" Suzy asks in amusement as we head to the ER.

I immediately stop and then smile.

"Huh, I guess I was."

I've been smiling like a lovesick fool all damn morning, and now I've started whistling catchy tunes like a fucking Disney princess. Even though the threat of my father still looms over my head, I can't help but be happy. DJ sent me a text on his way to work that said *I can't wait to have naked playtime with you again,* and I've pulled it out and read it about a hundred times. He even used a smiley face emoticon. A fucking smiley face! I'm in my own little bubble of happiness and not even the last secret I've kept hidden from him can mar that. I'll take it one day at a time and I'll ease him into it. Now that I've opened the floodgates and started being honest with him, explaining what it was like living with my father and showing him the proof of that life, I know I'll have the strength to talk to him about everything else when the time is right. I'll explain to him that he's the reason I no longer feel the need to burn myself. His love and his belief in me make that need a thing of the past. I feel like I can face anything as long as I have him by my side.

"Where's your guard dog?" Suzy asks as we get into the elevator and I press the button for the first floor.

I didn't really want anyone at the hospital knowing my business, but it was hard to hide the fact that I had a constant shadow in the form of a police officer. I told her the absolute minimum, just that I had gotten a few weird notes at home and the police wanted to keep an eye on me.

"He had to go to the bathroom. He's going to meet us downstairs," I tell Suzy as I let my mind wander back to DJ while we descend downstairs.

As soon as I can go back to my place, the first thing I'm going to do is throw away that fucking lighter and pack of cigarettes. I know doing that doesn't mean I'm completely healed. I know I should probably go back to therapy or some shit, but that can come in time. For right now, I'm going to let DJ be the healing balm to my wounds, mentally and physically. We can spend more time together getting to know one another, I can show him with my words and actions that I *do* trust him and I can finally remove that last burrier between us, confident that he'll understand and still love every part of me, fucked up or not.

"As much as I like this more chipper part of you, you might want to dial it back a notch. I heard this accident was pretty bad and the family members might not like you humming the song 'Happy'," Suzy says with a laugh.

Putting on my game face when the elevator doors open to the first floor, I push the blood cart out into the hallway and pick up my pace as we head to the ER. I hear Jackson yell my name to let me know he's right behind me when we turn the corner and see a madhouse of hospital workers, racing back and forth between curtained areas.

Suzy grabs a blood collection kit from the bottom shelf of the cart, but a worker stops us to let us know that only two patients were transported via ambulance instead of the original three we were told about.

"Well, that's good news, at least. You want me to take them?" Suzy asks.

I shake my head. "No, you go on back upstairs. I can handle it."

She shoves her tray back onto the cart and disappears down the hall. Pushing aside the first curtain, I head inside with my cart. There's a man lying in bed talking to a woman I assume is his wife based on the way she's fussing over him and kissing every inch of his face.

"Knock, knock," I announce, pushing the cart up next to the bed.

The woman moves back, but doesn't let go of his hand.

"I'm just going to take a few vials of blood to make sure everything is okay. How are you feeling?"

He starts explaining the accident to me and I keep him talking, asking a bunch of questions to keep his mind off of the needle prick while I fill up four vials of blood. It's over in seconds and I'm untying the tourniquet from his arm when he looks down in shock.

"Wow, you're fast. And that was pretty painless," he tells me with a chuckle. "Do you know how the driver of the red car is? I saw the whole thing happen and it was really bad."

I finish marking his patient information on the vials and stick them into the blood collection tray so they can be sent up to the lab for testing once I'm finished with the next patient.

"I'm not sure, but I think they're bringing her in next. I'll check and let you know," I tell him, disposing of the needle and syringe in the red biohazard container on the wall next to his bed.

Slipping off my latex gloves, I toss them into the trashcan before grabbing my cart and moving back out into the main hallway. The wife holds the curtain open for me and thanks me as I go.

I hear a loud commotion at the end of the hallway and move my cart out of the way. The doors to the ambulance bay have burst open and I see a gurney being wheeled in, surrounded by paramedics. Figuring this is the second accident victim, I start grabbing things off of my cart so I can be prepared when it's my turn. Glancing down at the fast moving bed as it whizzes past me, my supplies drop from my hand and clatter to the floor when I see who's on it.

My legs move on autopilot as I follow behind the gurney into an empty, curtained area. I push my way between the paramedics as they count to three and then lift Finnley from the gurney, moving her to a hospital bed. I immediately lean over my best friend, running my hands down her blood-covered face.

"What happened? What the fuck happened?" I cry as a doctor and two nurses rush in and get all of her stats from the paramedics.

"Phina, you need to move away," one of the nurses I've worked with off and on through the years says from behind me.

"Tell me what the fuck happened!" I bark at her.

"Car accident, that's all we know," she tells me as she hangs her IV bags on a portable stand and starts moving her stethoscope all around Finnley's chest.

While the doctor walks to the opposite side of the bed and starts checking her vitals and ordering things from the nurse, I press my cheek to Finnley's.

"You're going to be okay, honey. Please, just open your eyes," I sob.

I can't stop touching her as the doctor orders me to move back. I smooth her blood-caked hair away from her face, run my hands down her cheeks, throat and chest and breathe a small sigh of relief when I feel her heart beating strongly under my palms. I cradle her head to my chest and squeeze my eyes closed, praying that she's going to be okay.

The doctor keeps shouting at me to leave and I ignore him until the nurse grabs onto my arms and forcibly pulls me away from my friend. The tears fall steadily down my cheeks as I take a step back and watch them rip open Finnley's shirt and press heart monitors onto her skin. I hold my hand against my mouth to stop myself from sobbing as everyone barks orders and rushes around her bedside.

I finally notice Brad standing off to the side and he walks over to me.

"What the hell happened?" I ask him as we both stand there staring at Finnley.

"Ran a red light and some guy t-boned her," Brad explains quietly while the staff works on her.

I tear my eyes away from Finnley long enough to look up at Brad in confusion.

"Finnley wouldn't run a damn red light. She yells at me if I have the radio up too loud because I won't be able to concentrate on other motorists and she clears her throat in this really annoying way if I go one mile over the speed limit," I tell him.

Suddenly, I remember the page DJ got earlier and I realize this was the car accident he had to respond to. Jesus, he must have lost his mind when he got there and saw it was Finnley.

I quickly pull my cell phone out of my scrub pocket and realize I turned the damn thing off before I came down here. I turn it on and immediately see that I have a couple of missed calls from DJ.

"Shit, DJ tried to call me," I mutter.

"Yeah, he showed up a few minutes after I got there. Calmed her fiancé down and was going to bring him here in his own truck. That guy is one calm motherfucker under pressure," Brad tells me in awe when we hear Finnley's weak voice across the room.

"Collin?"

I race to her side and I almost scream in happiness when I see her brown eyes staring back at me.

"What happened? Where's Collin?" she asks with a scratchy voice as she tries to get up.

I gently press my hands to her chest and ease her back down on the bed.

"You were in an accident, sweetie, and Collin is on his way," I tell her, grabbing her bloody hand and holding it to my stomach. "Jesus, you took ten years off my life when they wheeled you in here."

She brings her free hand up to her head and groans. "Fuck, my head hurts."

I laugh in relief when I hear her curse as the doctor starts asking her some basic questions like her name, what day it is and what all she remembers. As Finnley speaks, more and more of the accident starts coming back to her and I hate that she remembers the sounds. She tells the doctor she just keeps hearing glass breaking, metal crunching and a loud bang. Working in a hospital and listening to patients talk after an accident, that's their major complaint – that they can't get the sounds out of their head.

"I tried to stop in time. I saw the light change red and I had plenty of time. I pressed on the break, but it wouldn't work. I kept pressing it and pressing it, but I couldn't slow down," Finnley tells him.

A strange feeling settles in the pit of my stomach, but I push it away, figuring the bump on her head might be messing with her memory a little bit. If she actually pressed on the break, the car would have stopped instead flying through an intersection at top speed. I start thinking about the call I accompanied DJ on the other night with Mrs. Martinez when she spoke about crashing into the front of a Red Lobster. Now that Finnley is alert and seems to be okay, I kind of want to tease her and ask her if she mistook the break for the gas like poor Mrs. Martinez did, but the doctor asks me to step away from the bed to give Finnley a chance to close her eyes and rest for a few minutes.

"She's stable. The laceration on her head is pretty bad and is going to require some stitches. The nurse is going to put a temporary bandage on her head so we can get her upstairs for an ultrasound and CT scan to check for internal bleeding. Her abdomen is soft and pliable right now, so I don't think we'll have to worry about that, but it's always better to be safe. If everything goes well with the scan, we'll keep her for observation just to make sure she doesn't have any swelling on the brain. All in all, I'd say she was pretty lucky. The paramedics out in the field did a great job."

My heart swells with pride when I hear this. Even though I'm sure it must have killed him on the inside, DJ did what he was trained to do and he probably saved Finnley's life. I want to kiss the hell out of him right now.

I walk back to Finnley's side and give her a kiss on the cheek and tell her I'll wait here for Collin and send him up to the digital scanning area as soon as he gets here. An orderly comes in then and pushes Finnley's gurney out from the curtain towards the elevators.

With a deep sigh and a quiet 'thank you' to God for keeping my friend safe, I push through the curtain and wait in the hallway for Collin and DJ. A few minutes later, the doors to the ambulance bay burst open again and I look up to see Collin running through them, his eyes anxiously searching all around the busy area until they connect with mine. I run up to him, throwing my arms around him and giving him a hard squeeze.

"She's going to be okay. The doctor said she's going to be okay," I tell him as I pull back to look at his face.

His tense shoulders sag with the news and he closes his eyes in relief.

"They just took her upstairs for a CT scan. She was alert and talking right before they took her and she was asking for you. I told her I'd send you right up."

Collin thanks me and takes off running for the elevators. Five minutes after he leaves, DJ comes through the doors and I run into his arms just like I did with Collin, but this time, I pull back and pepper his entire face with kisses.

"Thank you so much for taking care of her. I don't know what I would have done if..."

I can't even finish that statement. Thinking about losing my best friend is not an option.

"Where's Jackson?" DJ asks, looking past me down the hall.

"He was back there somewhere sitting in a chair last I checked," I tell him in confusion.

"Stay here, I need to talk to him," he tells me as he starts to walk around me.

I sidestep him and get in his way. "What's going on? Why do you need to talk to Jackson?"

He won't look at me, just continues to search over my head down the hall.

"Don't worry about it. Just sit here and wait for Collin and Finnley to come back down and I'll be right back."

He tries to get around me again, but I slap my palms against his chest. "Stop it! Talk to me! What the hell is going on?"

He lets out a huge sigh, tilting his head back to stare up at the ceiling. "Please, Phee, just let it go for now. I'm going to take care of it."

I shake my head back and forth. "No, absolutely not. We're in this together. If something is going on, I have a right to know."

Thoughts start screaming through my head, bad thoughts. Things I don't want to believe, but if DJ needs to talk to Jackson after just leaving an accident that my best friend was supposedly responsible for, there's only one reason for that.

"It was her fault, right? Brad said she ran a stoplight and even though she's the most conscientious driver I know, accidents happen sometimes. Tell me it was an accident, DJ," I beg, even though I know just by looking at the sadness and fucking pity on his face that it's not true.

He tries to wrap his arms around me, but I swat them away. I don't want his comfort right now, I want the fucking truth.

"The cop on the scene told us there weren't any skid marks from Finnley's car," DJ tells me softly.

Okay, so that could happen. Especially if she just wasn't paying attention. God, how bad of a friend am I that I hope she just wasn't paying attention as opposed to the alternative?

"And?" I prod.

He bites down on his bottom lip as if he's trying to shut himself up and stop himself from telling me more. I can tell by the conflicted look on his face that he really doesn't want to tell me more.

"DJ!" I shout in irritation.

He growls, throwing his hands up in the air in frustration, spitting out the next bit of information as quickly as he can.

"Dax called when I was parking the car after I dropped Collin off at the doors. He went to the accident site and checked over her car."

He pauses and I hold my breath, trying not to curse at him.

"Her brake line was cut."

My breath leaves me with a sob. DJ tries to pull me to him once again, but I back away.

"Phee," he pleads.

I shake my head back and forth as I continue walking away from him.

No! No, no, no!

This is my fault, all my fault. It should have been me today, but I've had Jackson on my ass since I left DJ's house and he couldn't get to me. He hurt my best friend because of *me*. He almost killed my best friend because of *me*.

I can physically feel my heart breaking in half. My chest hurts and I want to curl up in a ball and scream until my throat is raw.

DJ starts to head towards me when another paramedic grabs him from behind, pulling him down the hall away from me to help with another emergency that's coming into the hospital. I watch as he tries to struggle away from the guy, keeping his eyes glued to mine, waiting for me to call to him, to beg him to hold me and stay with me.

I close my eyes and turn away from him. There's nothing he can do to help me now.

26

DJ

I CURSE MY fucking job and the biker who was hit by a car that I needed to help move from the ambulance into the ER when I should have been racing after Phina. That goddamn stubborn woman is blaming herself for what happened to Finnley. I wanted to hold her and erase all of that blame from her head, but she wouldn't let me. I could see the exact moment she shut down and forgot about everything we'd promised each other. Her eyes became vacant and her face shuttered every emotion from me. There is no fucking way I'm going to let her shut me out. Not now. Not after everything that's happened and how far we've come.

By the time I helped move the injured biker, Collin and Finnley were back down from CT. I wanted to leave immediately and go to Phina, but my best friend clearly needed a little support. He was visibly shaken even though Finnley was still awake and talking both of our ears off about the accident. I stared at the huge bandage over her forehead, noting most of the blood had been washed away by one of the nurses and memorizing the irritated look on her face as she complained about the hospital food she would have to eat for the next twenty-four hours. I would much rather commit *this* face to memory than the one of Finnley unconscious and pale with blood covering almost every inch of her.

"Thank you for being there and making sure Collin didn't beat someone's ass," Finnley tells me.

Collin looks away sheepishly and I laugh, patting him on the back, figuring he must have come clean with her about his behavior at the scene. I try to keep the mood in the room light and purposefully avoid telling either one of them about what Dax told me. They'll find out soon enough when he comes in to question them. Might as well give them a few moments peace before the shit hits the fan.

"Go easy on the guy," I tell her. "He's a macho man and I don't think he liked the fact that he couldn't go in and save the day. Feel free to call me your hero any time you'd like."

Collin punches me in the arm as Finnley laughs, quickly stopping to hold her hand up to her head. "Uuuugghhh, get me some pain killers already. This headache isn't going to heal itself."

I reach over on the nightstand and grab the TV remote, pressing the red call button for the nurse.

"Relief will be here shortly, Crash," I tell her with a smile.

She closes her eyes with a groan and rests her head back on her pillow. "Get that nickname out of your system right now because you are never uttering it outside of these walls."

"Whatever you say, Crash," I repeat with a laugh.

The nurse comes in with some Tylenol and lets Collin know that they're going to be moving Finnley up to her own room in just a few minutes. Collin looks at me expectantly and, as much as I want to follow them upstairs, there's somewhere else I need to be.

"I need to leave. I'll come back later to check on you guys, okay?"

Finnley swallows the Tylenol and hands the empty cups to the nurse before looking at me.

"Is she okay?" Finnley asks softly.

Even though she's got a concussion and a massive head wound, Finnley didn't miss the absence of Phina in the room and I'm sure she wonders where she is. I don't want to tell her that she's probably drowning in guilt right now and I'm scared to death about what that's going to do to her, so I just shrug.

"Yeah, just a little shaken up at seeing you such a bloody mess, Crash," I tell her with a forced smile. "I'll go find her and bring her back to see you."

Collin perches on the edge of Finnley's bed and starts running his fingers through the mess of her hair. She curls up against him and closes her eyes again.

"Tell her to bring me a cheeseburger. I'm not eating any fucking hospital food," she grumbles.

I laugh as I walk up to the bed and kiss the top of her head, bumping my fist with Collin's before I leave. He calls my name as I pull the curtain back.

"Thanks, man. I owe you a lot for what you did today. You saved my girl," he tells me, trying to clear his throat to keep the emotion out of it.

I just nod at him as I leave, hoping I can save my own fucking girl, as well.

AFTER TAKING THE elevator up to Phina's office and finding it dark, I placed a quick call to Jackson and found out that he took her back to her place. When I pull into the driveway, I find him sitting on the front step.

"I secured the house before she went in. After that, she told me to get the fuck out and slammed the door in my face," he explains.

I thank him as I head inside and softly close the door behind me. Checking the first floor and not finding her anywhere, I head upstairs and see a light shining under Phina's bedroom door. I slowly push open the door and find her sitting on the floor with her back against the bed and her knees pulled up to her chest.

I quietly make my way over to her side so I don't spook her. Her eyes are squeezed tightly shut, one hand holding a cigarette to her mouth and the other flicking a lighter over and over, and she's clearly very deep in her own head. When the hell did she start smoking?

Squatting down in front of her, I gently place my hand on her knee as she takes a deep drag of the cigarette.

"Baby, what's going on?" I ask quietly.

She opens her eyes when she exhales the smoke, but doesn't look at me. Instead, she stares at orange glow burning at the tip of her cigarette and continues to flick the lighter.

"Do you know what it feels like to press something like this into your skin?" she asks in a monotone voice that gives me chills.

Jesus Christ, I don't want her thinking about her father right now.

"Phee, you don't have to tell me, okay? Not right now."

She either doesn't hear me or doesn't care, just continues talking in an emotionless voice, the fucking click of the lighter igniting repeatedly making me want to scream.

"Your skin is so tight, you feel so dead inside and you just want to feel alive. You don't think anything can make your heart start beating again, but then it does. It sinks into your skin like a hot knife going through butter and you can FINALLY get some relief."

She sighs audibly as she takes another drag and my skin crawls with fear. She quickly exhales and brings the butt of the cigarette close to her face, staring wide-eyed at the orange tip.

"I thought I found something to make it all go away, to make it stop because I thought I finally deserved to feel good instead of miserable," she whispers.

I slowly reach forward and take the cigarette out of her hand, stabbing it out in the ashtray on her nightstand. She doesn't even notice what I've done, transferring her gaze to the flame of the lighter that she's holding suspended in front of her face. Wrapping my hand around hers, I ease the lighter out of her hand, as well, and toss it to the side.

"Baby, let's get you cleaned up and out of these dirty clothes," I tell her softly.

She blinks a few times and finally looks at me confusedly, almost like she didn't even realize I was here. Then, she looks down at her hands that are still covered in blood, quickly moving her eyes to the front of her scrub top that is also stained red with quite a lot of what I assume is Finnley's blood.

She starts panting, whimpering with each exhale of breath as she quickly scrambles up from the floor and starts tearing at her clothes.

"GET THEM OFF! GET THEM OFF OF ME!" she sobs.

I jump up in front of her as she starts raking her fingernails down her arms to try and remove the blood on her skin, crying and screaming the entire time.

"OH, GOD, IT'S ALL MY FAULT! GET HER FUCKING BLOOD OFF OF ME!"

I wrap my arms around her from behind to try and stop her as she scratches and claws at her face, pulls her hair and tries to physically rip the clothes from her body, but she's like a wild hellcat. She rips her arms out from under mine and starts punching and kicking as I lift her in the air and move her over to the bed. The tortured screams coming from her make it sound like someone is killing her.

"Phina! Come on, baby, calm down and let me help you," I shout over her, my heart breaking with each painful cry from her mouth.

I toss her onto the bed and manage to get her onto her back without an elbow to the eye, bringing her arms above her head and securing her wrists in one of my hands as I push my body down on top of hers. The fight leaves her as soon as I get her in this position and she stops struggling. Quiet sobs leave her body and I bring my other hand up, using my thumb to wipe the tears off of her cheek that is still covered in Finnley's blood.

"I can't...I can't...get them off of me," she whimpers softly this time.

I nod my head even though she's squeezed her eyes closed and can't see me.

"Okay, okay. I'm going to let go and I'm going to get you out of these clothes and then we'll get in the shower," I reassure her softly, trying not to sob right along with her.

When I let go, she keeps her arms above her head as I ease off of her body and stand next to the bed, leaning over her. She stares up at the ceiling with tears streaming down her cheeks as I grab the hem of her bloody scrub top and slide it up her body. For the time being, I'm glad she's not looking down because as soon as I get her top off and unhook her bra, I see that her skin is stained with blood from it soaking through her shirt.

I move back and hook my fingers into the waistband of her scrub pants and her hands immediately come down to cover her face. Her shoulders shake as she continues to cry while I ease her pants down her legs and toss them to the side. I do the same with her lace boy shorts, quickly pulling them off and tossing them with the pants. My eyes roam up her legs and her thighs, stopping when I get to her hips. I slowly lean forward, pressing my hands to the bed on either side of her to get a closer look.

I know that when I look back on this night, I'm going to wish I could have stopped the gasp of horror that flew from my mouth. I'm going to wish I did a lot of things differently, but you can't go back in time to fix your mistakes, no matter how much you want to.

"That motherfucking piece of shit," I curse, bringing one hand off the bed to trace my fingers over a whole slew of burn marks that Phina never showed me.

She quickly sits up in bed and gently pushes my hand off of her skin. I meet her eyes and can't hide the obvious rage in them. She stares at me and, even though she's visibly exhausted from her freak out and all of the crying she's done, there's still a spark of hope in her eyes as she waits for me to say something else.

"I fucking *hate* the sick, fucked up bastard who did this to you," I growl.

Her eyes immediately lose their spark and she drops her head. I try to backpedal, thinking I must have said something wrong, but how could I? Of *course* anyone who burns someone's skin with a goddamn cigarette is clearly fucked up in the head AND a bastard.

"Funny, I hate that person, too," she says softly with her head still down.

I shake my head in confusion, wondering why she sounds so fucking dejected. It doesn't make sense. Nothing about what's happening right now makes any sense.

She pushes herself up from the bed and walks around me, heading towards the shower. It's then that I notice matching burns on her other hip and I growl and clench my hands into fists. She pauses halfway to the bathroom, but doesn't turn around.

"You need to leave."

I shake my head at her back and walk around the end of the bed, putting my hands on her shoulders to try and turn her around to face me. If she would just look at me and talk to me I could figure out what the hell is wrong.

"Phina, please. Talk to me," I plead.

She yanks her body out of my grip and continues walking towards the bathroom.

"Just go, DJ. I don't need you here."

"PHINA!" I shout in anger as she opens the bathroom door.

She finally turns around and stares at me with lifeless eyes.

"Get. The. Fuck. Out. Of. My House."

She slams the door closed and I hear her lock it behind her. I'm so frustrated and angry that I don't know what else to do. I stomp out of her bedroom and down the stairs, figuring I'll give her a little time to cool off. She told me to go, so that's what I'm going to fucking do.

As soon as I get outside and see Jackson sitting there, my anger goes up tenfold. No fucking way am I leaving her here with him. I don't care if he is her police protection and she doesn't want me here, I don't trust anyone at this point after what happened to Finnley. My escort, a ten-year veteran named Marcus Walker, is still parked behind my truck with his car running. I wave in his direction and point back to the house, indicating I'm staying and hoping he can see me, but the interior of his cruiser is dark.

"I just told him you might be a while, heard some shouting coming from upstairs. Everything okay?" Jackson asks.

"None of your fucking business," I growl.

Yeah, I'm an asshole. Sue me. The guy gets on my damn nerves. Collin told me he and Phina dated back in college and even though I've gotten over my issue with Dax, I'm still a jealous fuck at heart.

"Aw, trouble in paradise?" Jackson laughs.

"One more word and I'll kick your ass all the way to the curb."

He continues to laugh as he pushes himself up from the top step.

"No hard feelings, man. That one's a stubborn one," he says, jerking his head towards the house.

Don't I fucking know it.

Doesn't mean I have to like that this douchebag knows it, too.

Turning around, I go back into the house and try not to protest when Jackson follows me inside.

"Just going to grab a bottle of water from the fridge," he tells me, making his way around me and towards the kitchen.

I glare at his back until he disappears into the kitchen. I don't like how fucking familiar he is in this house. How the hell does he even know Phina *has* bottled water in her fridge? She does, I mean who the fuck doesn't in this day and age, but still. That fuck nut doesn't know that.

Jesus Christ, I'm losing it.

I hear the shower shut off upstairs and my stomach flops in anticipation of seeing Phina again, hoping the shower calmed her the fuck down and she's ready to talk. What the hell did I say that was so wrong? What did I do that forced her to put all those fucking walls back up around her heart, refusing to let me in? She opened up to me last night about her father, she told me about the burns and she showed them to me and even let me make love to her instead of fuck her like a crazy person. Something isn't adding up and my pea-sized brain isn't grasping it. Is she just upset because of Finnley's accident? Is the guilt she's feeling making her relive every horrible thing her father did to her and she's back to feeling like she's not worthy of my love? She's the only one who can answer these questions and she damn well better be prepared to open her beautiful mouth and start talking.

Jackson waltzes back into the living room, whistling as he goes and I want to punch him square in the mouth. Instead, I flop down on the couch angrily and clasp my hands together between my knees.

I hear footsteps on the stairs a few minutes later and my heart starts thundering in my chest. As soon as she gets down here, I'm going to grab onto her and kiss her, remind her of all the reasons why she can't fucking shut me out. I glance up as she pauses on the bottom step and looks at me in irritation. Her wet hair hangs down around her shoulders and her make-up free face that's been scrubbed clean of Finnley's blood makes her look much younger and more vulnerable. That is, until she opens her mouth.

"I thought I told you to leave?"

Every good plan swirling through my brain disintegrates into a pile of dust.

27

Phina

I STARE IN a daze at my feet as Finnley's blood mixes with the water from the shower and the pink-tinged liquid slides down my body, swirling around the drain. I should be crying. I have every reason to cry, but I feel so dead inside that nothing happens. I knew as soon as DJ started to remove my pants that he'd see. That stupid pep talk I gave myself meant nothing when it came down to it. I try to reason with myself that I just wasn't ready for him to see. If I would have just had a little more time to prepare myself and think about what I wanted to say to him, maybe it would have turned out differently, but I know that's a lie. If it happened tomorrow, a week from now or six months from now, I probably would have done the same thing – waited for him to look at those burns in horror and give me a reason to push him away. It's what I do. It's what I know, and no amount of pretending that I was this happy, well-adjusted person the last few weeks was going to change that.

I used his words of hatred for the man he thought was responsible for putting those burns on me against him. I know he doesn't hate *me*. He loves me and he would do anything for me. The problem is the woman standing in the shower right now watching her best friend's blood drip down her body. I hate myself too much to allow anything good in my life. It's just like the bullshit they feed to people at Al-Anon meetings. 'It's not that your loved one doesn't love *you* enough to stop their addiction, it's that they don't love *themselves* enough.'

It's almost funny when I think about it, but I'm so numb that I can't even force myself to laugh. DJ wants to tear the person who burned me limb from limb, assuming it was my father, when he was staring at the culprit the entire time. I'm sure it won't be long before he puts two-and-two together. He's a paramedic. He knows what fresh burns look like compared to fifteen year old ones. I can't blame him for not realizing it when he first saw the marks on my hip. I'm sure my freak-out confused him and he was still running on adrenaline from the accident. He immediately assumed he knew where the burns came from and I didn't correct him. If I was a different person, maybe I could have come clean, finally told him about the problem I have and what I do to myself from time to time. Maybe he would have pulled me into his arms, kissed away my tears and told me it didn't matter. Maybe I would have believed him.

I turn off the water and dry off robotically, throwing on a pair of yoga pants and a sweatshirt. Grabbing my cell phone out of my scrub pants, I close my eyes so I don't have to see the blood. I dial Finnley's number and breathe a little easier when I hear her tired voice on the other line.

"Did you get my cheeseburger?"

I try to laugh at her odd question, but it comes out as a sob and I quickly smack my hand over my mouth. She doesn't need to be burdened with my problems. Because of me, she's in a hospital right now and she could have died.

"Oh, honey, I'm fine," she tells me softly. "Just a bump on the head and all my tests came back good. I'll be able to go home tomorrow night."

I'm glad she's going to be okay, but that doesn't change the fact that she's in this position right now because of me. Her car flew through a busy intersection because my father couldn't get to me. She was covered in blood and Collin almost lost the love of his life, all because of me. I let my guard down and was fucking humming with happiness all morning while Finnley was fighting for her life.

"Listen, I know you heard about what happened to my car," Finnley states, interrupting my thoughts. "I want you to promise me right now that you don't blame yourself."

I close my eyes and she continues, not even waiting for a reply.

"It's not your fault, Phina. I know you and I know you're beating yourself up over this and you need to stop. The things he did to you, the things he's still doing...it's not your fault, do you hear me? What happened today, it could have happened to Collin, to DJ or to you."

"But it didn't," I whisper softly.

"BUT IT COULD HAVE," she replies loudly. "That sperm donor is the one who is responsible for this shit, not you. He's responsible for the shitty way you grew up, for making you think you don't deserve to be happy and for all of the crap that's been going on lately. HIM, not you. You didn't ask for any of this."

In theory, I know she's right, but it's impossible for my head and my heart to come to an agreement. I can still see the way DJ looked at my hips and I can still hear the hatred in his voice. My father might have started the ball rolling, but I took over his job for the next fifteen years and did a great job of fucking myself up.

"I love you, Fin," I tell her softly.

"I love you too, you big dummy. Oh, I almost forgot, Dax called here looking for you. Said he tried to reach you on your cell, but you didn't answer."

I noticed a couple of missed calls from Dax on my phone before I called Finnley, but she was my first priority.

"He said he found something out and needs to talk to you as soon as possible," Finnley finishes.

I end the call with a promise to come up and see her when I'm finished with Dax. Holding my cell phone in my lap, I stare at the ashtray on my nightstand with the lone cigarette in it, the one I lit earlier with every intention of pressing it into my skin. I try to go to that place in my mind, the one unconscious of everything around me but the need to feel pain. I close my eyes and concentrate, thinking about what it feels like to press the burning embers into my flesh. I imagine the smell of burning skin and the relief that washes through my body as it gets a new brand on my hip. My hands start to shake, not with the need to light up the cigarette, but with the fear that I don't have the desire to do this to myself anymore. I found something better to become addicted to, but I told him to leave. It was for the best, I reassure myself. As much as it hurts, it needed to happen. The pain of pushing him away is far greater than any burn from a cigarette.

I lift my phone from my lap and hit the return call button next to DJ's missed call. After a few rings, it goes to voicemail. I leave him a quick message letting him know that I'll just come up to the station to talk to him. I don't want to be in this house anymore. Everywhere I look, I see what happened between DJ and me and it makes me want to scream. I hope Dax finally has some good news for me. I'll never be able to look DJ in the eyes again now that he's seen my scars and knows what kind of a person I really am, but maybe I'll finally be able to finish this shit with my father and get on with my life. As miserable as that life might be without DJ.

Tossing my phone on my bed, I push myself up and head downstairs to find Jackson. I feel bad about yelling at him earlier when he tried to stay in the house with me, but I was not in the right frame of mind to deal with him following me around. I need to apologize and see if he'll be able to take me to Dax's office.

As I get to the bottom of the stairs, I round the corner into the living room and stop short when I see DJ still here with his ass parked on my couch. I try not to let myself feel relief that he didn't do as I asked and leave. I try not to drink in the sight of him and wish that I were a different person, worthy of the love I see shining in his eyes as he quickly jumps up from the couch when he sees me. I shut off every part of myself that he's touched with his love and concentrate on my anger. It's always been an easier emotion for me to handle, anyway, so why should this be any different?

"I thought I told you to leave?" I question him in a bored voice.

His happiness at seeing me quickly vanishes.

"I think you should know by now that I never do what I'm told, Fireball," he says sarcastically.

Folding my arms across my chest to stop myself from racing across the room and wrapping them around him, I stare at him blankly before turning my gaze on Jackson, who stands awkwardly by the front door with a bottled water in his hand.

"Jackson, can you take me to see Dax?"

He nods, opening his mouth to agree when DJ glares at him before turning that look towards me. "The fuck he will! If you need to go anywhere, I'M taking you."

I scoff, rolling my eyes. "Why are you still here?"

"Obviously because I'm a glutton for punishment!" he shouts. "Get your ass in my truck and I'll take you!"

"Fuck off! I'm not going anywhere with you!" I yell back.

"Then you're not going anywhere! If you leave this house, it's going to be with ME!"

Dropping my arms to my sides, I take a few deep breaths to calm myself. He's picking a fight with me on purpose. This is what we do. It's like fucking foreplay, but I refuse to play into it.

Luckily, I hear the buzz of DJ's pager attached to his belt. Without taking his furious eyes off of me, he yanks the thing off of his hip and brings it up in front of his face.

"Shit! Shit, motherfuck, shit damn!" he curses, pulling his cell phone out of his pocket and quickly dialing a number.

I listen to his one-sided conversation, finding out the page was about a huge warehouse fire on the opposite side of town and all paramedics needed to respond.

"Go be a hero for someone else, I don't need you," I tell him loudly so he'll hear me over his phone call as I walk over to the coffee table and grab my purse.

He covers the mouthpiece with his hand and stares me down.

"Don't fucking move!" he orders loudly.

He squeezes his eyes closed immediately and lets out a huge calming breath before softening his voice with his next words. "I love you, Phina. We'll handle Dax together. We will handle *everything* together."

He turns away from me and moves closer to the kitchen, quietly arguing with whoever is on the other line about how he can't make it into work right now, that he has an emergency of his own at home.

I feel myself wanting to give in, to forget about all the reasons why being with him is a bad idea. My feet start moving me in his direction when Jackson clears his throat quietly from behind me.

I can't do this. I can't keep bringing DJ into this shit. He wants to skip work when there are people whose lives he could save because of *my* problems. What happens after that? What happens when I have another issue he needs to deal with? Eventually he's going to realize I'm not worth all the trouble he has to go through just to be with me. I'm always going to have problems, and he's always going to want to save me.

While DJ is distracted on the phone, I quickly turn away, grabbing Jackson's hand and quietly pulling him out the door.

28

DJ

"No, DO NOT call Collin. He's got enough on his plate right now," I argue with my captain.

He continues to explain about the warehouse fire, telling me that without Collin there, he needs someone to fill in and take charge and I'm the only option. The warehouse is a huge manufacturing plant on the other side of town and it's full of workers who just got there for the next shift. The five-story building is over a hundred years old and it's going up like a fucking tinderbox.

I can't just NOT respond to this call, but I also can't leave Phina right now. I could see her wavering when I told her I love her. Running my hand through my hair, I stare up at the ceiling, trying to come up with a plan. If I have to, I'll tie her ass up and take her with me.

"Fine. I'll meet you there as soon as possible. My gear is still in my locker, make sure someone grabs it on the way out so I don't have to make an extra stop," I tell him before ending the call.

I turn around as I shut off my phone, gearing up to explain the plan to Phina without starting another argument. When I see nothing but an empty living room and a wide-open front door, I completely lose my shit.

"YOU HAVE GOT TO BE FUCKING KIDDING ME!" I yell to the empty house.

Racing across the living room and out the front door, I search the street and of course, Jackson's cruiser is gone. Making my way down the steps, calling Jackson every fucking name in the book for going against me, I hear the screeching of tires a few houses away and hope to God he had enough sense to turn around and bring Phina back. I watch an unmarked, black Crown Vic fly up to the curb in front of my truck and see Dax get out of the vehicle and race up the front walk.

"Where is she? Where the fuck is Phina?"

He tries to go around me into the house, but I stop him with a hand on his arm. "She's not here. She just left to go see you."

He takes off running towards Marcus' cruiser, which was parked behind my truck in the driveway and still running.

"I thought I told you to make sure she stays here!" Dax shouts as he flings open the driver's side door. "Oh, Jesus. SON OF A BITCH!"

Walking up behind Dax, I watch as he leans in and presses two of his fingers to Marcus's throat, which is pretty pointless because even I can see from over Dax's shoulder that the bloody hole in Marcus's temple would make it pretty hard for his heart to keep beating.

"Who the fuck did that?" I ask in shock as Dax steps back from the vehicle.

"Did Phina leave alone? Tell me she left alone," Dax says worriedly, ignoring my question.

I shake my head at him, wondering if he's been drinking tonight.

"Um, clearly she didn't go alone. She's got police protection on her ass twenty-four-seven, dumbass. Although by the looks of poor Marcus here, you didn't exactly hire vigilant guard dogs."

Dax curses, pulling a wad of napkins out of his pocket and wrapping them around the bloody shoulder piece still attached to Marcus's uniform.

"What the hell is going on?" I ask again as panic starts to set in.

He doesn't answer me, just pulls the radio off of Marcus's shoulder, careful to keep the napkins in place.

"I should have left both of you a more detailed message," he mumbles to himself. "Son of a fucking bitch."

"Dax, you better fucking start explaining things or I'm going to kick your goddamn ass!" I shout.

He holds his finger up for me to wait and I almost grab onto it and twist it off his fucking hand.

He holds his thumb and a corner of the napkin over the press-to-talk button and starts talking rapidly.

"This is Detective Trevino, I've got a 10-00 and need back-up assistance at 743 Vine Street. I need an APB and BOLO for badge number 29763, last seen driving a city-issued police Taurus, license plate Boy King Mary Yellow 324. Armed and dangerous, possible female hostage, thirty-four years of age, over."

He releases the button and I try to process what he's saying.

Female hostage, female hostage, female hostage…

Static comes over the radio seconds later and a tinny female voice replies.

"Copy that. APB and BOLO have been processed. Do you need medical assistance for the 10-00, over?"

Dax glances at Marcus sadly. "Negative. Officer is DOA, over."

"Copy that. Assistance is en route, ETA five minutes, over."

"Copy." Dax reattaches the radio to Marcus's shoulder and tosses the bloody napkins onto the floor of the car. He backs away from the vehicle and immediately starts dialing his cell phone while I stand there, trying to make sense of what's going on.

"I need deeds to any piece of property that Jackson Castillo and/or Anthony Giordano own. Text me the addresses as soon as fucking possible."

He ends the call and finally looks at me. I can do nothing but shake my head back and forth.

"This isn't happening. This is NOT fucking happening," I whisper.

"Do you have any idea what direction they went in?" Dax asks.

I continue shaking my head, wondering how in the hell this could happen. I shouldn't have let her leave. I shouldn't have taken that fucking call and turned my back on her.

"I was on the phone. She left when I was on the phone. She fucking left while I was on the phone," I repeat like a deranged idiot.

"This is all on me, do you understand? You had no way of knowing she shouldn't go off alone with him," Dax explains. "He's one of my fucking own. I put him in charge of watching her, dammit."

Pulling my fist back, I punch him right in the mouth, exactly like I wanted to do earlier. I shake out my hand as he shouts in pain, spitting a wad of blood out of his mouth and onto the sidewalk.

"I'll let you have that one shot because I know you're pissed, but that's all you get. You do it again and I'm hauling your ass in for assaulting a police officer after I beat the fuck out of you!" Dax shouts at me as he holds the back of his hand against his busted lip.

My entire body shakes with rage and I see nothing but red. I don't pay attention to his warning and I advance on him instead.

"What the fuck did you do? WHAT THE FUCK DID YOU DO, ASSHOLE?" I scream, shoving my hands against his chest.

He stumbles backwards into the side of his vehicle and then, faster than I can come up with another insult, he's got me turned around with my arms secured behind my back in the iron lock of his hands.

"Seriously, this is your last fucking warning!" he yells by my ear.

I struggle against his hold, but he just tightens it until my arms feel like they're being ripped out of their sockets.

"Why does my guard dog have a hole in his head and why the fuck did you issue an APB and a BOLO for Jackson? TELL ME WHAT THE FUCK HAPPENED!"

He shakes me roughly to get me stop struggling and I pause for a moment to let my anger simmer so he'll fucking speak. My brain has already caught up with all the shit happening around me, but I want to hear him fucking say it.

"I got an anonymous call earlier that there was someone on the inside making all those threats against you and Phina. Guy claimed he saw the person light the fire around the ambulance and cut the brake line on Finnley's car. Even saw him tape a few notes to yours and Phina's front doors," Dax explains. "I didn't want to believe it. I mean, for all I knew it was her fucking father calling it in trying to get us off of his tail, but I still had to look into it, just in case."

I've already put two-and-two together and I don't want to hear what he says next. I don't want to know that everything I'm thinking about right now could be a reality.

"I never actually worked with Jackson. He's a beat cop and I'm a detective, so our paths have never really crossed. My captain put out a few calls when Phina started receiving threats and the guy actually came to me and volunteered for the job. Told me some story about his cousin fucking up Phina's best friend's life and how he just wanted to do right by everyone for his family's sake. I didn't like it, but he came highly recommended from my captain. I trust that man, DJ. He was my fucking mentor at the police academy and he's been like a father to me since I graduated. I had no solid reason to think Jackson was anything but on the up and up even if my gut didn't agree. Besides, this city doesn't exactly have the resources to put a full-time cop on glorified guard duty. Jackson was on personal leave and we already had another cop filling in for him at the station, so it seemed like the perfect solution on paper.

Dax finally lets go of me when he's sure I'm not going to haul off and punch him again. I turn around slowly, waiting for him to tell me the rest, still unsure if I'm going to be forced to beat his ass.

"As soon as I got the call, I started discreetly asking about Jackson around the station. A lot of people don't like him. They think he's shady and there's been some complaints about his forceful tactics when he goes on calls. There were even some rumors that he's been taking bribes from prisoners to do favors for them on the outside. They said the captain refused to make any formal complaints until someone came to them with solid proof. Jordan's death was the perfect excuse for cap to ask Jackson to take a leave of absence and get his head on straight."

This is all just too fucked up. The man watching us day and night, following us everywhere we go, is responsible for all the threats and for almost killing us. And now he has Phina.

"I called Phina and told her to call me back right away and then I called Marcus and told him to make sure she didn't leave because Jackson could be a threat. I also called your stupid ass, but you didn't answer. I wanted to come here and question him myself and feel him out. You can't just go around accusing a cop of working on the wrong side of the law," Dax explains.

I don't want to hear anything else. Jackson could be the biggest threat to Phina, or if his co-workers are correct, he could have taken a bribe from her father and be delivering her to him right now. Either option is unacceptable.

"Move this fucking cruiser out of my way," I tell Dax, pointing to Marcus' car still blocking my truck as I pull my keys out of my pocket and head over to it.

"You're not fucking going anywhere, DJ. Back-up will be here any minute now and the cops will handle it," he tells me as I get inside my truck and slam the door closed.

With the window rolled down, I start it up and give him one last look. "Yeah, because the cops have done a SUPER fucking job of it so far. Move the goddamn cruiser before I run the fucker over!"

I rev my engine and put the truck in gear. We've already wasted enough time standing out here in the front yard talking when we should have been high-tailing it after Phina and Jackson.

"Goddammit, DJ! Don't make me do this!" Dax shouts, pulling his gun from his shoulder holster and pointing it right at me.

I smirk at him, taking my foot off the brake. "Go ahead, pull the trigger, dick fuck."

He can either let me go or shoot me. I'll do whatever it takes to find Phina.

Dax shakes his head at me and curses a blue streak as I press on the gas. As I start to turn around to look behind me and see how much room I have before I smash into the cruiser, the explosion from Dax's gun echoes through the night.

29

Phina

I LOOK OVER at Jackson questioningly as he makes a right instead of a left at the end of my street.

"Heard on the radio there was an accident on Clemmons Street. Going to take a shortcut to the police station," he explains.

Nodding silently, I rest my head on the seat back and stare out the window.

God, why does this have to hurt so fucking much? Me, the woman who loves pain, suddenly doesn't want to feel it any more.

"Hey, so how come things between us never worked out?" Jackson suddenly asks.

I close my eyes, really not wanting to talk right now, but I also don't want to be a bitch to the person who has taken time out of his life to keep an eye on me and keep me safe.

When I open my eyes again, I continue to stare out the window.

"I don't know, I guess we were just too different. It never would have worked out," I reply softly.

"You and DJ are pretty opposite, but that seems to be working out just fine."

At the mention of DJ's name, I press the palms of my hands against my chest, trying my hardest to keep my heart from jumping out and flopping like a dead fish onto the floor at my feet.

I don't respond to his statement. I definitely don't want to get into this right now. It's too soon and I'm too raw. It feels like someone has filleted my skin and then dumped acid over it. Everything hurts and I just want to curl up in bed, pull the covers over my head and sleep until I stop aching.

"Seriously, I just want to know why I wasn't good enough for you?" Jackson prods, the tone of his voice suddenly turning harder than it was moments ago.

Jesus, it was like twelve years ago. Get over it already.

"That wasn't it at all, Jackson," I tell him, trying to keep the irritation out of my voice. "It was me. I wasn't good enough for *you*."

He either doesn't hear me or doesn't care, continuing to talk nonsense.

"I know it was because of the shit that went down between Jordan and Finnley. You just couldn't handle being with a guy who had that kind of craziness in his family tree."

What in the hell is he talking about? We broke up long before Jordan and Finnley even got married, let alone finding out Jordan had boarded the crazy train headed straight to his death.

I notice a few things all at once as I stare across the console at Jackson. He's clutching the steering wheel so tightly that his knuckles are white, the armpits of his blue uniform shirt are stained with circles of sweat, and he keeps tipping his head from side to side to crack his neck like a nervous tick. My sixth sense kicks in and I subtly glance at the door handle and contemplate jumping out of the moving vehicle if things get any weirder.

"Jackson, we dated back in college. Finnley and Jordan weren't even married yet," I remind him, glancing at the door handle again.

He suddenly flips on the lights and siren and presses down on the gas, almost like he knew what I was contemplating. The car takes off so quickly that I'm thrown against the seat.

"Jordan wasn't crazy, he was in love and Finnley fucked him over," Jackson mutters, not even listening to me.

Cars, trees and buildings whiz by the window as Jackson continues to press down on the accelerator, going at least ninety miles an hour. I grab onto the center console and the handle above the door, hoping to God people move the fuck out of our way and we don't hit anyone.

"He was my fucking best friend and that douchebag you've been sleeping with decided to just let him burn in his own fucking house!" Jackson shouts angrily.

My blood turns to ice in my veins and my hands start to sweat so badly that I can barely hold onto the door handle as we make a sharp turn, barely slowing down.

I don't know what to think right now, my mind is going a mile a minute, almost as fast as this damn car. Did he suddenly snap and decide he's jealous that I was with DJ? That makes absolutely no sense. Jackson and I only dated for a couple of months and we didn't even sleep together. The guy couldn't have held a torch for me this long, that's just sad and pathetic. Him being angry about Jordan's death makes much more sense, but still, to blame DJ for it? That's reaching just a little bit.

"This all could have been avoided if you'd just kept your fucking legs closed and not been such a whore!"

His loud, booming voice screaming the word *whore* is what makes some of the pieces snap together in my mind.

"Oh, my God, it was you?" I whisper in shock. "You left those notes for me, didn't you?"

How? Why? This can't be right. It couldn't have been Jackson all this time. My father called me. He admitted to leaving the notes and he told me I was going to burn the same night DJ and I were trapped inside of the ambulance. And yet, Jackson had been there every time something bad happened. He was at the fair when I was given that dose of insulin, he was parked outside my house when it was broken into and the living room was trashed, and he was watching the ambulance when the fire started out all around it. He was there, each and every time.

The only time he wasn't around was this morning, when DJ and I were getting dressed for work. He sent me a text saying he was running to get coffee and asked if we wanted anything. He was only gone for five minutes tops since there's a coffee shop a block away, but it would have been long enough to get to Collin and Finnley's house the next street over and cut her brake line.

"Jackson, what have you done?" I ask in horror.

He lets out a cold, calculating laugh and shakes his head at me.

"Someone needs to pay for what happened to Jordan and since you're the whore who has taken up with his killer, I've decided it should be you. Paybacks are a bitch."

His right hand jerks off of the steering wheel and his fist slams into the side of my head. The force of the blow knocks me roughly into the window and I see stars before everything goes black.

30

DJ

"I CANNOT BELIEVE you shot my fucking tires!" I shout at Dax as I jump down from my truck and he holsters his weapon.

He shrugs his reply as a whole caravan of cop cars with lights and sirens blazing come flying up the street, blocking the driveway, pulling up onto the lawn and stopping wherever the hell they find a space. It looks like every law enforcement official from the entire city has shown up, and Dax immediately starts explaining the situation and issuing orders.

I walk across the lawn, wondering how much trouble I would get into if I stole a cop car. Standing right next to one idling by the curb, I hear Dax shout my name.

"Don't even think about it, asshole. Do you really want Phina to have to visit you behind bars when we get her home?"

I roll my eyes and look away from him. He said "when," not "if." That's got to be a good sign. I want to be positive, I know I *have* to be positive for her sake, but I'm dying inside right now. I don't know where she is, what she's thinking or if she's hurt. Instead of focusing on all the horrible things she could be going through, I think about something good, instead. I think about her smile and her laugh, about how amazing she is with my nieces and nephews, how she stretches her entire body when she first wakes up in the morning, groaning "strrr-reeeaaaaaach" while she does it. I think about the scent of her shampoo and how my pillows always smell like it. I think about how much it turns me on to fight with her and how fucking fantastic sex is after a good screaming match.

I rest my palms on the roof of the running cruiser and let my head drop down to rest my chin on my chest. I think about how she trusted me with the hardest part of her past and let me kiss those painful memories away, even if I couldn't erase the faded, old scars from her body.

Faded old scars...faded old scars.

Goddammit! Goddammit all to hell! I'm a fucking paramedic, how did I not put this together until right now? My head jerks up and I slam my fist onto the top of the car.

"Hey, that's taxpayers money. Don't break it, or you buy it," Dax warns me as he comes to stand next to me.

"Tell me there's a fucking plan! We need to get her back right the fuck now," I tell him as I start pacing back and forth.

"We're working on it. I have men checking out the properties that are on file and we should know something soon," he tells me.

Those fucking burn marks on her hip...some of them looked exactly like the ones on her back, but most of them were angry, red and fresh.

"I fucking hate the sick, fucked up bastard who did this to you."

"Funny, I hate that person, too."

My hands grab onto handfuls of my hair and I tug as hard as I can as I continue to pace.

I told her I saw her. I told her I saw everything and that I loved it all, but I missed the most obvious fucking thing. I run through the things she said when she was in a daze when I first got here earlier, the cigarette in her mouth and the lighter in her fucking hand. It all comes together in one horrible, messy picture in my mind as I remember the look in her eyes, begging me to see that final piece of the puzzle and still keep my promise to love her no matter what.

One of the cops comes up to Dax, gives me a nervous look and then leans in to whisper something in his ear. When he's finished, Dax gives him a nod and the cop scurries back to the rest of the group on the lawn.

"What's going on? Did they find her?"

Dax pulls his keys out of his pocket. "A report of a house fire was just called in. The property is registered to Anthony Giordano."

I can't lose her. I can't fucking lose her now when I have so many things I need to say to her.

"I'm fucking going with you," I tell Dax.

He nods. "I figured as much, but if you get in the way of police procedure I'll-"

"Toss my ass in jail," I finish for him. "You already covered that a few times tonight."

Dax shakes his head in irritation at me, but doesn't say another word as we jog across the yard and hop into his car.

31

Phina

I BLINK MY eyes rapidly as I open them, the bright light making the pounding in my head a thousand times worse. I groan and shut them again when a sharp, stabbing pain rockets through my skull.

"Ahhhh, you're awake."

A voice close to my ear makes my skin crawl, but I slowly open my eyes anyway. I find Jackson squatting down in front of me with a huge smile on his face. I try to lunge towards him to smack the smile right off of his face, but my body jerks to a halt and it feels like I pulled every fucking muscle in both of my arms. Looking above me, I realize my arms are tied over my head, the rope completely wrapped around a refrigerator. Ignoring the pain in my shoulders and arms, I start tugging frantically against my bindings.

"There's no point in hurting yourself more, I was a Boy Scout back in the day. That right there is a double constrictor knot," he informs me proudly, pointing to the thick, white rope that holds my arms secure.

"I see tying knots is the only thing you were good at. Did they kick you out for being a sick, twisted fuck?" I ask him sweetly through clenched teeth.

The smile falls from his face and he quickly pushes himself up to tower over me. "The only sick fuck in this room is you, my dear. Do you have any idea what it was like to find out you were fucking the enemy? The man who tore my family apart and took my best friend away from me?"

He starts pacing back and forth agitatedly in front of me, and I suddenly stop trying to tug against my bindings when I get a look at my surroundings. Lime green, rusty appliances, wood paneling on the walls, stained Formica countertops and a rickety blue plastic table against the wall. How many times did I get shoved face first onto that table so a cigarette could be jammed into my lower back?

"I see you finally recognize where we are," Jackson says when he sees me glancing nervously around, his smile back in place. "Luckily, the place had been paid off before your parents moved in since they inherited it from someone in the family and your dad had enough money socked away to keep paying the taxes on it. It's been sitting here unoccupied for fifteen years"

I notice dust and cobwebs on every flat surface and I try not to imagine myself as a little girl, cowering under the table when I'd hear the flick of my father's lighter.

"I thought it would be fitting to take you on a trip down memory lane. Did you know I've been in contact with dear old dad for a few months? Nice guy, a little bit of a Jesus freak these days, but what can you do?" Jackson asks with a shrug. "He told me all about your rough childhood and let me tell you, my heart just broke for poor little Seraphina Giordano. He was a wealth of information on you. Had an entire notebook filled with facts about your life. He's been keeping an eye on his little girl all these years even from prison, isn't that sweet?"

I feel bile rising in my throat knowing that Jackson has been speaking with my father. Who knows what kind of shit that man told him?

"Did you help him get out on parole?"

Jackson tips his head back and laughs. "Oh, you have too much faith in me, Phina, if only that were possible. No, he really did get out on good behavior, but what a nice coincidence for me, wouldn't you say? He's been a big help."

It's bad enough knowing Jackson is insane and has me tied up in my childhood home. If my father suddenly shows up here, my life is officially over. How the hell can I take a cop AND a man who hates me and has spent fifteen years in prison learning how to fight dirty, all with my hands tied to a fucking refrigerator?

"This plan of mine only had a few snags. Lucky for me you and lover boy had a little fight tonight, or I wasn't quite sure how I'd get you alone," he tells me. "I tried to get to that asshole Collin, but that fucker is always looking over his shoulder and he's always surrounded by fucking firemen. I didn't really intend for Finnley to get hurt, but imagine my surprise when I cut the brakes on the wrong car? That whore finally got to feel a little of the pain I've felt since she allowed Jordan to burn to death inside their house."

Obviously, bat shit crazy runs in the Castillo family.

"My best fucking friend!" he screams suddenly. "Do you know there wasn't anything left of Jordan after that fire? That they had to use my best friend's dental records to identify his body? It should have been Collin and the man you've been fucking. THEY should have been the ones to burn!"

I really don't want to piss him off any more, but I can't just sit here and let him excuse the man who tried to kill Finnley and place all the blame on Collin and DJ.

"You have lost your fucking mind!" I yell back. "Jordan doused her carpets in gas and lit the place on fire while she was inside. Collin and DJ did what they had to do to get Finnley out. They tried to save him, but he refused to leave. Did you know that? He backed away from the window in a room surrounded by flames and wouldn't let Collin pull him out. He knew what he did was wrong and he wanted to die!"

Jackson screams at the top of his lungs, throwing his fist into the fridge above my head before walking over to the cupboards and ripping half of the doors off their hinges. I duck and hold my arms over my head as best I can as wooden doors start flying at me, bouncing off of my legs and crashing into walls.

"YOU'RE LYING! YOU'RE FUCKING LYING! HE WOULD NEVER DO THAT! JORDAN WOULD NEVER LEAVE ME ON PURPOSE! I WAS LIKE A BROTHER TO HIM!"

He continues to rage and scream as he tears apart the kitchen, toppling over the kitchen chairs and pulling dusty plates and bowls from the doorless cupboards, shattering them on the kitchen tile. When he's cleared out the cupboards, he rushes out of the room and comes back seconds later with a huge red gas can in his hands. He mutters to himself as he flips the top of the spout and begins pouring it all around me. My heart drops and my eyes go wild with fear as I watch him douse every bit of the kitchen, from the ceiling to the walls to the floor. Gas drips from the ceiling and makes puddles all around me.

When the can is empty, he tosses it across the room and stalks over to me, his shoes crunching on the broken ceramic and glass that covers the floor. He gets down on his knees in front of me and quickly pulls his gun out of his holster, pressing it right into my forehead.

"You're a liar and a fucking whore! I'm tired of listening to your bullshit. This all could have been avoided if you would have just stayed away from Taylor! Now it's HIS turn to lose someone he loves!" he shouts, shoving the barrel of the gun harder against my skull.

"If you pull that trigger with all the gas in here, you're going to kill both of us," I try to reason with him.

He laughs maniacally before leaning down to get right in my face.

"Do you think I give a shit? Do you honestly think I would make it out of this alive, anyway? I'm a cop, Phina. Cops don't survive very long in prison."

I squeeze my eyes closed and pray to God that DJ isn't the one who finds me here. He'll never forgive himself for letting me walk away from him tonight and finding my charred remains in this kitchen would haunt him for the rest of his life. This fucking kitchen…where all my nightmares began and I guess they are going to end, as well. I wish I could tell him I'm sorry. I wish I could tell him that I never meant to push him away, that I love him more than I ever thought possible. He's the missing piece I've been looking for all my life, the only one who could've stopped the pain for good. I feel like I'm starring in a fucking Lifetime movie. The idiot that's about to die always realizes her mistakes at the very end.

I start to whisper DJ's name, over and over, mixing with my quiet sobs. Just the sound of his name in my ears makes me regret everything I did wrong with him and wish I had a chance to do it over. I would never push him away and I would fight to be good enough for him. Even though he's not with me right now, I can feel his arms around me, telling me everything is going to be okay.

I suddenly hear the slide of the release dropping the bullet into the chamber and I'm surprised I don't feel an ounce of pain when the gun explodes.

32

Anthony Giordano

I KNEW THAT little weasel was trouble. There was somethin' off about him when he came to visit me in the pen, fishin' around for information about my baby. I was stupid in the beginnin', enjoyin' the first visitor I had in fifteen years and I talked his ear off about her. I shoulda known better. You can never trust the fucking cops.

I wasn't a good man before I got locked up. I made a lot of mistakes. When I die, the pearly gates will be locked tight and I'll be headed somewhere much warmer, and that's okay because it's what I deserve. The good Lord giveth and the good Lord taketh away. He gave me a good life and I pissed all over it. The only reason I didn't mouth off at my parole board hearin' was because of this moment, right here. The one where I could make amends for my mistakes. I been prayin' over this for weeks, lookin' for direction from Him on what I should do to earn forgiveness from the one person still on this earth who means something to me and He finally answered my prayers. Lord knows the cops didn't answer them when I called earlier and told them one of their own was a turncoat.

I've spent every wakin' moment since I walked outta the pen followin' my baby, tryin' to find the right time to talk to her and tell her how sorry I am for the man I used to be. I saw that little fucker light the fire around the ambulance and then play it off like someone else did it. I watched him cut the brake line on someone's car around the corner from my baby. I coulda taken him out both those times, but I'm a changed man. The Lord says thou shalt not kill.

I stand here now lookin' through the window of the back door to my old house and I wonder if God will forgive me just this once since I'm doin' it to save Seraphina. I'm sure it won't get me into the Kingdom of Heaven, but at least when I die, I'll know one person I killed deserved it. I don't like bein' back here at this house. Too many bad things happened under this roof and there are too many ghosts hauntin' these rooms. If it's this hard on me bein' back here, I can only imagine what it's like for my baby. Must be like a whole herd of demons nippin' at her heels. I wish she coulda had a better childhood. I wish I coulda been a better father and I wish she didn't have to add another bad memory to her time spent in this house. So many things I wish coulda been different, but wishin' is a waste of time. Shoulda burned this damn house down a long time ago.

As quietly as I can, I turn the handle to the back door and open it, surprised the hinges don't squeak. I'm not sure the crazy cop with a gun pressed into my baby's skull would notice it, anyway. I look around the man's shoulder and get a good look at my daughter. She's so pretty, even with tears runnin' down her cheeks, that it makes my damn chest hurt. I shoulda seen just how perfect and pretty she was when she was little. I watched her so much lately that I memorized every beautiful feature of her grown-up face, even though I could never get close enough to really look at 'em.

I turn off the sappy shit when I see the cop pull the slide release on the gun and I whisper a prayer into the quiet night.

"Lord, forgive me."

I aim, and pull the trigger.

33

Phina

I REALIZE I'M not dead when I hear screaming. My eyes fly open and I see Jackson standing in front of me, staring at the ceiling. I glance up and find it covered in flames, quickly spreading towards the back door. Something out of the corner of room catches my eye and I see the ghost from my past waltz through the open back door with a gun in his hands. He's aged a great deal and his brown hair is now white, but I would recognize him anywhere.

"Hi, baby," he tells me with a smile. "I was aiming for his head but I guess I'm a little rusty in my old age. Guess I should have recognized the smell of gas before I fired."

I immediately start fighting against the ropes, twisting and turning my body as hard as I can, screaming for someone to help while the fire quickly spreads across the cabinets, licking against the walls.

Jackson takes off running in the direction of the living room and I watch in shock as my father flies across the room, much faster than I would have ever thought possible considering his age. He jumps over my legs and tackles Jackson with his arms around his waist right in the doorway. Both men crash to the floor with a loud thud and immediately start wrestling. I turn away from their fight as the crackle and snap of the fire spreading echoes all around me. Smoke fills the room and I try to take low, shallow breaths as I pull so hard against the rope that my wrists burn and I can feel blood dripping down my arms.

The blast from a gun makes me scream and I whip my head back to where my father and Jackson were fighting.

My father straddles Jackson, still holding the gun towards him. I glance down and see a bloody hole blooming on Jackson's shirt right over his stomach. I look up and my father's eyes meet mine for the first time in fifteen years and I can't stop the scream that flies out of my mouth. I know I said I wanted him to just fucking show himself after all these weeks of notes and threats, but I immediately want to take it all back. When I look into his eyes, I see him coming after me with a gun in his hand the day I saw him murder someone in his bedroom. I see him charging towards me, wanting nothing more than to end my life and relieve himself of the burden that was me. I see the hatred when he glared at me across the courtroom the day I testified against him and I see every single time he dragged me out of my hiding places, held me against the table and burned me with his cigarette.

As he gets up from Jordan's body and walks towards me with the gun while the fire rages out of control around us, I'm not quite sure which is scarier. He quickly steps over my legs to get to the other side of my body, putting himself in between the fire and me as he squats down next to me. I pull my legs up to my chest and bury my face in my knees so I won't have to look at him when he kills me. I don't want my last sight to be his face. I hear something click, feel my arms jerking back and forth and then suddenly, they drop down to my sides. I look up in confusion to see my father holding a pocketknife in his hand.

I quickly scramble away from him, my arms screaming in protest as

I move my feet and legs as fast as I can, coughing from the smoke as I get to my feet and jump over Jackson's body, refusing to look down at him.

"Seraphina, wait!" my father shouts as I make it to the doorway to the living room.

I slowly turn to face him even though every instinct inside of me is telling me to run. Run from this house and never look back.

My father stands and takes a step towards me, stopping when he sees the fear on my face. His frame is silhouetted by fire as it spreads along all of the cupboards and most of the walls and ceiling.

"I'm so sorry, baby. I'm sorry for everything I ever done to you. You never deserved any of that shit. You were a good girl. God blessed me with the most beautiful little girl in the world and I never appreciated it."

My eyes fill with tears from his words and the smoke making its way towards me. Is this some kind of joke or a dream? Why is he saying these things to me?

"I know you never read none of my notes, but I wrote you one every couple of months just to tell ya how sorry I was. God is good and He made me see the light."

The phone call he made to me suddenly makes sense now. The notes he was talking about were the ones he mailed to me in prison and the *burn in hell* comment clearly had to do with his newfound religion. My father did nothing but curse God my entire childhood.

I hear a groan and I look down at the kitchen floor ten feet away and scream, jumping back and throwing my hands over my mouth. Jackson opens his eyes and coughs, blood dribbling down the side of his mouth.

Just then, a fully engulfed beam from the ceiling rips away and crashes down in front of me, blocking me off from Jackson and my father. I jump back as sparks and cinders swirl around the room.

I watch through the flames as my father quickly turns around to go out the back door, but it's now completely surrounded by fire. The ceiling above it, the frame around it and the door itself are raging out of control. He's completely trapped. He turns back towards me and shouts over the roar of the fire.

"You go on and get out of here now, ya hear? I'll make sure this little fucker doesn't go anywhere," he yells, pointing to the floor in front of him where I know Jackson still lies.

Even though I can barely see him through the smoke and fire, something makes me stay right where I am. Something makes me look at him, really look at him for the first time in fifteen years. The fire is getting too close and I feel it on my face and skin, my body dripping with sweat from the heat. I take another step back to get some relief, but keep my eyes locked on my father.

"I'm really sorry, baby. If I could take it all back, I would. You get the hell out of here and you go have a good life. You forget all about me because I'm not worth another second of your time and neither are all the bad memories in this house. You deserve to be happy. I'm gettin' what I deserve and it's okay. It's okay as long as I know you're happy."

I sob and choke as I move back further into the living room and away from the fire. I stumble over a piece of musty furniture and fall on my ass as I watch more pieces of the burning ceiling rain down on top of Jackson and my father. I cry harder when I hear my father scream out in pain, knowing that he's burning to death. It was what I always wanted. I wanted him to feel the burning agony of fire and ash and I wanted him to regret every time he forced me to feel the same. I hate that I want to run back into the room and try to save him, even though I know it's useless. I can't see anything inside the kitchen but the orange glow of angry fire. I hate that he chose *now* to say all the words he should have said to me a long time ago.

Flipping over on my hands and knees to try and stay below the smoke that is billowing above me, I hack and cough and cry as I crawl through the living room where I used to dream about having a father who loved me enough not to hurt me. I can barely see anything in front of me when I get to the front door and I run my palms blindly up the wood and feel for the handle. I turn the knob and fling the door open, stumbling out onto the front porch, trying to take huge gulps of fresh air.

I hear a horrifyingly loud crash behind me and I grab onto the railing, staggering down the stairs, running as fast as my legs will allow to the woods bordering our old property. I don't know anything about house fires aside from what I've seen on TV. On TV, they usually explode, and I'm not going to take any chances. I clear the first cropping of trees, tripping over vines as I try to put as much distance between the burning house and myself as possible. My body wracks with coughs and I stumble over a large tree root, face-planting right into the ground. I can't stop coughing and I can't stop crying. My lungs burn with smoke and my eyes are so swollen I can barely see out of them. The shadowed woods quickly grow darker and darker and everything around me starts spinning like I'm on a tilt-a-whirl. I close my eyes and drop my head to the ground.

34

DJ

I SEE AN orange glow of flames in the sky a few miles in the distance and panic ricochets through my body. Dax floors it, the speedometer reaching a hundred, but it's still not fast enough. Phina's childhood home was the furthest away from all of us when we were in school – twenty minutes by car and an hour and ten minutes by bike. Not that I was ever invited over...or rode my bike past her house a million times, searching for a glimpse of her.

Dax finally pulls up to the burning house at the same time as two additional fire trucks, joining the one that is already here fighting the fire. Dax slams on the brakes in the middle of the street and I jump out of the car before he puts it in park, racing towards the house. I'm tackled from behind halfway across the yard and my body slams against the ground as Dax shouts in my ear.

"WILL YOU STOP DOING STUPID FUCKING SHIT?! Let them put some of the fire out and get in there before you try to be a damn hero! We don't even know if she's in there!"

I shove him off me and get back up on my feet, not giving a damn about what he said. Firemen are racing around me, dragging hoses around to the back since the first truck has already started spraying down the front. I begin walking towards the house again when a loud explosion booms all around us. I instinctively duck and cover my head as debris and ash rain down around us and men start shouting. When I look back up, I see part of the front of the house is now missing, the skeleton inside the house completely engulfed in flames as the firemen work tirelessly to put it out.

"NOOOO!" I scream, the flames growing so high that I have to take a step back when I feel the heat of them licking my face. "OH, GOD, DON'T LET HER BE IN THERE!"

I feel helpless. I feel useless. I'm a goddamn fireman, but I know I can't go in that house right now. It's minutes, maybe even seconds from collapsing, but everything inside of me is telling me to just run in there. Who cares if I burn? Who cares if I don't make it back outside? I know if anyone is in that house, there's no way they're making it out alive, and if she's in there, I don't fucking care what happens to me. I will go in there with her and I will never leave her side again. As I stare at the house, the images that flash through my mind are like the worst horror movie ever made. Her gorgeous red hair burning away, her smooth skin melting from her body, her full, pink lips that kissed mine so many times pulled back and frozen in a scream of pain.

Oh, God, I can't take it! It hurts too much!

Dax tugs on my arm, pulling me further away from the fire, and I stare powerlessly at the house where Phina grew up as it burns to the ground. She'd be happy about this if she were standing next to me now. She'd be overjoyed that the place of her nightmares was finally going to be gone for good and she wouldn't have to think about it ever again. I can almost hear the sound of her laughter telling me it's about fucking time someone torched this place to the ground. I try to laugh, but it comes out as a sob. I need to hear her laugh again. I *have* to hear her laugh again, there's no other option.

The cop from earlier at Phina's house runs up to Dax and I force myself to turn away from the fire to hear what he has to say.

"Sir, we found Castillo's cruiser parked next door. We already checked inside and canvased most of the houses in the vicinity. A neighbor across the street said she saw a man carrying a woman inside about thirty minutes ago."

The confirmation that she was in that house a half hour ago doesn't mean anything. I won't let it mean the worst. I hear shouts coming from the back of the house and I head off in that direction, refusing to believe that she's anything but okay. She's strong and she's a fighter. There is no way she would put up with fucking dying. She'd stomp her foot, look death in the face and tell it to fuck off.

Dax runs after me, shouting my name, but I ignore him. I come to a dead stop at the edge of the lawn when I see two firemen covered in black soot carrying a body bag between them as they race away from the house.

I won't panic. I won't fucking panic!

It could be Jackson. It better fucking be Jackson in that bag.

Please, God, don't take her from me.

I hold my breath and stare around the corner of the burning house, waiting to see a glimpse of her gorgeous red hair and her beautiful, unhurt body being carried in a fireman's arms. My heart beats erratically and I clench my teeth to keep my screams at bay, squeezing my arms as tightly as I can to the sides of my body to stop it from shaking. Seconds pass, but they seem like hours before I finally see the bright yellow reflective stripe of someone's turnout gear. He's walking backwards in this direction and I start moving towards him. I watch as one man suddenly morphs into two when they both turn their bodies sideways, another black body bag suspended between them.

My legs give out from under me and I don't even feel Dax's arms go around me to stop me from hitting the ground. My screams finally let loose and I close my eyes, turning my face towards the sky as I let the sound of my heart breaking in two fill the night air.

I KILLED HER.

The beautiful, smartass firecracker that exploded into my life with the force of an atomic bomb – she's gone because of me.

All those moments spent fighting with her were a waste of time. Time that could have been better spent getting one of those rare laughs that were just for me, memorizing every freckle on her nose and showing her just how much she meant to me even though I fucked it all up in the end when she needed me the most.

From the very first time I tasted her lips, she was mine. With that cherry red lip-gloss and her hands on her hips, all sass and snark and attitude – she was mine but I fucked things up with her *that* time too and that damn graduation party.

Who the fuck knows at eighteen-years-old that the girl he felt up at a party would turn out to be his entire world years down the line? I sure as hell didn't. I drank too much and I didn't even get to remember what should have been the best fucking night of my life. I kissed those perfect lips, slid my hands up her tight shirt and tried not to blow my load when she moaned into my mouth. Then, I blacked out, forgetting all of the important things and walked away the next morning like the cocky little punk I was and tried to forget about her. I thought I'd done a pretty good job of it until four and a half months ago, when I saw her again. All that bullshit I'd spouted off to my best friend about how it's unnatural to spend your life with one woman…fuck, what I wouldn't give to go back and beat the shit out of that stupid asshole who thought he knew everything.

Eighteen weeks spent fighting her continued brush-offs and fighting with *her* when I should have been on my knees begging her to never leave me.

Eighteen days spent learning about what made her into the woman she was and trying my hardest to prove to her that she was worth more.

Eighteen minutes spent praying to a God I'd never believed in, begging Him not to take her from me.

Eighteen seconds too late.

It seemed like an eternity waiting on that front lawn for one of the firemen to carry her alive out of that house, but it only took eighteen seconds. Eighteen seconds between the first body bag and the second that ended my life as I know it.

I've counted each and every minute with her these last few months, the good and the bad. 181,440 minutes that I would give anything to do over. Sitting here with a half-empty bottle of whiskey and some dive bar I don't even remember the name of, I count the drops of condensation on my glass as they slide down, each one fading away and disappearing into the napkin underneath it just like every moment I spent with her. I had her and I let her slip through my fingers. I should have held tighter, fought harder, gotten there sooner.

I'll never run my fingers through the long, crimson hair that reminded me so much of fire when the sun hit it. I'll never feel the heat of her body pressed to mine again or the way she'd whisper my name against my lips right before she came.

Fuck, that goddamn sigh…it was like she just *breathed* my name, as if it were the oxygen in her lungs that gave her life. I can still hear that fucking sound every time I close my eyes and it completely guts me.

She branded her name on my heart and I know I'll never be the same. I'll never get the chance to tell her that I don't fucking care about the scars on her body. I don't care about anything but seeing her smiling and hearing her laugh.

Staring up at the clock on the wall behind the bar, I realize it's been eighteen hours since I last saw her alive. In my mind's eye, I see her standing there, a flush on her cheeks and determination in her eyes as she told me to go. I did as she asked because I was angry and I knew she was hurting. I couldn't stand the thought of hurting her any more than I already had. It seems that all I've ever done is hurt her.

She told me to go, and I did. I left her alone in that bedroom and I didn't fight for her. I should have stayed in that damn room until she finally talked to me. I let my anger get the best of me and I turned my back on her to be taken by a sick fuck looking for revenge.

If only I would have stayed.

35

Phina

"JESUS CHRIST! GET me a gurney and some oxygen! MOVE, MOVE, MOVE!"

I hear shouts and the rustling of leaves from somewhere in the distance, but it feels like a dream. The voices are muffled, like people are shouting underwater. I don't want to open my eyes. Everything hurts. My head is pounding, my skin feels raw and my throat burns. I can feel someone poking and prodding at me and I want to scream at them to stop, but I can't make any words come out. Each time I try to speak, it feels like someone is rubbing a hot coal against my vocal chords.

I just want to sleep. I want to stay in this beautiful oblivion between sleep and waking up where I don't have to think about everything that's sitting right at the edge of my mind, waiting to take over – rope, threats, kitchen, fire, guns, daddy…

"It's okay, Phina, try not to move. We need to make sure nothing's broken."

I must have made a noise of pain. I want to tell the voice it's not the physical pain that's killing me right now; it's the mental pain. I see his face through the fire, the one that haunted my dreams and called me so many bad names. I see him in a different light, one filled with love and regret and apology. He traded his life for mine, the ultimate act of love. I don't want to think about it, I don't want to remember. It's so much easier for him to be a monster in my mind than a savior.

I'm gently rolled onto my back and something hard slides under me. I finally open my eyes, hoping the memories fade as I let go of the darkness.

I blink rapidly when someone shines a light into my eyes while my arms and legs are strapped to something hard and uncomfortable.

"Hey, there you are! How do you feel? Can you speak?" Brad asks as he leans over me with his stethoscope, pressing it against my chest.

I look down and notice my sweatshirt has been sliced in half right up the front of my body. Before I can say anything to him, a plastic oxygen mask is pressed against my nose and mouth. Brad gently lifts my head to slide the elastic band around my head to hold it in place.

"Just breathe normally and take it easy," he instructs me as I feel cool air inside the mask begin to float down my throat and put out the fire in my lungs.

I feel a prick in my arm and have the sudden urge to start giving Brad instructions on how to properly start an IV. That makes me want to laugh, which immediately makes me start to cry. I cough into the oxygen mask as my eyes sting with tears and my throat swells with emotion.

"It's okay, you're going to be okay," Brad tells me softly as he continues to move the stethoscope around my chest.

I'm lifted suddenly and I stare up into the trees, watching them float above me as I'm moved until the night sky filled with stars is above me. I hear the rumbling of trucks, the wailing of sirens and so much shouting when we break through the trees that it makes my head pound.

"Oh, my God! Get out of my way! GET THE FUCK OUT OF MY WAY!"

A face comes into my line of sight, blocking out the stars, but it's shadowed in darkness. All I can make out is short hair and I start to cry harder.

"DJ," I croak with a raspy breath, my voice sounding like Darth Vader in my ears with the oxygen mask over my face.

I try to speak again, to tell him I love him and how sorry I am for everything I put him through. I want him to know that I was never really alive until I found him again. I want him to know that I can survive anything because of HIM. Because of his love and his belief in the type of person I could be.

"Sorry, princess, you get the consolation prize."

I blink through my tears and the flashing lights from one of the vehicles illuminates Dax's face as he stares down at me.

"Jesus Christ, I can't believe you're alive," he whispers, resting his palm on top of my head as he shuffles along with the group carrying me.

Reaching up, I pull the oxygen mask away from my face as I suddenly stop moving and Brad leans over the opposite side of me, tightening straps and pulling blankets tighter around me.

"DJ," I whisper, wincing at the pain in my throat. "Where's DJ?"

I'm lifted away from Dax and pushed into the back of an ambulance, but I didn't miss the look of sadness and worry on his face when I asked him where DJ was.

Once I'm inside the ambulance and locked into place, I twist my head to the side to look down beyond my feet where Dax is still standing by the ambulance doors.

"He thought...we saw...it didn't look good, princess. They brought two body bags out of the house and, well...he pretty much lost it," Dax tells me as Brad and another paramedic jump up into the ambulance with me and start hooking me up to all sorts of equipment.

Oh, God, DJ. It would have killed him to see something like that.

I don't let myself think about the fact that one of those bags would have been filled with the remains of my father, the man I hated for most of my life, but who tried as best he could in the end to make up for everything.

"Don't worry, I'm going to find him and get his ass to the hospital as soon as I can, okay?" Dax reassures me.

I nod and close my eyes as Brad presses the oxygen mask back to my face.

I just need DJ. I need the sound of his voice and the feel of his arms around me to make everything okay. My heart won't hurt with the memory of the look on my father's face when he told me I deserve to be happy because DJ will erase all of that pain with just his smile.

I just need DJ.

"YOU CAN'T LEAVE," Collin argues with me as I rip the heart monitor stickers from my chest and pull the surgical tape holding the IV in place off of my arm.

"I can't stay here. You idiots already let me sleep through the night," I complain, wincing as I gently pull the IV needle out of my skin.

"Look, I'm going to find him. I've been to almost every fucking bar in the whole damn city and anywhere else I thought he might go. When I find him, I'll bring him right to you. After I kick his ass for turning his damn cell phone off."

Jumping down from my hospital bed, I grab the pair of jeans, tennis shoes and t-shirt that Collin brought from my house in the middle of the night and head towards the bathroom.

"I'll find him myself. You've already spent enough time away from Finnley and she's going to be released in a couple of hours," I remind him.

When I arrived at the hospital last night, I had Brad go to Finnley's room, find Collin and explain to him what happened. I didn't have the strength to go through it all over again. He came right down to the ER pushing a sobbing Finnley in a wheelchair in front of him. We hugged and cried while the doctors checked my lungs and looked over my body for burns. They commented on the marks on my hips and Finnley stared at the burns in shock. I knew she could tell I didn't sustain them during the fire, they were too round, too perfect and nothing like the scars she has on her body from her own experience with a house fire.

I promised her I would talk to her about them later, and it is a promise I plan to keep. It's time for me to start being honest with the people in my life, ALL of the people in my life.

I finish dressing in the bathroom and come out to find Collin still standing by the bed with an irritated look on his face and his arms crossed. Tossing my hospital gown on the bed, I turn to face him and mirror his pose.

"I don't like this. The doctors wanted you to stay here another night," he complains.

"And I don't like the fact that I've been sleeping all through the night and no one has been able to find DJ," I fire back.

"You weren't sleeping, you were heavily medicated after a TRAU-MATIC EVENT," he argues, raising his voice at the end. "DJ stole Dax's car, believe me, Dax is pissed off enough that he'll probably find him before anyone."

Dax got a ride to the hospital behind the ambulance and questioned me about what happened before they shot me full of painkillers and I passed out.

I really wish I had been high on morphine when I had to relive all of those details without DJ by my side.

I made him tell me what happened with DJ even though he didn't want to. He said it was the most painful thing he'd ever witnessed and he didn't want me to think about it, but I had to. I put him through this shit by sneaking out of the house with Jackson instead of waiting for him to end his call. I hurt him when I went off on my own and he found out that Jackson had been the one threatening us all along. I broke him when he got to the scene of the fire and had to watch the firemen carrying two body bags out of the house, believing one was me since he had no idea my father was in the house, as well. I put myself in DJ's shoes, thinking about what I would have done if the roles were reversed and I thought he was dead. Just thinking about it makes me want to die. I have to find him. I have to fix him. It's my turn to pick up *his* pieces and hope to God he forgives me for what I put him through.

I lean up on my tiptoes and kiss Collin's cheek, thanking him for running to my place to grab some clothes and for leaving Finnley for most of the night to search for DJ. He opens his mouth to argue with me again about staying, but he can see that he's fighting a losing battle. Nothing can stop me from going to DJ right now. My blood work came back fine, and even though I breathed in a lot of smoke, my lungs are clear. They only wanted to keep me another night for observation because of the blow I took to the head when Jackson hit me in the car. My head still throbs from the goose eggs on either side of my skull, I feel like I have the worst case of strep throat ever and I swear there are knives scraping around in there whenever I swallow, but it's nothing I can't handle.

Holding my hand out in front of me, Collin sighs regretfully as he drops the keys to his car into my palm.

"Be careful, and call me as soon as you find him," Collin tells me as I walk around him towards the door.

I nod my agreement, keeping my head down as I sneak around the nurse's station and make my way to the elevators.

A FEW MINUTES later, I pull into DJ's driveway and shut off the car. I probably could have taken up where Collin left off and started searching bars, but it would be like chasing my own tail. DJ has to come home eventually and I'm going to be here, waiting for him when he does. I overheard Collin and Dax talking quietly last night when the morphine began to pull me under and they were worried that he might do something stupid and reckless. Something permanent that would take him from this world so he wouldn't have to deal with the pain of thinking that he'd lost me. The only thing keeping me calm at this moment is the knowledge that he would never hurt his family like that. He would never put his parents, his sisters and his nieces and nephews through something so horrible.

Getting out of the car, I head up to his front porch, cursing myself for not being smart enough to realize his door would be locked. Turning around, I lean my back against the front door and slide down to my butt. Hugging my knees up to my chest and resting my chin on top of them, I close my eyes and think about all the things I want to say to DJ when I see him again.

36

DJ

"Buddy, wake up!"

I jerk awake, wiping the drool from my chin as I take in my surroundings. Ripped and stained black leather seats, window partition splattered with fluids I don't even want to know about and an irritated man staring at me through the dirty window.

Shit, taxi.

Leaning to the side, I grab my wallet out of the back of my pants and toss all the bills I have through the open section of the partition and get out of the cab as fast as I can. Thank God I slept for the entire hour and half ride or the smell coming from that thing would have made me throw up the entire bottle of whiskey I consumed through the night that is currently churning in my stomach.

I stand on the curb in front of my house, staring after the cab as it pulls away, squinting in irritation at the bright sunlight that amplifies my headache. When I turn around, I groan at the sight of Collin's car in my driveway. I don't want to fucking see him or talk to him right now. I don't want to be around *anyone*, which is why I threw my cell phone to the ground as soon as I got to the bar last night and stomped the shit out of it until there was nothing left but teeny, tiny broken pieces.

Just like my goddamn heart.

I don't want to walk in that fucking front door. She lived in that house with me and everywhere I look I'm going to see her, smell her and remember her. I'm going to picture her curled up on the couch watching a movie, standing in the kitchen loading up the dishwasher or lying on my bed, tempting me as I tried to get dressed. I'm going to see her in the shower, in the hallway, in the reflection of every motherfucking plate. I could walk away and never step foot in that house again, never have to feel the pain of losing her breaking apart my chest every time I take a breath. I seriously consider it, just walking away from my house, wandering aimlessly down the sidewalk until my legs give out. Not packing up my things, not saying good-bye, just disappearing into the wind like *she* did. I think of my mother, my father, my sisters and their children and I know that as much as I want to leave, I can't. They love me, they depend on me and their hearts would ache as much as mine is right now if I did that to them.

Like the dumb fuck I am, I turn and make my way slowly up the driveway, giving Collin's car the finger as I walk around it. I'm a glutton for punishment. Even though I don't want to go inside that house, I *have* to go inside. I have to smell her on my sheets one last time, I have to pick up the clothes she strewed at the end of my bed, lift them up to my nose and let the scent of her skin and perfume surround me. There's also extra strength aspirin in the kitchen that will hopefully put an end to the marching band that's taken up residence in my head.

I try not to, but I silently curse Collin in my head as I go up the walk, digging through my pockets for my house keys. He's going to tell me how sorry he is, he's going to tell me it wasn't my fault, and then he's going to go home to Finnley and get to touch her, hold her and stare at her as much as he wants.

My feet angrily stomp up the steps and I stare down at them as each one pounds into the wood, wishing I could rip my heart out of my chest and do the same to it. Just pound it to dust like my phone so it didn't have to sit there like a half-dead fish inside my chest, coming back to life every few seconds to flop around and remind me it's trying to live, but is missing the one thing it needs the most – oxygen. Phina was my oxygen. I don't want to breathe without her. It hurts too much to even try.

I get to the last step and pause as I finally manage to pull the tangled set of keys out of my pocket, flipping through them to find the gold house key. When I finally find it, I look up, and the keys slip through my fingers and clatter to the floor of the porch.

Goddammit. God fucking dammit.

I knew walking up to this house was going to be hard, but I thought I'd have at least a few minutes before I started to lose my fucking mind. I see her, clear as day, curled up on her side at the foot of my door, fast asleep.

I clench my eyes closed as tightly as possible and bring my fists up to rub them angrily. When I open them again, she's still there, looking more beautiful than anything in my memory. Her knees are pulled up to her chest and her hands are tucked under her cheek just like they always are when she sleeps.

Oh, God, it hurts. It fucking hurts so much!

I close my eyes again, rubbing my palms over my face, begging the image go away. I can't do this right now. I can't stand this pain. I just want it to go away. Just like before, when I open my eyes, she's still there. My legs give out and I drop, my knees slamming into the wood. My arms hang uselessly at my sides as I slump my ass back on my feet and stare at the vision in front of me. I watch as her chest rises and falls with every breath she takes, I watch as a small gust of wind blowing though the porch plays with a piece of her hair, lifting it off of her cheek and swirling it around before it drops back down like a feather. Her lips twitch and she sighs softly in her sleep. The sound guts me and my useless arms finally move, wrapping themselves around my waist as I rock back and forth.

"I can't do this, I can't do this. I want you to be real," I whisper as I finally let the tears I've held back slip down my cheeks.

I see movement behind her eyelids and then her eyes flutter open. I wonder if I'm making this happen by sheer will alone. I need to see her eyes. I don't *want* to see her fucking eyes that have been haunting me through the night. I can't tell what's real and what isn't. I feel the cold, hard wood beneath my knees, I feel the wetness on my cheeks and I hear birds chirping and cars driving by. I know those are real. I can feel and hear that they are real. What's happening in front of me can't be real. She's dead. She's gone. She can't be waking up on my front porch, her green eyes locking onto mine as she quickly pushes herself up into a sitting position.

"*DJ.*"

She breathes my name and it tortures me. Her voice sounds real, but I know it isn't. I close my eyes and shake my head back and forth, trying to make it all stop.

"Open your eyes," her voice commands softly.

My head keeps shaking back and forth. I won't do it. I *can't* do it. It's too much, too hard. Goddammit, it's too hard!

I hear something sliding against the wood and I squeeze my eyes closed tighter when I feel the warmth of her body right in front of me.

"Drake, please. Open your eyes and look at me," she pleads with a sob.

I feel her warm hands press against either side of my face and it throws me. Warm, not cold like a fucking ghost or whatever the hell this is.

"I can't, I can't...you can't be real," I mumble even as my face turns into her palm and I nuzzle her skin with my nose and breathe her in.

In the next second her lips are against mine, warm and soft and so fucking real. I taste tears on her lips and I wonder if ghosts have the ability to cry and then realize I don't fucking care. I don't care if my mind is completely gone and I'm so fucked up in the head that I'm imagining this. I'll stay a fucked up mess the rest of my life if I can have her lips on mine and it can feel this real.

Over and over she smacks her lips against mine and I finally open my eyes.

"I'm real, I love you, I'm so sorry," she repeats in between kisses.

Even though I don't want to, I move back from her lips, just enough to really look at her. Her hands stay on my cheeks and she holds my head in place, staring into my eyes. I see the flecks of gold in her eyes and the tiny black ring around the green. I see every freckle on her nose and I feel her breath floating against my mouth.

My arms move on their own until my hands are cupping her head. I tilt her face up and turn it slightly from side to side, looking at her chin, her cheeks and her lips. I see a horrible purple bruise under her left eye that I know I wouldn't imagine if she were a dream and suddenly, everything she went through last night and *survived* makes me equal parts horrified and grateful.

"Oh, my God," I whisper, sliding one hand down the side of her face, the warmth of her skin telling me that this is not a dream, it's not some fucking illusion. It's real. *She's* real.

I trace my fingertips over her eyebrow, her nose, her flushed cheek and her lips. I touch each part of her that I can't stop staring at.

She moves her hands away from my face and presses them to the top of mine, pushing my palms more firmly against her cheeks.

"Do you feel that?" she whispers. "I'm real. I'm right here and I'm okay."

A strange mixture of a sob and a laugh flies out of my mouth and I quickly lean forward and kiss her. I laugh and cry against her lips and she moves closer, crawling onto my lap and wrapping her legs around my waist. I feel the weight of her on my lap, the strength of her thighs squeezing around my hips and the warmth of her body so close to mine and I finally let go of the last of my doubt.

"I thought I lost you. How is this happening?" I ask her as I rest my forehead against hers and her thumbs gently rub back and forth over the top of my hands that are still pressed against her cheeks.

"I'm so sorry, DJ. You have no idea how sorry I am that I put you through this," she cries softly.

"Shhhh, it's okay, baby. Please don't cry. Just let me keep touching you to make sure you're real," I tell her softly, trying not to cry like a fucking baby right along with her.

I run one hand through her hair over and over, letting the soft strands tangle with my fingers. I run my palm against her cheek again, careful of the bruise, down her neck, over her collarbone and rest it against her heart. I feel it beating strongly and I finally let my own start beating again right along with it.

37

Phina

DJ EASILY LIFTS me up into his arms and carries me into the house and up to his bedroom. I've apologized to him so many times, but it will never be enough. The anguish and torture I witnessed on his face out on his front porch almost killed me. I did that to him. This strong, amazing man…I brought him to his knees and it hurts everything inside of me.

He gently puts me on my feet at the edge of the bed and we undress each other without any words. There's so much I need to say to him, but right now it needs to wait. He needs this reassurance that I'm here and I need his comfort and his love to take away all the pain.

With the bright afternoon sun streaming through his bedroom window, he peels off all of my clothes, kissing his way up and down my body as he goes. For the first time, I don't try to hide my hips from him. I let him stare at me as he pulls my underwear down my legs and I'm not ashamed when he runs his palms over the scars. I'm standing naked in the bright light, in front of a man and I'm letting him see *all* of me. It doesn't matter that he saw everything the other night because it was wrong then. I pushed him to look so that I could push him away because I didn't feel like I was worthy of him.

I finally believe that I deserve this. I deserve to be happy and nothing makes me happier than having his hands on my body and his lips on my skin.

He lifts me up into his arms again and then lays me down on top of the bed, quickly covering me with his body. He kisses every place on my face that he can reach while I wrap my legs around his waist and pull him closer. He enters me slowly and I sob against the side of his neck when he's finally right where he belongs. We fit so perfectly together that I don't know how I lived my life before he came back into it.

He moves against me and I lift my hips to meet him. We rock together slowly until I have no idea where he begins and I end, like a perfect circle. Everything about this moment is perfection and I never want it to end. When he's inside me, I let go of everything that causes me pain and let him fill me with everything that brings me joy. He is my heart, my soul and my reason for breathing and I tell him that over and over each time he pushes into me.

"You are everything to me...*everything*," he whispers against my lips.

"I love you," I reply, wrapping my arms tighter around his body.

He kisses me and never stops, continuing the unhurried movements as I pull him deeper inside of me. The build is slow and perfect, my release climbing at an unhurried pace until my scalp starts to tingle and it works its way down my body and flows out of me. It's magic and bliss all rolled into one big wave of pleasure that makes me feel like I'm floating on a cloud.

He pulls his mouth away from mine to stare down into my eyes as he follows right behind me, breathing my name and words of love when he comes.

"Don't ever leave me again," he whispers against my lips.

"Don't ever let me go," I whisper back.

"I SHOULD HAVE been there," he tells me as we lie naked in bed facing one another, our arms and legs tangled around each other.

I've spent the last twenty minutes telling him what happened, ending with my time in the hospital, and I hate that he feels even an ounce of guilt.

"Stop, you had no way of knowing. I hate that you had to see what you did. I hate that you thought the worst."

He sighs, pulling me closer until every inch of our bodies are touching. His chest is pressed against mine and I feel his heart beat thumping against me.

"How's your cheek? And your wrists? Fuck! I didn't hurt you, did I?" he asks in a horrified voice, pulling back slightly to run his fingers over the white bandages covering the rope burns on my wrists.

Pulling my hands away from him, I wind them around his neck and pull him back closer. "I'm fine, I promise."

He sighs, resting his chin on top of my head. "I still can't believe your dad got you out of there. I can't even imagine what you're feeling right now."

I shrug as he rolls to his back, pulling me with him. I rest my cheek against his chest.

"I don't know *what* I'm feeling. I was so scared after I got out of that house I just didn't *want* to think about it. I keep seeing his face through the fire, telling me he loved me and he was sorry. I hate that I feel bad that he died like that."

"You can't feel bad about what he did, Phina. He made a choice and he chose *you* over himself for once. He chose *your* happiness instead of his own. It doesn't make up for all the shit he did to you, but it's okay to be sad about losing him. No matter what kind of a father he was for all those years, he was still your father. He was a part of your life and a part of your blood. In the end, he finally did right by you," DJ tells me softly.

I snuggle into him and wrap my arms around his waist.

"Listen, I need to get a few things off my chest, so I want you to just lay there and be quiet for a few seconds," he says suddenly.

I smile against him and let him continue.

"I shouldn't have reacted the way I did when I got to your house after Finnley's accident."

I quickly lift my head and open my mouth to protest, but he places his finger against my lips.

"Shush. I said no talking," he tells me with a smile.

I raise my eyebrow at him in irritation, but he keeps his finger pressed firmly against my mouth.

"I'm a dick. I reacted without thinking, and I should have known something else was going on. I know I didn't say the words you wanted to hear and that snowballed into you being hurt and lashing out. So, I'm saying the words now. I love you. I love every part of you. I don't care if you have scars on your body from someone else or from your own hands. None of it matters to me. Whatever happens, I'm not going anywhere. The only thing that matters is that you talk to me. You tell me if you have the urge to do something like that. I might not know what the fuck to do, but I'm not going to walk away. I will help you and I will be here for whatever you need."

I blink back tears, reaching up to gently remove his finger from my lips.

"Can I speak now?"

He laughs nervously before nodding his head.

"I had a problem."

I think about that for a minute and then shake my head.

"Correction, I *have* a problem. I haven't done it since before we got together, but it's always there in the back of my mind, even if I don't have the urge to do it. I wasn't angry with you about the things you said. I knew what your reaction would be and I knew what conclusion you would jump to. I was angry with myself for being so weak and for doing whatever I could to push you away," I explain.

He brings my hand up to his lips and kisses my palm, but he knows I need to keep going so he stays silent.

"I don't even know what made me start doing it exactly. One day I just felt so much pressure and so much anger and I needed to release it. I was banging around the kitchen and I burned my hand on the stove. It just… did something to me. The pain in my hand made me forget about the pain in my mind. I did that a few times whenever I felt my anger brewing inside of me, but Finnley started to notice the blisters on my fingers and she asked questions that I didn't know how to answer."

I take a deep breath and look away from DJ to trace circles with my fingertip onto his chest.

"I decided to start hiding what I was doing. The most logical place was on my hips where no one would ever see it. That's why I've always kept my underwear on or the lights off during sex. I did whatever I could to hide what I did. I was ashamed, but that didn't stop me from doing it. Pain got confused with pleasure. It made the anger go away and it helped me breathe. I felt so constricted and so torn up, and burning myself was the only thing that gave me any relief."

I finally look up at him and shrug. "It's pretty fucked up considering that's how I spent most of my childhood. The exact thing I feared and hated growing up turned out to be the only thing I could do to make the fear and the hate go away."

DJ leans forward and kisses me. "I wish you would have told me. I wish I would have known."

I shrug again, resting my chin on my hand against his chest. "No one knew. I never even told Finnley. Like I said, I was embarrassed, especially with you. I didn't want you to look at me and see how messed up I was."

He shakes his head. "You're not messed up and I would never think that."

"I AM messed up, but it's okay. I'm going to get help. I'm going to talk to someone. Even though I don't have the urge to do it anymore, I want to make sure I never do again. I want to be good for you, I want to be a whole, healed person for you."

He wraps his arm around me and hugs me tightly. "I just want you to know, you're already perfect for me. Everything about you is exactly what I need, but if this is something *you* need, I fully support it. Don't do it for me, do it for yourself."

I smile up at him. "I love you, Drake Jefferson Taylor. I will do it for myself, I promise. You put a mark on my heart that will never go away. You branded me with your love and I know it's the only thing I'll ever need to keep the pain away."

"A mark on your heart, huh? So it's sort of like I pissed on my territory," he says with a laugh.

I smack his chest and laugh with him. "You're an ass!"

He moves quickly, flipping me over onto my back and resting his body between my thighs. "I'm *your* ass, my little Fireball, and you're stuck with me. I just need you to promise me one thing."

I slide my hands through his hair and feel him harden as he presses himself against me. The smile slips from his face and he looks down at me seriously.

"Never, ever die on me again. My heart can't take losing you a second time."

I look up at him, this man who fought for me, believed in me and saved me from myself. I look at him and I know that I'm the luckiest woman on earth.

"I promise," I whisper softly as me slips inside of me. "No more dying, no more branding, nothing but this."

He moves inside of me and I sigh in relief, having him right where I need him.

"This is all I need to breathe," I whisper.

EPILOGUE

Phina

Six months later...

"I CAN'T DO this anymore," DJ tells me in a frustrated voice.

I put my hands on my hips and glare at him. "Yeah? Well, I can't either!"

He throws his hands in the air and stomps away from me while I cross my arms in front of me waiting for him to say more. I just know he wants to say more. Clearly, he hasn't pissed me off enough in the last hour.

"You can't keep doing this to me. It's killing me. KILLING ME!" he shouts to the wall.

"Oh, my God, quit being so dramatic."

He whirls around and stomps back to me, grabbing the binder from the counter on his way. He holds it in front of me and stabs at the open page.

"Five times. FIVE FUCKING TIMES you've changed the backsplash in this kitchen and now you're telling me that THIS is the one you have to have."

I stare longingly at the Tuscan marble tile that he's pointing to and sigh. "It's so beautiful."

He growls, tossing the binder back on top of the counter. "The crosshatch silver was *gorgeous*, the Murano Mosaic was *stunning* and the brushed nickel was...I forget, what was the brushed nickel again?" he asks in annoyance.

"Complimentary to the appliances," I reply through clenched teeth.

"Killing me. Motherfucking killing me," he mutters before pulling his phone out of his pocket and calling the contractor.

I smile in victory, bouncing over to him to kiss his cheek while he tells the contractor that I've changed my mind. Again. He smacks my ass when I turn away and head out onto the front porch.

Flopping down on one of the Adirondack chairs, I kick my feet up on the railing and look out at the yard.

The last few months have been a whirlwind of emotions. I started seeing a new psychologist and I really like her. I still see her once a week and she's helped me get to the root of my issues and learn how to transfer the anger and hatred I sometimes feel into something healthier. I go outside and scream, I take a walk or I beat the shit out of the heavy bag DJ hung in the garage. Most importantly, I talk to him about everything. Nothing is held back, and he always knows what's going on in my mind and my heart. He even accompanies me to some of my appointments so he can learn about my problem and understand how to help.

I thought telling DJ everything was hard, but it was nothing compared to telling my best friend. Finnley cried silently when I told her about my burning addiction and how I'd used it to cope through the years. She had a hard time forgiving my father once she knew the extent of his abuse, but she knew I wouldn't be alive today if it weren't for him. It felt good to finally confide in her and I know our friendship is stronger because of it.

I'm still working at the hospital after a short medical leave and taking time to bury my father. DJ is still working full time as a paramedic, telling me he might go back to the fire department in time, but for right now he's happy where he's at. When he has to transport someone to my hospital, he always sends me a text on the way so I can meet him downstairs for a quick kiss. He tells me it's because he can't get enough of me, but I know a part of him still thinks about that day on his front porch when he couldn't believe I was alive. Even six months later, he still needs the reassurance that I'm here, I'm okay and I'm real.

As I stare out at the trees around the property, I think about our future, once so uncertain, but now so perfectly clear. It might seem like the strangest decision to a lot of people, but it felt right to me. The land my childhood home was built on transferred over to me after my father died, and when the attorney called to ask me what I wanted to do with it, I knew the answer immediately. I would rebuild on this land, the one that housed all of my nightmares, and with DJ by my side, I would make new, better memories. I would erase all the sins of my past and I would start over with a clean slate.

"We might have to hire a new contractor," DJ tells me as he joins me outside and sits down in the chair next to mine. "He made me promise him that this would be the last time you change your mind about the backsplash."

I smile over at him. "This will definitely be the last time."

"Oh, thank God," he groans.

"I'm not so sure about the tile in the bathroom, though."

He stares me down for a few seconds while I fight to hold back a laugh. He leans across the arms of our chairs and rests his hands on my huge stomach and puts his mouth right against it. "Your mother is killing me. Do you hear me, Shaleh? I hope you appreciate the shitty

Italian marble in the kitchen when you get here."

When we found out we were having a girl, we chose the name Shaleh because it means *flame*. She was conceived in the midst of fiery, all-consuming passion, so it seemed fitting. We'll most likely never tell her that, though.

I smack the back of his head. "Language! We don't want our daughter's first word to be s-h-i-t-t-y."

He grins at me, lifting away from my stomach to kiss me. "She's your daughter, her first word will probably be f-u-c-k."

"Speaking of f-u-c-k," he continues. "They delivered the bed earlier, how about you and I go test it out."

I run my fingers through his hair and smile. "I think that can be arranged. Go on upstairs and I'll meet you there in a minute."

He stands up, placing a kiss on my belly and then one on my lips. "I'll meet you up there, Fireball. Do NOT look at that damn tile binder on your way."

I laugh when he walks inside and take a few moments to relax, rubbing my hand over my belly and staring out into the yard. I can picture myself as a little girl, running out here to hide or to escape from the pain that awaited me inside the house that used to stand in this very same spot. My plan of building a home here wasn't a way to keep me tied to the past, it was a way for me to look forward to the future and change things for our new generation. I can look at our home and our yard and I can also see our daughter running out there some day, happy and full of life and confident that she will never, ever be hurt by the ones who are supposed to love her.

I will brand her with words of love and encouragement instead of cigarettes and hatred. I will give her the kind of childhood that I always dreamed of having.

It will be perfect and it will be beautiful…

Because I deserve it.

The End

Look for *Scorched*, the conclusion to the Ignite Trilogy, coming Spring 2015! You don't want to miss Dax and Harley's story!

To stay up to date on all Tara Sivec news, please join her mailing list:

http://eepurl.com/H4uaf

ACKNOWLEDGEMENTS

Thank you, as always, to my publicist Donna Soluri who lets me send a book to her one chapter at a time as well as a billion text messages at all hours of the day and night. Thank you for your friendship and for not wanting to kill me (much) when I send you a chapter that ends on a cliffy and you have to wait for the next one.

Thank you to my editor Nikki Rushbrook, bless your heart for putting up with me and the Tara Fucking Sivec tenses.

A HUGE thank you goes out to Patrick Stork from the Cocoa Beach Fire Department and his wife Suzy for helping me with the paramedic questions. Thank you for the job you do and for taking the time to help me with mine!

Thank you to my sister-in-law, Janet Sivec for answering my nursing questions and for not being offended when I called you a whore in all my text messages. I love you.

Thank you to my beta readers, Michelle Kannan and Stephanie Johnson for loving DJ and Phina as much as I do and for always being excited when I say, "Hey, want to read something?"

Thank you to all the bloggers who take time out of their day to read and promote my books. Your support means the WORLD to me and I love you all!

2113

Made in the USA
Lexington, KY
13 January 2015